A Jury Of One's Own

by Dan Bell

To Tim & Lanie
Any friend of welcome
Steinguss is welcome
at my house
Dan Bell
23 November 2003

www.thebookden.com

Library of Congress Cataloging-in Publication Data
ISBN: 0-87714-307-2

For my daughters Colleen and Lara, Ms. Chris and the Lady in Red

CHAPTER ONE

Gant parked his plum-colored Porsche under an ancient oak next to a rusted van with no plates. Two Rottweilers growled from their run at the side of the converted farmhouse. A hand-carved wooden sign reading "Vipers" hung above the door. Deeper into the driveway, near the garage, he could see cycles ready for their riders. The air stank of grease and dog feces. Gant worried about his Italian leather shoes as he picked his way to the door.

Mouse stood in the entrance, eclipsing the interior light. At six foot five and a beefy three hundred pounds, he was five inches taller and one hundred pounds heavier than Gant. They both had thickened and sagged since Gant, a year out of law school, convinced a jury that Mouse acted in self defense when he busted the face of an undercover cop in a bar fight. With formality, they nodded and shook hands across the clubhouse threshold. Mouse wore his customary pin-striped bibs, and Gant was attired in a tailored, silver-gray suit which matched his eyes.

The Vipers relied on Gant as their legal mechanic. His name and number were magneted below the plumbers on the "who to call" list on the side of the fridge. Gant flaunted the biker gang as a trophy client, never missing the opportunity to walk the middle of the main corridor in the courthouse, bikers rattling and clomping on each side.

"Wine, Jake?" Mouse said facetiously. "For special guests, we have a nice Chardonnay. Hairball picked it up accidentally on his last run to the liquor store." He nodded at the fat man on the leatherette sofa.

"Yeah, the owner told me I could take whatever I could carry if I'd just leave the store. Surprising how often it works. This look drives them crazy," Hairball said, rubbing his bare, furry belly. "You here for Willie? It's a bad scene, man."

Mouse walked into his office, a small former extra bedroom furnished with a stained mattress, an old card table and two stuffed chairs which had been badly abused during a knife sharpening contest.

"You be careful of that beautiful silver suit, Mr. Gant," Mouse said. "Cost more than everything in this place." He laughed at his own joke. "I'll get Willie."

Strangely empty with expectation, like the first moments alone in a doctor's examination room, Gant casually gazed at the centerfolds of bikes and women on the walls. He paired himself with May's topless brunette, confident she'd get wiggly over the dimpled charm of his smile rather than hesitate because his complexion resembled wood, rough sanded and lacquered. He could hear the shouts from pool players and the rattle of the rock and roll from the next room reverberating in the tinny table legs.

Willie crossed the filthy carpet warily as if at a bar in a strange town. Gant found his handshake soft with disdain. With the controlled tension of a coiled spring, Willie sat in the other chair. He was bald as a plucked chicken and pockmarked as an old dart board. He wore the standard issue gold skull earring on the left side and his face was shaped like one of those furry animals built close to the ground, a ferret or weasel, maybe. It was distrust trimmed with hostility. Gant felt a small surge of adrenaline. Bikers — always a special challenge.

"I got to know about my bike," Willie said.

You have to love it, Gant thought. A girl is dead, this cue ball is looking at ten years in prison, and he's thinking about his bike. Gant carefully wrote "Willie Rotten" at the top of the yellow pad followed by "bike" which he underlined four times. He slowly recapped his fountain pen and looked as deep into Willie's eyes as he could get.

"We'll get there, Willie. Trust me," Gant said.

Willie didn't blink.

"You ever been in trouble before? Where you needed a lawyer?" Gant began his indoctrination routine. An oft-used and often successful package of an intimidating tone, self confident language, and inclusive gestures given to new clients who exhibited uncertainty about their choice of attorneys.

"No way, man. I never wanted nothing to do with lawyers."

"Yeah, well, it happens. Even to the best of people. Now listen up. You must do exactly what I say and you must say exactly what I tell you to. If not, your bike gets sold at a police auction and you start counting days at the governor's hotel upstate." Gant stood quickly, banging his words down hard on Willie's hairless dome. "You got your mind in gear now?"

"Yeah," Willie said.

"All right, I'm going to tell you how it works and the best shot we got to get you off. I can tell you that without even knowing what the facts are. You know why?"

"No."

"Because I'm the lawyer. More than that, I'm the best lawyer in Madison. Top ten in all of Wisconsin. Make that top five, I don't care about the facts. You know what I care about?"

"No."

"All I care about is what the district attorney can prove in court. You know how that works?"

Willie shook his head.

"Okay, I'll explain it to you," Gant said. "You look like an intelligent guy so I'll run it straight through. You read that complaint there where the district attorney says you should go to prison for ten years because you ran your motorcycle off the road while you were drunk and your passenger got killed? Well, he's got to do more than just write those things on a piece of paper. He's got to call witnesses and introduce exhibits. That's called evidence. He's got to get enough evidence to prove all those things to the jury beyond a reasonable doubt. If the jury has any reasonable doubt, then they have to find you not guilty. That's my job — to make sure the jury finds a reasonable doubt. It doesn't matter whether you actually committed the crime. That's irrelevant. That means it has nothing to do with it. I don't care about that and I don't want to know about it. So don't tell me whether you think you did it or not. Ever. It'll screw up the case. Got it?" Gant said.

"Yeah, but...." Willie said skeptically.

"Do it any other way, and you'll do time. Do it my way and you have a chance of making the Labor Day run."

"Maybe." Willie nodded.

"Don't get me wrong. I'm not asking you to lie. Whatever you say will be the truth. I'm telling you not to admit to anything in the complaint. Let me give you an example. They say you were intoxicated, don't they?"

"Yeah."

"If you were intoxicated, I don't want you to tell me. Understand?"

"Yeah, I guess."

"If you tell me today that you were intoxicated, I can never let you get up on the witness stand and say that you weren't. I'd be doing what's called 'suborning perjury.' That means letting you lie under oath. I could lose my license. If you don't tell me one way or the other, then we keep all our options open. Okay?"

"You mean you don't want me to tell you whether I think I did anything they said," Willie said.

"You got it. Just tell me what happened. Start with when you got up that day."

"What difference does that make?" Willie said, defiantly.

"I won't know until you tell me," Gant said. "Believe me, I know you don't want to be here. The sooner we get done, the sooner you're out of here. So let's go."

Willie nodded. "Probably seven, seven-thirty. I don't exactly remember."

"Okay. Then what did you do? Just keep going. I'll interrupt when I have a question," Gant said.

"Like I say, it's hard to remember exact. It being Saturday, I probably ate breakfast, played with the kids, helped the old lady around the house. She always has stuff she wants done. Then Hairball called to say there was a party at Freed's farm, and did I want to go."

"What time was that, about?"

"Morning sometime, maybe nine, nine-thirty."

"What's Freed's farm?" Gant said.

"What do you mean?" Willie said.

"Is it a farm, or...?"

"Yeah, it's on County H, near Linden. This guy, I don't know, he likes to have bikers around. A weird shit. We party there because no one hassles us."

"Did you tell him you'd go?"

"Yeah, I remember now. I was doing the storms. I'd promised my old lady I'd get them down and the screens up. She likes them up early. I told him it'd be eleven or so before I was done. We agreed to meet at eleven-thirty at the club. But the fucking ladder broke and I had to find a neighbor who was home to borrow one.

So I didn't get there till closer to noon. He was ready to roll and I took some shit for being late."

"Did your wife go?" Gant said.

"Oh, no, man. It wasn't that kind of a party. My old lady and I, we got an understanding. I've got the club, and she's got the house and kids. Maybe a couple times a year, on weekend runs, she'll come, when I need her to help with the cooking and shit like that. But that's it."

"Did you have anything to drink before you left for the party, any alcohol?"

"Maybe a couple of beers while I was doing the storms. Yeah, probably. But, you know, I don't really remember," Willie said.

"No more than two, right?"

"Yeah, as best as I remember," Willie said.

"Any drugs?" Gant said.

"No, man. Don't do much of that shit."

"What happened after you met Hairball?"

Willie described the party, a great ride, beer, music, catching up with a winter's worth of news, old friends, softball, dancing, laughing young women.

Gant's thoughts drifted parallel to Willie's in a vague and barren search for the last real party he had attended. Instead of good times, he recalled a long string of boring, stand-up affairs full of lawyers talking about their cases.

"It was a blast," Willie said. "We left about six. It was getting dark."

"How many beers did you have at the party?" Gant said.

"I don't know, man. I wasn't counting."

"I understand. Why would you? Let me ask you this, how many beers can you actually remember drinking?"

"I don't —."

"I'm talking about those you actually remember. What, maybe two, three, four?"

Willie snorted.

"Let's replay it. Tell me the first beer you can remember having, can actually picture yourself drinking," Gant said.

"Let me think. I had one with Hairball and some guys from

Milwaukee, right when I got there. Standing by the bikes," Willie said.

"Good. What's the next one you actually remember?"

"Some guys from Milwaukee brought some new shit. I had one of those," Willie said after additional thought. "One during softball. I remember that because the ball knocked it over before it was empty."

"How much was left?"

"Not much. Quarter maybe."

"Any others that you actually remember?" Gant said.

"We all had one just before we left. Sure there were others, but —."

"Wait. Listen. You've told me you actually remember having four beers, correct?"

"Yeah, but —."

"Now you want to tell me you think you may have had more. Correct?"

"Yeah, man, I mean I know —."

"I'm only interested in the truth, Willie. The truth is what you remember. You may think you had more than four beers, but that's speculation because you don't actually remember having any others. Four beers. That's all you actually remember. You hear what I'm saying?"

"Yeah," Willie said.

"So, if we're at trial and the district attorney asks you how many beers you had at the party, what are you going to tell him?"

"Four. Almost four."

"Good. You got it. We set on that now?"

As Willie nodded, Gant saw the first spark of recognition in his eyes.

"Who was Sherry Dobler?" he said.

Willie jumped like he had touched a hot exhaust pipe. "This chick," he said quietly.

"She was at the party?" Gant said delicately.

"Yeah. Needed a ride home. I said okay," Willie said.

"She asked you?"

"Yeah."

"You're sure?"

"Yeah. I'm sure."

"Did you know her previous to the party?" Gant said.

"I don't understand," Willie said.

"Had you ever seen her before the party that day?"

"Yeah. I mean...yeah."

"Where had you seen her?"

"Clubhouse. Parties. Shit like that. She, uh, she liked the Vipers."

Gant leaned back in his chair and massaged his face hard with both hands hearing the rasp of his whiskers and feeling the blood redden his face. He wrestled with recurring fatigue caused by years of digging for information in the rock-hard minds of the guilty, the injured, and the frightened.

"You two have anything going?" Gant said.

"Like I said, she'd come around. Liked to get it on," Willie said.

"A punch board." Gant grinned.

"What'd you say?" Willie said amazed.

"A punch board. She liked to do a lot of guys in a row."

Willie gave a raunchy barroom hoot. "Yeah, that's right, man. Sherry, she liked that. Pulling the train, we call it. You —."

"You ever on that train, Willie?" Gant said sharply.

"Oh, shit, man. My old lady.... Do I have to tell you?"

"You just did. Tell me this — was it a regular thing, or only a couple of times, or what?"

"Yeah, maybe a couple," Willie said. "She'd be at the club passing it around. I thought, shit, why not? If my old lady finds out —."

"Anybody know about this except for Vipers? As far as you know," Gant said.

Willie shook his head, shoulders drooping.

"All right. Now, let me tell you this. Nothing you've told me leaves this office. If your wife gets the news, it won't be from me. Got it?"

"Okay," Willie said without conviction.

"Tell me about the accident. Run it straight through."

"We were coming down Highway H. Hairball took point. He likes to be first, man. Then VD maybe ten yards behind him. Then me and the broad another ten yards back. We're all steady at the speed limit. Five five. Then that quick I'm on the shoulder. Don't know what happened. Trying to keep the bike up. Front wheel all over the place. Down in that little ditch. Hit something. Stump maybe. We both flew. I went out. When I came to, my brothers had their lights shining down on us. Her head was close enough to touch. Eyes wide open. But her body, man, her body was far away. She hit a guy wire and ..." Willie drew his hand across his throat from ear to ear. "Fucking blood, man."

Decapitated. Photographs, Gant thought. Tabloid stuff for the DA. What a thing to wake up to. Gant looked at the clock. They'd been talking a little more than an hour. It was time to wrap it up before Willie became defiant again.

"We're almost done. Tell me what happened next," Gant said.

"We went to my cycle. It was all fucked up — front wheel twisted, forks splayed, bars bent, scratches. Then the cops came."

"You tell them anything?"

"No," Willie said.

"Written statements?"

"No way."

"Tests?" Gant said.

"Yeah. At the scene, and at the hospital," Willie said.

"You hurt?" Gant said.

"No. Scratches and bruises. Just wanted to check me out, I guess," Willie said.

"You blew a point one three on the breath test. Not terrible, but the limit's point zero eight, you know," Gant said, looking at the complaint.

"What can I say?"

"Well, all we can do is deal with it. Okay, that's it for now. Except fees."

"What about my bike? I want it back."

"I'll see what I can do. But I've got to be straight with you here. If the DA considers it evidence, there's no way you'll get it back until after the trial," Gant said.

"What do you mean? He can keep it? That's bullshit. It's my bike, man. What am I going to do?" Willie said.

"The law says that anything seized by the police as evidence in connection with a crime — an alleged crime — is held until the case is over. In this case, the bike is part of the alleged crime. So, I can guarantee you that no judge will order its release if the DA objects. Understand?"

"It's still bullshit."

"That may be. I want to look at the cycle anyway. Maybe there's something there that will help us. I'll talk to the DA. Maybe I can work something out. Who have you talked to about this?"

"The old lady. Couple brothers. That's it."

"I advise you not to talk to anybody else. Nobody. If anybody asks, tell them your lawyer said you can't talk about it. Got it?"

Willie nodded.

"About fees — five grand up front, ten more before trial, if we go to trial. Fifteen thousand max."

"Shit man, that's a lot."

"True. But so is ten years in prison. This is a serious charge. It's not some barroom fight. If you weren't a Viper, the fee would be more, a lot more. Ask Mouse, or your other brothers I've represented."

"I ain't got five," Willie said.

"Can you get it?" Gant said.

"I don't know. Thinking about the public defender."

"As a carpenter working full time, you make good money. I doubt you'll be eligible. You'd have to check it out. Some are very good, some aren't. It's the luck of the draw who you get. Or you could find someone cheaper. Maybe a kid out of school. You'd pay less, but you'd get less. I'm telling you straight up, I'm your best chance to stay out of prison. And, like I said, I'm giving you a good deal on fees."

"I don't want to do time, man. Shit. No choice, I guess. Can I bring the money in a couple of weeks?"

"I'm not doing anything on your case until I get some money, Willie." He looked through the papers Rotten had given him. "Your preliminary hearing is set for April twenty-sixth. Little over two weeks. That doesn't give me enough time. And there's evidence out there that might disappear if I don't get right on it."

"Shit man..."

"Didn't you bring any money? Gant said impatiently. "I can't understand why Mouse didn't tell you to bring some."

"He did, but I ain't got no five grand."

"How much do you have?"

"Twenty-five hundred."

"Well, Christ, why didn't you say so earlier?" Gant said, exasperated. "All this screwing around. Give me the twenty-five hundred now and the other twenty-five hundred in two weeks. That's fair, right?"

Gant traded one business card for twenty-five, one hundred dollar bills which he neatly slid into his inside jacket pocket. He wanted no more of Willie Rotten today.

"I'll see what I can do about your cycle first thing tomorrow," Gant said.

Willie escaped with the sidelong glance of a frightened dog.

As Mouse escorted him to his car, Gant explained the fee arrangement. Mouse accepted responsibility for it on behalf of the gang. He understood Gant set fees at the low end of fair based on the continued expectation that all members of the gang's extended family of friends injured in accidents would be strongly encouraged to hire Gant.

"How's it look, man?" Mouse said as he closed the Porsche's door with exaggerated gentleness.

"Not good. I'll look at the police reports tomorrow. Check the bike. I'll find something. But this one's extra tough. If I save his ass, you guys owe me something extra."

Mouse laughed. "Like what, a case of Chardonnay?"

"I'll think of something," Gant said

"That we can fucking count on."

Cigarettes, then The Dew Drop, Gant decided. Willie Rotten — what a perfect name for that scrawny weasel. In regular clothes, nobody even looked at him. Put him in leather on that chromed-up gleaming black Harley, and he became his own irresistible vision of something special. The biker mystique. He recalled years ago cruising down Highway 17 to Charleston. Suddenly fifty bikers appeared in his rear view. All he could think about was getting out of their way. He bounced onto the shoulder as they roared by without looking at him, like he didn't exist.

Gant drove three times around the block in search of a parking spot near his cigarette store. His cigarette store. His liquor store.

His gas station. Unless he could get deliveries or office calls, like from the dry cleaner and tailor, he did all his business like that. Gant wouldn't chance buying at some unknown convenience store because he thought that somebody dark who knew twelve words of English would stare haughty and hostile, then make him repeat 'Camels' three times before giving him the wrong brand. At his stores, the clerks called him by name, or at least 'sir', and, upon request, would exchange pleasantries about the weather or the weekend. Gant sent them flowers at Christmas.

Soot from a city bus blasted through the open window and settled on Gant's carefully coifed blond hair as he made another turn around the block. A pickup's brake lights signaled imminent departure. A mini-van, stopped in front of the departing truck, claimed the space with its flashers. Gant ignored the van and slipped into the space nose first, trailing the departing pickup as tightly as grocery carts in the check-out lane on Saturday afternoon. He hauled himself up through the door and stood eye-to-eye with the driver of the mini-van.

"You..." she said, her brain unable to communicate to her mouth the degree of betrayal turning to rage. "My space...."

Gant declined to acknowledge her existence and strode toward the store. Unwilling to temporarily abandon her vehicle, kids and dog, she loudly abused Gant's sex and race with such strident foulness as to bring reproachful murmurs from the small crowd. The van's open door and empty driver's seat attracted the attention of a passing squad car.

As Gant tossed the carton of cigarettes onto the passenger seat, the woman interrupted her discussion with the officer to point at Gant with emasculating ferocity, triggering gestures of male solidarity between the officer and Gant.

I am the king of my domain, Gant thought as he followed the officer's signal to merge with traffic. The best there is, as good as there ever was. Let the challengers, the pretenders, come with their lasers and swords, their motions to dismiss and demands to admit. Let me get them to the jury. Mano y mano. Mano y womano more and more these days. Dumb broad. Probably yelled her way into a ticket, he thought. Juries love me. Clients love me. Women love me. His feet tap danced lightly on the clutch and gas pedal. Me. Me. Me.

The charm of the Dew Drop Inn began with its gravel parking lot. Gant discovered the tavern several years ago. No ferns hung by the lighted beer signs and no video games cluttered the worn tile floor. The beer was cheap, the lights low, the music traditional, and the booths and bar stools genuine Naugahyde. Cell phones were banned. For Gant, the bar served as a refuge, a lawyer-free zone where regulars, like Lola, tolerated him.

Lola wasn't a woman of mystery — bleached blonde hair stiff with spray, watery blue eyes dominated by twin towers of black mascara and flaccid breasts escaping from a cheap knit top. She looked her part of bartender by trade and part-time hooker by profession. Gant slept with her as he needed, comfortable because Lola knew how to get up, get dressed, and get out well before the sun came up.

Gant hadn't started his day with a woman since Rebecca moved out nine years ago. Assistant District Attorney Rebecca Varner was a volcano of passion beneath a polar cap. For fifteen months, they tried to keep the professional conflict between prosecutor and criminal defense lawyer out of the bedroom, the kitchen, and the car on the way to work. They talked about changing jobs to avoid the conflict. Rebecca blinked first, offering to quit the DA's office if he'd commit to her forever. Gant declined. Shortly afterwards, for reasons known only to Gant, he accused her of passing information about one of his cases to another assistant district attorney. She hadn't done it and told him so. She also told him he was vain, selfish, and crude. Since then, although they worked in the same courthouse, it was like one lived in Bangor and the other in Bangkok.

As Gant straddled a barstool, Lola gave him a sweet smile younger than her years. The platform sandals accentuated the roll of her hips as she walked down the bar, slowly drying her hands on a white cloth. She made him a vodka gimlet, no ice, and watched him drink it while she refilled the two beer glasses of the only other people at the bar. Lola made him another and came out from behind the bar to sit next to him, putting her hand lightly far enough up inside his thigh to make him tingle. He inhaled, her cut-

rate perfume not masking the faint sweet smell of stale alcohol.
Gant waited, knowing she wanted something.

"Mr. Gant," Lola said, "I need some advice. Well, it's not for
me, actually, it's for my friend Rita."

"What's your friend's problem, Lola?"

"Well, she.... Mr. Gant, I can't lie to you. It's not her problem,
it's my problem. Will you still help? I don't want you to think bad
of me. That's why I said about Rita."

"You know I won't think bad of you. What's the problem?" Gant
said.

"Well, this boyfriend, this old boyfriend and I bought a car, in
both our names because he didn't have any credit. When we split
up, he kept the car. Now he's stopped the payments and the finance
company has been calling me. It's seven hundred and fifty dollars.
I can't pay. I tell them I don't have the car, but they keep calling.
Home. Here. They say it'll ruin my credit. Driving me bonkers.
What am I going to do?"

"Your boyfriend, your old boyfriend, has the car?"

"Yes," Lola said.

"Car worth at least seven hundred and fifty?"

"Oh, yeah, it's —."

"Don't do anything. It's his problem," Gant said.

"But my credit. If he doesn't pay...."

"Listen. If you don't pay, they'll go get the car. They'll sell it for
more than you owe, then you're free," Gant said.

"You mean they'd just take the car from him?" Gant said.

"Boom, just like that. Unless he pays."

"Oh, I can't let that happen to him. He couldn't live without his
car."

"Lola, Lola, Lola. You're too nice. You let people use you. You
should get tough. Be strong. Say no to these guys. And mean it.
Okay?"

"I know, Mr. Gant. You're right. Oh, well." Lola smiled
seductively, "You want to take me home tonight? Monday night
special. White meat platter. Plenty hot. I love the way you do me,
Mr. Gant."

"Not tonight." Gant held up his empty glass. "You do me again."

Pensive, Gant crossed the linoleum floor to the bowling machine stretched out next to the Wurlitzer in an alcove behind the booths. This dignified predigital and precomputer chip pair served as heart and soul of the Dew Drop's ambiance. Two players, both regulars, stood at the business end of the machine with their hands wrapped around thick-bottomed draught glasses. Gant watched the men take turns sliding a chrome piece, more like a hockey puck than a rice cake, toward the triangular set of ten teeth which protruded out of the hardwood alley. The machine chimed as the piece passed over the teeth and bounced off the far wall back to the players. It registered strikes and spares on a scoreboard so low-tech as to be one rung above done-by-hand in the evolutionary hierarchy of gaming devices. The game progressed steadily, but unhurriedly, reminiscent of pruning, carving, sewing. The players conversed more with themselves than their opponent. Gant watched, but didn't play. He couldn't stand the pace.

The machine's manufacturer had painted a black foul line across the alley. Without electronic sensors the machine knew nothing. It left it up to the players. Whether a hand crossed the line or not became a judgment call, an ambiguous situation, Gant thought, not unlike whether or not a person entered an intersection on a red light or consented to intercourse or intended to murder their spouse.

Ambiguity — the by-product of the daily experience, the foundation of reasonable doubt, the sanctuary for the criminally accused. Ambiguity meant accepting of the possibility that each witness could give a different account of how an event occurred. During voir dire, as he questioned potential jurors, Gant sought to eliminate those who saw life with the certainty of electronic sensors. In court, Gant used the fallibility of the human experience with the same sly skill the priest used the infallibility of the scriptures. He wanted open-armed jurors willing to embrace his client's version of reality.

Not that Gant didn't appreciate the power of technology. On the contrary he accepted it because he understood that technology, like religion, rewards its most devout disciples with the power to control the less devout. He intended to use technology, not become its victim.

One player dropped another quarter in the machine, asking Gant with his eyes if he wanted to play. Gant shook his head and looked at the bar clock, its neon frame long dead. It was nine thirty-eight.

"Another, Lola." he said, marching on the bar with glass held high like a scepter. "Lola, Lola. What a beautiful name. Lo. La. See. Say it with me. Lo. La. That's it. You have a beautiful tongue, Lo. La. Pink and broad and hard. When you lick me —."

"Mr. Gant! Shh," she said.

"Shh? Why shh? It's true. Beautiful eyes. And breasts. Beautiful breasts. Come here,

"Oh, I love.... No. Not here. Can't," she said. Lola, let me put my face between them."

"No one's watching. Anyway, no one cares. Come here, Lo. La. You're so beautiful," Gant said.

"Not that I don't want to, Mr. Gant. It's just...." Lola said.

"I'll be quick. Honest. Now come on."

"Oh...."

"Now, Lola. Get over here."

Lola stood patient as a nursing ewe in front of Gant's barstool. He hoisted each breast, exposing more overripe flesh, and buried his nose in the crevasse. He slowly drew his tongue between her breasts, across her throat, under her chin, and plunged it into her mouth. She sucked on it. He pulled away.

"Mr. Gant!" she said.

"I think you've gone far enough, young lady. Behave yourself."

"Me? You're the one."

"I'm the one?"

"That's not fair." Lola sniffed. "I...You ... Don't play with me that way. I can't take it. Not from you, Mr. Gant."

"I feel the same way," Gant said sharply, spinning a one eighty, afraid he'd laugh if she cried.

"I'm sorry, Mr. Gant," Lola said softly, a few minutes later. "Please don't be made at me. Please. I didn't mean anything."

Gant sighed. "I don't want to be mad at you." He reached out his right hand, almost touching her. "Friends?"

Lola immediately grabbed it with both hands. "Oh, yes. Forever."

"But I want you to do me a favor."

"Oh, anything."

"I need you to make a phone call."

"No, not that. I hate to play that game," Lola said.

"It's a joke, Lola. Bruce will know that." Gant imagined Bruce and Lydia reading in bed. The perfect marriage, Bruce claimed. Stronger than Wakmart.

"Those calls aren't very nice, I don't think," Lola said.

"Do it for me. I won't ask again. Honest," Gant said.

As he listened to Lola, low and sexy, Gant imagined how the look on Lydia's face changed as she handed the receiver to Bruce. After the first few words he'd treat it as something poisonous and reach over his wife to hang up the phone. Gant knew Bruce would tell him what happened afterwards.

"Thanks, Lola," he said, sliding her two twenties. "You were great."

CHAPTER TWO

Exactly two months after he met Willie, Gant watched the after lunch promenade from his corner office four floors above the square, Cheeseheads on parade. Men's jackets fell down their backs from crooked fingers and women's coats rode folded and slung like saddlebags across their arms in homage to the heat of early summer. The deep green leaves of the maples and giant oaks contrasted with their dark trunks and limbs. A profusion of petunias hung heavily over purple pansies in the city's flower beds. An elderly woman fed bread to pigeons which marched at her feet like windup toys.

The Harley kept him at the window. The biker balanced the heavy machine between his legs with the nonchalance of familiarity, watching over his shoulder as he stepped backward until the wheel gently bumped the curb. The big bike roared its arrival with each flick of the man's right wrist. Pointing at the street, its ready-to-roll position mocked the cars sedately parked nose to tail around the square.

The man killed the engine. Straddling the cycle with hands resting loosely on the grips, he moved only his head, deliberately like a lizard, seeking the people nearest him who happened to be Bruce and Lydia walking hand in hand. In one thoughtless movement, he kicked the stand down onto the gutter, lowered the bike, dismounted, and sauntered toward Bruce and Lydia who had stopped smiling.

Away from his bike, the man seemed shorter and smaller. He stopped two feet in front of the couple and dug his right hand in his jacket pocket. Bruce stepped slightly forward and to his right in front of Lydia.

Very manly, Gant thought, his lips parting in a slight sneer, but I bet your lunch is turning to liquid.

The man quickly withdrew his hand. Gant watched Bruce flinch, then relax with relief when he saw it only was a piece of paper. The man handed it to Bruce who nodded with a big grin and pointed precisely at Gant's window. The biker waved in dismissal and started across the street. Bruce laughed and put his arm around Lydia as if he had done something wonderful.

Gant clapped four times in mock applause. Bruce, Bruce, Bruce, he thought. You are so straight.

"Hey, Joan, hide your purse and keep your knees together," Gant said to his secretary. "Here comes Willie Rotten. He's a half hour early. Try the DA again."

Joan's tenure as Gant's secretary predated the partnership. Her physical appearance matched her temperament. Shaped like a palm tree - tall, skinny, with a huge thatch of frizzy red hair - Joan bent as Gant's tropical storms raged around her, but never broke. She equally distributed her life between her job, caring for her disabled husband, and wine making. She spoke seriously of the first and sadly of the second. The third made her freckles dance in animated delight.

She touched the soil of each plant on her way to Gant's desk. "He's still not in. I'll keep trying. Here's that invitation. You told me to remind you."

"Not now," Gant said without looking up.

"You told me to ignore you if you said that. So here it is." Joan dropped the folded paper in the middle of the desk and walked away. "Plants need water. If you don't do it today, I'll do it tomorrow."

In or out, he thought. The invitation to his twenty-fifth high school reunion had stuck with him like a splinter since he brought it from home three weeks ago. He wanted to go, but.... The invitation reminded him of his teenage years, a mixed bag of little victories and large embarrassments. He did not want to replay his high school years. Gant studied the names of the reunion committee members. Only one was familiar —Andrea D'Oreo. Great name.

"Give me a bite, D'Oreo, please." All the guys said it. Senior year he ate pizza with her one night while her folks were out of town. In between pieces, she plopped on the couch, dropped her shorts, and pointed at the area between her legs. "There's D'Oreo, Jake, take a big bite." He couldn't remember all he said, but part of it had been that he had to leave right away. After that night, he never said anything but "Hi, Andrea" which made her laugh. It'd be different now, Gant told himself.

She's probably baked plenty of pizza since then. Twenty-five years — He hadn't seen or spoken to any of them since he left for college, but why would he? He hadn't been back since his parents left North Carolina the year after graduation. It was a quarter century so linear as to appear digital. He was the pampered only child of a couple who knew what they wanted of their son. He was a driven undergrad and a voracious law student who tasted the blood of competitive success in mock trial wins.

Having found something he was good at for the first time in his life, he gratefully allowed his work to consume him. He became a trial lawyer with a lusty appetite for notoriety and with the ethics of a great white shark. His parents told him they were proud that he was the founding partner of an envied law firm and the inhabitant of a movie set condo. I've done it all, he thought.

Watching his city through the window, he ran his fingers over the invitation as if the printing hid additional information. Three days in August. Please join your classmates for a weekend of memories and fun. Golf. Barbecue. Dance. Tour of the high school. Day care. Bring your spouse. Official prizes for the one who traveled the farthest, has the most kids, has been married the longest, looks the youngest, has moved the least.

Gant visualized himself standing on a hotel terrace, clean shaven, maybe wearing shorts, but probably slacks and polo shirt. He holds a glass wrapped in paper napkins wet with condensation. He is telling a group of classmates about his practice, his car, his latest vacation in the Seychelles. They half listening, bored, and wait their turn. All lawyers, they radiate confidence, power, and domination. The terrace became their stage. The conversation shifts to war stories about trials, corporate takeovers, large sums of money. From one of the chairs near the pool, he hears a classmate say, "Jake Gant. Didn't he turn out just like you thought he would?"

Now if I rode up on that Harley, Gant thought looking down at Willie's bike, that would be different. They'd find out I was lawyer and I'd be a lawyer on a Harley. Big deal. No, it's got to be better than that. More real. Maybe a woman. Black jacket…

"DA," Joan said from across the office.

"Bartley, my man," Gant said. "Ready to get your ass kicked again? Yes, Bartley, don't get mad. But it's true. When was the last... Don't yell. When was the last time your office beat me? Ringsvold? You're either desperate, deluded or kidding. You charge her with murder one. She pleads to involuntary manslaughter with straight probation, and you consider that a win? I'm speechless, Bartley, I really am. Maybe you need some time off, or maybe a career change."

As the district attorney loudly defended his office, Gant paced the perimeter of his private preserve, straightening framed copies of newspaper articles about his million dollar verdicts and photographs of him spending his money skiing at Aspen and catching tarpon off the Keys.

"Wait, Bartley, don't get me wrong. I meant you should consider moving up. I hear Judge Horton is thinking about retiring. I'd support you. Think about it. Yeah, yeah, I know. Now, what can we do with Rotten?... No, he's not going to plead guilty... Yes, I know you think you have a good case. The breath test and the decapitated girl. You're right, terrible photographs. Can't imagine you'd want to show them to the jurors. Give them chronic nightmares... No, I won't agree he committed a crime. You see, Bartley, and I don't mean to lecture you here, but you see, you guys never understand that not every death is a crime. Sometimes people get killed by accident. That's what happened here... No, it's not bullshit. His tire blew out which caused the crash. Drinking had nothing to do with it. No question her estate will get a bunch from his insurance company. Too bad it won't help her any, but her dad will get a new Caddie. That's how it works. Rotten may not be a paragon of good citizenry, but he's no criminal."

Many times in their careers, Gant and Bartley had similar conversations in search of a plea bargain. The district attorney, without the staff to try every criminal case, traded a lesser punishment to the defendant for a guilty plea. Gant always pushed hard for the best deal, then let the defendant decide. After all the client would be the one sharing the ten by ten cell, not Gant. Gant knew Willie would not accept the DA's final offer.

"No deal," he said to Joan. "That's okay. I'm ready. Trying a case against Bartley is like playing tennis against a five-year-old. I'll eat him up. Let's get on with it. Send Willie in. Call our expert witnesses. I want to talk to both of them today. Then tell Larry the

Law Clerk to get me some cigarettes, and both of you get in here as soon as I'm done with Mr. Rotten."

Gant didn't speak, blink, or move as Willie, with increasing discomfort, took the long walk across the extra plush carpet past the round walnut conference table, the Remington statute, and the avocado tree to the burgundy, brass-tacked leather chair. The chair sighed when Willie sat down and murmured as he squirmed nervously. Gant waited until the biker dug at the floor with his boots in irritation. He clattered his reading glasses on the desk and spoke, his voice as flat as a snake on a hot rock.

"How much did you bring?" Gant said.

Willie swallowed. "Nothing."

"I must be missing something here," Gant said very quietly. "I give you a deal on fees — twenty-five hundred, twenty-five hundred and ten thousand. You pay twenty-five hundred, a late fifteen hundred and zip. Let me ask you this, Willie, how come you brought nothing?"

"Ain't got it," Willie said.

"Mouse know about this?"

"Yeah."

Gant buzzed Joan. "Try Mouse, now." He pointed at the window. "Who's cycle?"

"VD's."

Mouse didn't answer, Joan said. Keep trying, Gant told her.

"Pretty good of him to loan you his cycle," Gant said.

"He's my friend, man," Willie said.

"If he was really your friend, he'd sell that bike so you could pay your lawyer."

Willie snorted. "No way."

"Let me see if I've got this right," Gant said, his voice rising. "You get in trouble, you hire me, you break our agreement, and you expect me to work for free and pay for expert witnesses out of my own pocket to keep you out of jail so you can ride with your buddies, that about right?"

"Man —"

"You shut up. I'm talking." Gant loved these moments of controlled rage. He used the power of his profession to penalize wayward clients by pulverizing their spirit, sometimes for a purpose and sometimes just because it felt good. He had different techniques to exploit their vulnerability. Guilt and logic worked effectively on those who professed a set of principles. Willie, he wanted to bludgeon. Gant seasoned his language with profanity because it temporarily unbalanced clients.

"You're fucking with me and I don't like it. I'm going tell you what's fucking going to happen and you're fucking going to listen," Gant said.

"Man —" Willie said.

"Don't give me that 'man' shit. Just shut the fuck up and listen. First, you find Mouse and tell him to call me. Today. Got that?"

"Yeah."

"Second, your trial starts one week from today. Whether you pay or not, I do that trial the best I can, like you were my son. Not because I care about your fucking ass, because I don't. I do it because I care about my reputation. Nobody's going to say Jake Gant rolls over if his clients don't pay. No fucking way. Understand that?

"Yeah, hey...."

"I said shut up. You got a hearing problem?"

Willie shook his head.

"Third, you do these things by Monday. No, make it Sunday. You get clean clothes. You clean your nails. You shave that scraggly fucking beard. You get some shoes that don't look like they were meant to kick the shit out of somebody."

"Man"

"Just fucking do it.

"Fourth, I need to see each one of the Vipers who was at that party. You make sure they get here. Fifth, I just talked to the DA. He wants you to plead to a felony and do hard time. I told him to stick it up his ass. You change your mind about that?"

"No," Willie said.

"Finally, I'm going to give you a letter today that says everything I've told you so you don't forget anything. You be here on Sunday to go over your testimony. I'm going to do all I can to keep you out of prison. But, win or lose, understand I'll be coming after you for the money, even if it means taking your cycle, your house, your wife, your kids. Whatever's worth anything. Got that?"

Willie raised his arms as if in surrender. "Sorry about the money, man. You ain't got no need to talk to me like that. I'm doing the best I can. I didn't mean for any of this to happen. I know I fucked up."

"What do you want me to do, feel sorry for you? You broke our deal. Be here Sunday. That's all," Gant said. Willie stood up and walked out.

Gant paced the thick carpet in front of Larry the Law Clerk. Good kid, he thought. Smart, quiet, respectful. Full of the ignorance, innocence and faith in the law which had been undisturbed by his formal education. A student's typical bi-polar view — black or white, good or evil, right or wrong. After two years here, Gant knew, he'd understand lawyers keep these ideas displayed on a shelf like precious antiques, well-cared for but rarely used. He'd learn to use instead the gray-colored tools of the trade such as mitigating circumstances, ambiguities, and reasonable doubt.

When Gant spoke to students, one invariably asked: "How can you defend someone who is guilty?"

He thought he had a polished answer. "I believe the jury represents the most important part of the American legal system. I trust it completely. The jury decides who's guilty. Not me, not the district attorney. The law says everyone is innocent until proven guilty. If the jury doesn't think that the district attorney has presented enough evidence to prove him or her guilty beyond a reasonable doubt, then he or she isn't guilty. What I think, or the DA thinks, doesn't matter. My job is to make sure my client gets a fair trial by presenting evidence of his or her side of the story. Then it's up to the jury."

Gant was certain that he'd be accused of malpractice if he did nothing more than present the facts. If he served the jury nothing but bare truth his client would be convicted, no doubt about it. Gant knew he had to season the truth sufficiently to create uncertainty on the palates of the jurors. The legal term for uncertainty, he always told them, was reasonable doubt.

"Now," Gant said to Larry, "we'll admit that Rotten tested a point one three. It is what it is, get what I mean? In fact, I'll tell the prospective jurors right away that he had some beers. They'll get the impression I'm being straight with them. The question is, what does it mean? Same thing with those photos. Take the moral high ground. You've seen them, right? Jury will be dying to see them. They'll be repulsed. Then we want them to blame the DA for showing them the pictures. Make the DA look like a thrill-seeking pervert for unnecessarily showing those godawful things to the jury."

"They are really gross. The one of the head," Larry said.

"Ever seen shots of burn victims? They're the worst. I had a guy who torched his ex-wife's house with the kids in it. A bad man. His might be the only case I regret taking."

"What happened?" Larry said.

"I got him off. Jury found temporary insanity."

"Was he a biker?"

"Hell, no," Gant said. "You being smart?"

"No, no," Larry said. "I just wondered."

"I'm trying to teach you something. Photographs are powerful evidence because the jury always believes photos are true. Never try to tell jurors otherwise, or you will lose them. At least, you have to neutralize the photos. The best thing is to work the photos into a positive context," Gant said.

"What about videos? And tapes?"

"Same thing. If a jury hears a person say something in their own voice, you've got to really work to overcome it. Understand?" Gant said.

Larry nodded.

"Fortunately, we've got a tire instead of a tape in this case. That tire will make us a winner. You seen it yet? No, well, go look at it. Today. DA's got it. It blew out. Who knows when it happened. Maybe before he left the road, maybe when the bike crashed. Willie doesn't remember it blowing before he left the road. DA doesn't know that. Willie's memory will return Sunday when we practice his testimony. You can bet on it. Our expert will say it blew out because of the way the cords are torn. Consistent with internal failure rather than external trauma. And our other expert will swear — assuming the tire blew on the road — that Willie handled the cycle like a teetotalling pro, all based on skidmarks, gouges, measurements, and Willie's testimony. Where do these guys come from, brothels? But, hey, they're ours, right? Reasonable doubt, that's the name of this game. We're not asking the jury to find him innocent, just not guilty."

Gant instructed Larry to immediately prepare a brief for the judge establishing Rotten's right to an affirmative defense based on an intervening cause.

"Find some cases that say the defendant's not guilty if the death would have occurred even if he were sober," Gant said as Larry scribbled the instructions on a yellow pad. "That's where the blown tire comes in. Death by chance, I call it. Do another one on the photos. Not long. Judge Harris lets in everything, so she'll let them in. I don't really care, but I want the DA to think I do. Then do the usual challenging the constitutionality of the statute, in case we lose. Got all that? Good. You're not doing anything important this weekend, are you?"

"Well, actually —" Larry said.

"Good. Be here Saturday and Sunday. Help prepare witnesses. And then sit with me at trial."

"But I've got classes and —" Larry said.

"Classes?" Gant snorted. "Come on, you'll learn more watching me than you will from a month of classes. I thought you wanted to be a lawyer."

Larry swallowed with difficulty. "I'll be here. That's great. Thanks, Mr. Gant." He hurried from the office.

"No calls, except Mouse and the experts," Gant said to Joan. Alone in his paneled office, he felt the glandular quickening which signaled an approaching jury trial. It's a climactic event. Except for the extremely rare occasion of a successful appeal, the loss is final for client and lawyer.

Although five years had passed since Gant, drained and helpless, last watched sheriff's deputies haul a client from courtroom to jail, the accompanying public display of failure remained fresh. After his client left, people fled his presence as if he were contagious. Because he abhorred appearing as a loser, Gant vowed to try only winnable criminal cases and cut plea agreements on the others. Willie's case, he recognized, was a macho saunter to the far edge of winnable. Willie needed a good jury, strong testimony from the experts, and a brilliant performance from his lawyer.

As he kneaded the facts and law into his trial strategy, Gant tended his impressive collection of plants — the giant red amaryllis in full bloom on the antique pedestal by his desk, the ficus trees, their trunks braided, as greeters by the door, a hanging pothos in each window, the prayer plant, which Joan periodically removed for a dose of stinky fish emulsion, on the conference table. The plants gave Gant fresh air and were his sole source of inner peace in his isolated and insular world. He watered, fed, and spritzed them with the care of a dutiful parent.

Shortly before five, Joan interrupted his trial preparation to remind him of the partnership meeting.

"You're a sweetheart. Always good news," Gant replied sarcastically. "What are my messages? Important ones." He listened until she held up the last slip like it was trump.

"And? I can tell by your look. What is it?"

"She's called three times this afternoon. A Joy Friendly. Said she'd take you to small claims unless you paid her ticket. Something about a parking place. It didn't make much sense." Joan looked confused.

"You're kidding." Gant snorted. "I don't believe it. Dingy broad. I don't have time for this."

"What do you want me to tell her? She will call again."

"I know what I'd tell her. I don't care. She's nuts. God. Try Mouse again." Gant searched for a pad to take to the meeting.

The partnership resembled the relationship of a couple who married for love and stayed together because of the kids. The more successful the firm of Gant, Johnson and Jones became, the more money they made; the more money they made, the more they bought and so on. The daisy chain lengthened constantly, each knot the shape of a dollar sign.

Gant defended the criminally accused and represented those injured by the negligence of others. Rich Johnson specialized in commercial litigation, protecting the interests of business in the courtroom, and Jeb Jones took care of businesses outside the courtroom, making sure they made as much money and paid as little tax as possible. As friends, the men formed the firm a few years after they graduated from law school. Through the years, their personal relationship spiraled down from friendship to acquaintanceship to mere civility. Equally successful and distrustful of each other, they were as mutually dependent as the legs of a tripod. The partners convened for necessary business once a month under a white flag.

"It's Mouse," Joan said, holding out her phone as he passed her desk on the way to his partners.

"What are you trying to do to me here?" Gant said into the receiver. "Yeah? Hang on, I'm changing phones."

He listened as Mouse explained the Vipers' attempts to raise money. Five thousand, maybe six thousand by trial time with the rest indefinitely later. Gant suggested selling a cycle and said he'd take Willie's, if it was whole. Mouse didn't respond.

"Maybe this works," Gant said. "Maybe. I got this idea. Twenty-fifth reunion this summer. Thinking I'd go as a biker."

Mouse was silent for awhile. "You shitting me?" he finally said.

"Just a maybe. Depends on whether I decide to go."

"What is it, a costume party?"

Gant ignored him. "Vipers owe me money. Maybe they would fix me up with a bike. Clothes. Everything. We'd be even on fees. Not sure. Idea only."

"You mean you'd forget five grand in fees if we made you a biker for, what, a weekend?"

"Yeah, maybe. I want to make an impression, you know, shock everybody," Gant said.

"Sounds fucking crazy," Mouse said. "Which high school?"

"Not around here. North Carolina."

"Well, shit, man, we can't that far —"

"Details. Let's be clear. Win or lose, Willie owes me money. If he doesn't pay, I'm all over him. I'll take his bike, his truck, his dog, whatever. I know the Vipers take care of their own.. Maybe you know someone out there. Might work for everybody. Just think about it."

"Yeah, why not," Mouse said.

"Most important now is the trial. You make sure everyone's here over the weekend. Their stories have to match or the jury will never believe Willie. All right. Got to go. My partners are waiting to ream me out over this case," Gant said and hung up.

CHAPTER THREE

Check out that body language, Gant thought, entering the private and soundproofed small conference room. Jeb's arms and legs were crossed as tightly as cooked pasta. The close-cut pepper hair framed a face of cardboard, sunken eyes guarded by black, fat-rimmed glasses. A blue and yellow striped tie was snug against the top button of his white shirt.

Rich dressed like a man comfortable with his body. The coat to his stylish suit hung neatly from the back of the chair and the sleeves of the blue button-down shirt were rolled up twice, exposing the muscular forearms and the big Rolex. Gant remained standing, his hand resting lightly on the burled oak cabinet.

"Glad you found time to join us, Jake," Jeb said sarcastically as Rich ran thumb and forefinger around the outside of his watch.

"Pretty clever. Think up that routine by yourselves?" Gant replied. "Let's get on with it."

"My secretary saw a biker in the reception room," Rich said. "Said she could smell him. What was he doing here?"

"We agreed, Jake," Jeb said. "No more bikers. They make other clients, good clients, nervous."

Gant stepped forward, challenging both of them. "First, Jeb, screw your clients. Second —"

"Now, wait...."

"You wait. You talked. My turn. Second, Rich, your secretary is so scared she needs an escort to go to the bathroom."

"Leave Carol out of this."

"She is out of it. Always has been," Gant said.

"This is a serious matter," Jeb said, red drifting across his face and intensifying. "We must guard our image. We know sometimes your personal injury clients are, well, not the people we'd like in our waiting room. But they've been hurt and their cases bring the firm substantial fees, so we tolerate them. But the bikers —"

"The bikers," Rich said, "are nothing but nostalgic playthings for you. They're lewd, dirty bums and I don't want them around. The firm is beyond that now."

"Tough. They've sent us a lot of good cases...." Gant said.

"Christ," Jeb said. "Give it a rest. Bikers, smikers who gives a shit. The problem is you two are in each other's face every time we meet. We used to be friends, remember? Then we became successful. Now each meeting reminds me of a bad movie. I agree with you, Rich, the bikers are a problem, but let's not bust up the firm over it."

"We've been through this," Rich said. "He agreed to see them away from the office."

"That's true. And I have been," Gant said. "But this guy's trial starts next Monday. I needed him to come in. Gives him confidence in me when he sees the office. And me control. We all do this. If I need to see a client — biker anybody — in my office, I will. If your clients have a problem with that, you deal with it."

"Hey, we're your partners here," Jeb said. "Listen, you're right. The bikers have sent us a lot of good cases. At one time we needed them. Obviously, they are still important to you. Personally, I don't care as long as they pay their bills. But my clients, Jake, they don't like to be in the same room as those guys. And they don't like it that their lawyer's law firm represents bikers."

"What?" Gant said. "Your clients are going to decide who I can represent?"

"No, I'm not saying that," Jeb said. "I'm saying we have to think what works for the whole firm. Just think about it. We know you have a case to try. Tell us about it."

Gant summarized the case, emphasizing its difficulty. He explained about the need for experts, the number of witnesses, the photographs, and the breath test.

"Who's trying it for the DA's office?" Jeb said.

"Bartley, himself. Surprised me. Rotten caught a break there," Gant said.

"It could have been Rebecca. I'd pay to watch you two in court," Rich said, smiling. "I always liked her."

"Rich, you know...," Gant said.

"How about fees," Jeb said, quickly.

Gant told them about the status of the payment of fees, omitting his discussion with Mouse about bartering fees for the reunion. Jeb and Rich berated him, complaining that he didn't charge enough, that he should have gotten more money up front, that he probably wouldn't get paid, and that he was giving away valuable time free.

They might need to talk about adjustments, they said, in Gant's slice of the profit cake.

"Then, Jeb," Gant said evenly, "you'll want to talk about the same adjustment to Rich's share for the free time he gives his black organizations."

"Wait a minute," Rich said, glaring at Gant. "That's different."

"Why? Because they're black?" Gant said. "And, Rich, what about the time Jeb spends on the golf course with his business buddies? The only money changing hands is bets."

"Nice try, Jake, you dog you," Rich said with a chuckle, "but Jeb and I are together on this one. His business people, my organizations, represent high quality clients, the kind of clients we want for our firm. The bikers are scum, bottom feeders that belong downtown at one of the legal clinics. You want to be their attorney for nothing. That costs us money. If it keeps up, we may have to take this money from your share. We're not threatening. We want what's best for the firm. And can we agree, after this case, no more bikers in the office?"

"You guys. What, you've been to some office management seminar? Trying to squeeze me. I can't believe it." Gant laughed. "What are you going to do? Leave? Give me a break. I bring in millions of dollars in fees. You couldn't make it without me. The bikers are good clients and I'm their lawyer. Now excuse me, it's poker night." He left without closing the door.

"He doesn't get it," Jeb said. "He'll never give up those bikers."

"Yeah," Rich said. "And he has plenty of good clients without them. I think he keeps them to piss us off."

"He's right about the amount of fees he brings in. Damn good lawyer. Be tough to meet overhead without him."

"I agree with all that. But sometimes I think he's out of control, like a flooding river. I hear things. Some attorneys settle because they don't want to go to trial with him. He's too crazy, they say," Rich said.

"What's wrong with that?" Jeb said. "That's good for us."

"Yeah, but being crazy lives right next to being out of control. I don't want my ass washed away because of him." Rich hesitated and leaned toward his partner. "Do you have a minute?"

Jeb checked his watch. "I've got about twenty minutes. I have dinner with clients at the club. Power company people. What's up?"

"I want you two to buy me out," Rich said.

"Why?" Jeb walked to the corner and picked up a putter which he balanced lightly in his hands.

"It's a political matter. You and I have an understanding it goes no further, right?"

"Sure."

"They have selected me as their optimum candidate for the Seventh Congressional District next year. I want to do it," Rich said.

"Congress? Against Calkins? He's a perennial lock. They've put stars in your eyes," Jeb said.

"I don't agree. He's old and out of touch. If I run, they promised no primary and full financial support. I'll go door-to-door. You know how hard I work. I believe I can win."

"You know better than me. Let me think about it. But why leave the firm?"

"It's Gant," Rich said.

"Gant?" Jeb said.

"They say I'm in his shadow."

"Figuratively, of course."

"He gets the press. His clips hang in our lobby. Our lobby. How are we known? As 'the Gant firm'. Here is their point. I'd be 'Rich Johnson, an attorney with the Gant firm.' Think about who he represents. How could I be tough on drug dealers when he's getting them off? How can I extol family values when he hangs out with motorcyclists in the courthouse? Besides, he's become a real egotistical, racist, son of a bitch.."

"What do you want from me?"

"Your support on the buy-out. With Rachel not working, I'll need the cash to support us and pay for Keesha during the campaign."

Jeb recalled the Monday night thirteen years ago. The three partners were at Rich's watching the Packers play the Bears on a snowy Monday night. Rachel, deep in the eighth month of her pregnancy, screamed from the bedroom. Jeb and Jake followed the ambulance and waited with Rich while the doctors performed an emergency cesarean. Keesha had twisted in the womb causing the umbilical cord to tighten around her throat and restrict the flow of oxygen to her brain. The surgery had saved Keesha's life, but did not prevent severe, permanent brain damage. Rich and Rachel raised Keesha at home, despite the urgings of doctors and social workers to transfer her to a care center.

"I'm willing to sell out for a quarter of a million. That's less, I'm quite sure, than the value, which would be set by an appraiser. I'd take half in cash and a two-year note for the rest," Rich said. "Time is important to me."

"We don't have that kind of money," Jeb said.

"I know we may have to borrow. The money will continue to roll in. You'd be paying the bank every month instead of me. You know that. Will you support me?" Rich said.

"You've got my vote at the polls, but not for a loan. I like being debt-free. I don't care for Jake any more, either. But life is good for me. I play golf with clients who pay me. One day I'll get the proverbial offer I can't refuse. Or Jake will self-distruct. Until then I support the status quo, even if it means being known as a partner in the Gant firm," Jeb said. "But if Jake will agree to a loan, I'll go along to help you out."

"I'm in a bind. I'll talk to Gant. You in the office tomorrow?"

"Everyday. Give my best to Rachel and the kids."

*

Keesha slept in a crib specially constructed to accommodate her height. The multi-colored nightshirt covered the bulky diapers and disappeared under the light quilt which hid her feet. Every day, Rachel dressed her as if she would be joining her friends at school. Rich set up a television that ran constantly because she appeared to respond to the flickering light. She had greatly outlived her doctor's expectations.

As he did every night, Rich released the side of the crib and sat on the bed. He gently wiped a string of saliva from his daughter's chin. Her breathing was slow and regular. Rich rested the back of his hand on her cheek. She did not respond. In this room he thought only of his wife and their children.

Rachel interrupted to tell him a supporter urgently needed to speak with him. Reluctantly, he wished the girl he called "my living doll" good night and quietly closed the door, as if he could disturb her sleep.

*

Gant was still thinking about his partners when he arrived at the restaurant for his regular pre-poker game dinner with Bruce. As he had hoped, Lydia wasn't there.

In the last fifteen years, Bruce had aged from the inside out, as men often do. His skin was unwrinkled except for smile lines at the eyes, and his hair color was unchanged. He listened to oldies and wore his clothes until Lydia discarded them. Years ago, Bruce installed home security systems to supplement his pay as a high school English teacher. Gant had used the fee from his first big personal injury case to buy a condo and decided he needed security. Bruce lacked a necessary switch box. While they waited for the part, Gant told stories about his cases. One involved a football player accused of betting on games. Their discussion of games of chance led to Bruce's invitation to his monthly poker game. Gant became a regular at one of the very few social events he wrote in his day book. Although the stakes were low, he played seriously and aggressively as if he were in a Las Vegas casino instead of Bruce's rec room. The men often met for dinner before the game. Gant got to unload into a safe ear. Bruce listened, attentive and fascinated, and took notes with the thought of writing a TV screen play.

"No Lydia?" Gant said, sucking on an olive. "Glad you're back together. I saw you two on the square today, with the biker. Looked like you were going to lose your lunch."

"I'm used to seeing kids dressed like that, not grown men on the square. I admit I was intimidated. He wanted directions to you. For some reason, I didn't think bikers asked directions. He a client?" Bruce said.

Gant careened through the story of Willie Rotten, describing himself as the champion of the underdog. Alone, he faced the wrath of the DA , his partners and, next week, that of the judge and jury.

"Speaking of wrath,' Gant said, "how's Lydia?"

"Still not right between us." Bruce recounted how her anger heated faster than grease on a grill after Lola's telephone call. The more he denied the affair, the more convinced Lydia became of its truth. She had left for her sister's so quietly Bruce didn't think she was gone. He'd call, she'd hang up. She threatened him with the cops if he didn't leave her alone. He missed classes. The whole thing went on for almost three weeks.

"Finally, you told me you had the call made," Bruce said. "She didn't believe me. You had to call her and explain. And Lola, too. Remember? Lydia won't forgive you."

"It was just a joke. She overreacted, the way I see it. I'll talk to her," Gant said.

"No, no. You stay away from her. No joke, Jake," he paused while the waitress brought their order. "I thought about our relationship, you and me. Strange, we meet so you can tell me your stories. Don't get me wrong, I've liked them. But...strange. Your joke did me wrong."

"Lighten up," Gant said.

"I'm serious. Someday, you'll be in a relationship and someone will do you back," Bruce said.

"No way. I don't get into relationships I can't control. Never."

Bruce's head jerked as if slapped. "Thanks. I feel a lot better," he said dryly.

The men moved briskly through their meal discussing, as if it mattered, the crispness of the greens, the lightness of the Alfredo sauce, the fullness of the wine. Gant mentioned his plan to possibly attend his reunion as a biker.

"What do you think?" Gant said.

"Another joke?" Bruce said.

"Maybe. Harmless, though."

"Yeah, I guess it sounds like something you'd do."

Bruce declined dessert, saying he wanted to get home to Lydia before the game. On the sidewalk he said, "Can I ask you a personal question?"

"Sure. Why not?"

"Is there anything you care about?"

"Nothing," Gant said, his eyes cold and hooded, "nothing except who I've become. Why?"

CHAPTER FOUR

Mirrors covered the walls of the living room in Molli's small apartment. Mismatched, cracked, and chipped, the mirrors hung with an anarchistic disregard for symmetry and meandered around windows and behind the ratty blue couch where Meryl the cat slept.

When Molli practiced her lines in the middle of the room, the mirrors critiqued her performance with the same range of expressions as a live audience. One four-foot mirror in the corner by the door to the kitchen devilishly compacted all six-feet of Molli submissively inside its frame. In the floor-to-ceiling mirror in the opposite corner, she towered enraged over her imaginary husband.

She read her lonely woman parts naked and saw her whole body flush as she uttered protestations to her demon lover before he took her in the hayloft of her father's barn. Her long muscled legs danced a rectangular chorus line around her and the invisible count as they waltzed across the oval rag rug from her mother's living room.

After high school, Molli had gone on the fantasy circuit where stardom arrives with the frequency of a lunar eclipse. She bounced back and forth between broken promises in New York and Hollywood until she understood that success was nothing but a word on someone else's lips.

As she was the victim of her dreams, so was she their student, learning self-preservation, persistence, and patience.

Against her mother's wishes, Molli had driven to Miami with a girl friend because she had heard that it would be next hot spot in the movie industry. She discovered that she was in demand by certain segments of the film producing community because she had fair skin and blonde hair, and could actually act. When Molli's boozing and abusing father filed for divorce, her devastated mother called for help. Molli immediately returned to coastal North Carolina, reserving the pursuit of a career in foreign films for another day.

She held her mother's hand during the divorce, enduring vicious accusations by her father. The trial left her mother financially crippled with only a small sum to supplement her social security.

They found her a first floor efficiency she could afford not far from the church and hauled the keepsakes over in her car. They slept together on the fold out until her mother stopped crying herself to sleep. Their daily conversations became unnecessary as her mother grew accustomed to the sights and sounds of city life, including a infestation of insects, in a deteriorating neighborhood. Molli still visited every Saturday afternoon and promised she'd buy her mother a house in the country when she became a star.

Molli temporarily reconciled herself to establishing a career in Wilmington, grateful for the city's bigtime movie studio. In early years, her hands advertised soap and her calves a razor. Her face, Nordic white skin stretched tight over high cheekbones and beaked nose, was proud as a prow on a Viking ship. She competed with beauty pageant contestants for bimbo parts, but she had the wrong body shape. Molli gained experience playing the supporting roles. As Molli plowed into her mid-thirties, she experienced a slight upturn in the demand for a woman formidable in appearance and delivery. She won bigger parts more frequently and reviews mentioned her by name. Audition and perform. Persevere and achieve.

It took Molli years to discover that she and her teachers sought the same goal - the creation, by speech and manner, of the perfect illusion. After additional years, she realized perfection was unattainable and, like Japanese potters, accepted the flaws as tributes to the gods. She held herself out as a sculpture and let her teachers chip and polish with criticism and praise. Molli had faith that these classes were connected with the same certainty as links on a chain. At the end of the chain she'd find a key to a room with a dressing table and a mirror and her name above the star on the door.

She understood why her mother couldn't understand her obsession .

"You go to church, Mom. It's the same thing." That always ended the conversation.

The money she earned from acting and from waitressing at the gay sports bar fed her personal needs, Meryl, and an old Buick named Ingrid. After the necessities, all money went for acting classes.

Molli found the ad on the board at the academy. "Filmmaker needs good-looking woman strong enough to handle Harley," and the phone number of some place in the next county. She hadn't driven a cycle since her friend's little Honda in high school, but figured, like cars, they'd be pretty much the same. In front of her mirrors in a leather jacket borrowed from costume with a black wig over her ultra-short white-blonde hair, she decided she looked the part.

The directions took Molli thirty minutes from her apartment near the university to where the country fell into the Atlantic. Cycles haphazardly parked outside a converted filling station identified Straight Ahead Cycle. Molli went through the door marked "Repairs and Sales. Harleys Only." Conversation stopped. Five men stared at her like they had heard about women, but never seen one. She asked for Mr. Flick. One of them pointed at the back door. Another, wiry with an amused expression, offered to guide her and put his arm around her waist. Molli introduced the steel toe of her boot to the inside of his left ankle. He yelped and bowed in pain.

The door opened into an immaculate shop area filled with Harleys in various stages of assembly. Blackened fingers pointed her to another set of doors. Inside, a huge man, at least eight inches taller than Molli, with a gray beard to his stomach, photographed a formidable and pristine motorcycle which stood in the center of the sparsely furnished, large, windowless white room. The commercial camera looked the size of a tourist's point-and-shoot in his enormous hands. She held her questions until he turned off the camera.

"Mr. Flick?"

"No 'Mr.' Just Flick. You the woman for the ad? You're big enough." Molli's hand was large, but Flick's covered hers like it was a piece of gum going into a purse. His brown eyes, glittering with curiosity, clinically appraised her body, like a woodsmen measuring a tree. He appeared to be smiling at her. "You're tall for an actress."

Oh, no, Molli thought, not this.

"I collect movies. I've noticed actresses are mostly short. Wonder why?" he said.

"Yeah, I wonder," Molli said scornfully.

"What kinds of tall woman things have you done?"

"Is this like an interview, or are you fooling around?" she said.

"Like an interview. You got a problem with that?"

"I've done ads, for the money. I've done serious theater, Chekov, Ibsen, like that, and comedies and musicals although my singing isn't the best. I've won some awards at local theaters. A few years ago I was an extra in the Eastwood film at the White House. I don't do bimbos or porn. I've been acting since high school. One day I'll be a star. What else do you want to know?"

"That Eastwood film, it wasn't his best. I collect films. I've got all of his."

"Really," Molli said, disinterested. "So, do I pass?"

"What, you don't like films?" Flick said.

"Oh, no, I like them a lot," Molli said.

"But you don't like Eastwood?"

"That's not it. I watch a film for the acting. You know, like you said, it wasn't his best."

"That's cool. Who do you like?"

"Meryl Streep. I'd give it all to spend time with her."

"Sit," he said, arranging two white plastic porch chairs.

He gave her his right profile, sitting expectantly as if waiting to hear a cue from some unseen director. A scar, jagged as lightening, traced a path from the bridge of his nose to his right cheek. He wears a mask, Molli thought, as she realized the permanency of his half-smile. She also noticed the blue beginning of a tattoo on his bicep below his shirt sleeve. His right leg stretched out so the foot rested against one of her chair legs.

"What's your name?"

"Molli."

"Last name?"

"No," she said, surprised he put it as a question.

"Like Madonna."

"Not quite. So, what's the deal?"

He took a breath out of sequence. A new motorcycle clothing company wanted low-budget shots for ads, he said. They wanted a woman driving the bike, not riding behind. He said they'd take some still shots inside, then go outside for the action shots. He'd pay her cash at the end of day.

"You've driven Harleys, right?" Flick said.

"No," Molli replied, detailing her experience with the Honda.

Flick leaned close enough that Molli could smell the tuna on his breath. He yelled at her, sounding like full bass at eighteen inches.

"Why are you here? The ad said you had to drive," he said.

Molli escaped by taking the Harley, swinging her leg over it and squeezing the cycle between her thighs. From her notebook, she read the ad to Flick. "'Filmmaker needs good looking woman strong enough to handle Harley.' It's ambiguous at best. Look, I'm handling it. Show me how to start it and I'll ride it out of here."

So this is what it's about, Molli thought. The power and weight and heat of the machine pounded between her legs as she followed Flick on her check-out ride. It was nothing fancy - down the quiet country road through the gentle "S" to the stop sign. Going the other direction, Molli couldn't keep up in the tight turns and dropped her foot when she traced Flick's U-turn. Otherwise, she knew she did better than okay. She shut it down next to his bike and straddled it aware that some of the men turned their backs at her approach.

She batted at a bee buzzing her right ear. It immediately sought refuge inside the front collar of her jacket. Startled, she yanked it open and brushed it free. This disturbed her delicate balance sufficiently to cause her left foot to slide on the thin layer of loose gravel on top of the asphalt. The bike tipped and wanted to lie down. Molli quickly swung her right leg over and caught the six hundred pound bike as it fell to a seventy degree angle. She closed her eyes, held her breath, and strained against the dead weight of the hot hunk of metal, but couldn't raise it. The engine heat slowly toasted her hands. The soles of her feet were slipping, and her shoulders burned and she choked on fear-induced phlegm. None of the men moved to help her.

Molli bent until her jeans bound her knees, dipped her shoulders, pushed from the bottom of her feet and groaned with concentration, transferring all her power to the points where her hands pressed against the motorcycle. The beast moved easier as it approached upright. Flick waited until the last five degrees before grabbing a handlebar to help.

"That's my son's bike you almost lost," he said.

Molli stumbled wheezing and coughing into a sitting position on the hot gravel, with the exhilarated exhaustion of a marathon winner. She squinted through perspiration at him like he were an alien.

Flick leaned against the bike. "You're damn strong. Stronger than some men I've ridden with. They'd of let it drop. Of course, it would have been their own bike. Get the lady some water, one of you, before she dies on us.

"As far as I'm concerned, women don't belong on a Harley unless they're behind their man. Nothing personal. Of course, I feel the same way about the stockbrokers and doctors and lawyers riding around in their short sleeve shirts. Don't know the difference between a panhead and a shovelhead. I even saw one wearing shorts last week. At a stop sign he grinned at me like we shared a secret. I wanted to take him out. Right then and there. I really did.

"Only a certain kind of people deserve Harleys. Matter of karma. Takes a commitment to a way of life. Like knights, or the samurai. Like me. I've been racing with the wind for thirty years. Gangs. Solo. I've done it all. I'm bragging, because I can prove it. Have to kill me to get my colors.

"True American phenomenon. Sometime maybe I'll tell you about this film I want to do. Right now the ad. You up to it or not?" he said.

"I need the money." Molli went to redo her face and reset her wig. Crazy samurai filmmaker, she thought. God, that bike was heavy. They stand around waiting for me to drop it. Then that asshole brings me hot water to drink. Get done, get paid, get out of here, she concluded.

Flick imagined Molli acting like calendar art cheese and Molli, snarly as a bull dyke, wanted to portray the get-out-of-my-way attitude of someone just in from East L.A.. Over Diet Cokes they agreed the part called for a fun-loving biker babe able to take care of herself. Molli finally smiled as Flick's rough looking friends, with chilly respect, delivered to her various jackets and assorted accessories like clerks in a boutique. She chuckled at the contrast between their scrubbed hands and arms and their dirty jeans and black T-shirts. She actually enjoyed their unabashed, open-mouthed admiring stares as she stretched her arms putting jackets on and off in front of the full length mirror in the large room.

Flick recruited someone from his shop to help move the inside lights around to eliminate shadows on Molli. Outside, he paid particular attention to camera angle relative to the changing light of the late afternoon sun.

"Cool," Flick said after he got his last outside shot of Molli driving by looking independent and stunning in wrap around sunglasses and a fringed pink leather jacket. "I enjoyed working with you. You are a pro."

"Thanks. It was okay. You're good with the camera" Molli said.

"Keep the jacket. My client will never miss it."

"I couldn't."

"Call it a bonus. It looks good on you. Not many women could wear it."

"Pink's not really my color. Oh, okay, I'll take it. Just for fun. Can I get paid now? I need to go feed my cat."

Flick reacted as if she hadn't spoken. "Here, let me show you what I got here for a studio." Molli saw the stack of twenties interwoven between his fingers, shrugged, and followed him on his tour through the back of the building.

Crude magic marker signs identified each room in the complex. Two more studios, dressing rooms, wardrobe room, screening room, office, conference room, spaces for the lighting and sound technicians. Designed as a birthplace for innovative sounds, the complex stood silent. Created as the home of action, it remained empty. The complex waited with the stoic hollowness of a hotel without guests or furnishings, its rooms vanilla shells destined either as virginal containers of fulfilled dreams or grim caskets for stillborn visions.

Molli listened as Flick explained how he had used the money from his motorcycle repair business and other unspecified endeavors to finish the complex. He unlocked a huge padlock on the storage room door to show her the equipment he had acquired. From the latest cameras for studio work to the smallest hidden microphones to capture the memories and opinions of the difficult and the wary.

"I know this may be a dumb question, but why? What's all this for?" Molli said.

"For my movie, about Harleys and the men who ride them. About death and comradeship and having something to believe in. About Sturgis and Daytona. About gangs and the initiations and riding one hundred in formation flat out across the desert. About the women and the kids. It's American, like rock and roll and apple pie. It'll be far out. It's a great story. Beautiful faces. Action. Amazing characters. Fascinating. I mean nothing has to be made up. And you know what? It's never been done.

"And I'm the one to do it. I know everybody. Every gang. Every event for the last thirty years. I attended all the big ones. And I've taught myself about films. I've studied the great ones. Peckinpaugh. Ford. Tarantino. I know I'm an artist. I could be right up there with them," Flick said.

"Are you serious? You are serious," she said.

"More than serious. It came to me like a revelation. It's my life's work."

"How far along are you?"

"I haven't started. I need bread. Financing. It'll be expensive because it's mostly on location. Once they see what I've got, investors will line up like bikers at the beer tent. Financing. I'll get it, whatever I have to do. Almost whatever. Here, dig this."

"I should go," Molli said.

"You know who would do this?" Flick said. "Honda, that's who. My son told some people he knows at Honda about my idea. I can see it — 'Riceburner Productions presents The Story of the American Biker' or some soft shit like that. No fucking way. I'll do anything but that for the money."

"That the son with the bike I used?"

"No, that belongs to the youngest. The oldest is a lawyer. This year he's teaching something to do with securities law at Kyoto University in Toyko." Flick shook his head. "Don't think he's been on a cycle since he was eight or nine."

"How many children do you have?" she said.

"Three. Daughter's a psychologist in the Air Force. She calls once a month to tell me I'm crazy," he said.

"And the youngest?"

"He's around." Flick looked away. "Got to find financing soon."

"Yeah, money's always the thing," she said. "Well, say, when you get it, give me a call. I'll be your star."

"That's cool. Ah, you know, July Fourth ride this weekend," he said. "My old lady's going, but if you want to come along, Molli, I'll find you someone to ride with."

"Thanks, I've got plans. And I don't do back seats."

"I dig it," he said.

"I've got to go," she said.

"I've got something to do tonight."

"So?" Molli said, gesturing at the money in his hand. "You going to pay me?"

"We're a cash operation. You don't mind, do you?" Flick said as he dropped bills on the seat of the motorcycle in the main studio. Molli nodded, mouthing the increments. At one hundred twenty, he quit counting to answer the phone. Flick was screaming by the second sentence.

Give me eighty dollars more and I'm out of here, Molli thought. Flick's rage reminded Molli of her father. She was almost ready to walk out with the one hundred and twenty dollars and forget the rest when his voice died down like the wind at dusk..

"Stay cool, Dannyboy," Flick said into the phone. "Don't do anything stupid, like talk to the wrong people about this. I can always find you. Yeah, later."

Molli eyed the money. Count out four more and let me out of here, she thought. Christ, he's walking away, mumbling to himself about a truck, a job, being a man short, and who's he going to find this late in the game.

"Come on, Flick, give me the rest of the money. I need to go. Please," she said.

"Yeah, hey, dig this. For a month I'm counting on this guy to help me out tonight. Big money. Now, what time is it? Six-fifteen. An hour before we're supposed to split, he calls to say something came up with his family. Old Dannyboy better not be messing with me or his family will be very sad. Where am I going to find someone else?" Flick said, looking at her like he found the answer.

"Don't even think it, Flick. I've got to go. Honest."

"Two hundred and fifty, Molli. Help us load. Couple hours, maybe three."

"Do I look like a mover? Sorry. No way. Give me my money and I'm gone."

"All right, five hundred dollars. I'm in a bind."

"Five hundred dollars?"

"Five hundred dollars."

That pays for a class, Molli thought. "I'm not saying yes, but what exactly would we be loading?"

"Bikes."

"Whose bikes? Details," she said.

"They belong to these guys."

"Stop it. I'm not doing twenty questions here."

Molli listened detached, like she was watching a film. Look what's going on up there. What an adventure. I wonder what it would be like to do something like that? That couldn't really happen.

"Like I said, I'll do almost anything for financing," Flick said. "Dig this. Everybody wants a Harley, especially a new one that's got the improvements and not the maintenance hassles. You have to love your bike to own an old one. They can only manufacture so many. They're sold before the dealer sees them. But the demand is still there. High demand means high prices which means high profits for a risk-taking opportunist like me. Where to get more bikes, that's the question. I could give you some pseudo revolutionary crap about liberating Harleys from the wannabes —"

"Spare me," Molli said.

"Right on. From time to time we rip off a bike, not from any brother, of course. One here and there is tedious. Tonight we're going to get a dozen from a parking lot of a rich church in Cary. They belong to a group called the Christian Wheelmen. I filmed them in a parade. I can't believe they're part of Harley history, but I'm fair and in the end, everybody winds up in the movie. Anyway, these bikes get new owners. I get some financing. The owners wind up mildly inconvenienced. Who cares? They'll live. The insurance companies take the hit. That's cool. I mean anytime you can make an insurance company pay, that's cool. They've got all the money." He paused. "You're in, right?"

"Not for $500, I'm not," she said.

"What'll it take?"

Be strong, girl, Molli thought. Twenty five hundred dollars had a good sound.

"What?" Flick said loudly.

"Twenty five hundred. Cash. Upfront. Plus the ad money."

"You're ripping me off. Fifteen hundred. That's it."

"Listen," she said, "I've never been in trouble before. You want me to commit a crime. What if I'm caught. It would absolutely kill my mom. My, god. My career. My future. I can't believe I priced myself so low."

"Here's your eighty dollars. I'll find someone else. See you," he said.

Both disappointed and relieved, Molli got to, but not in, her car before she heard the big boots on the gravel immediately behind her. She spun around, her knee ready. Flick pulled her hard to him with one arm and jammed a stack of bills into the top of her shirt with the other hand, his rough knuckles scraping the top of her breast. She tensed, feeling his thigh tight against her and his fingers resting on her ribs. What the hell, let him kiss me, she thought. Molli relaxed, eyes closed, and waited. She opened her eyes to a crocodile grin and her nose to his tuna breath.

"That's fifteen hundred dollars. Another grand when we're done. Let's play poker sometime," Flick said. "I bet you're one far out kind of player."

Flick, she thought. That name. The way he talks. The beard. Perfect throwback. Probably has a wife called Sue and kids named after spices.

CHAPTER FIVE

The truck side vibrated against her back. Molli recalled trips to the feed store with her brothers in the back of the pickup, her mom and dad quiet in the cab. Instead of sunshine and the smell of fresh cut hay, Molli rode in utter darkness with the odor of sweat and tuna. She used the silence to consider her set of new options provided by the afternoon's events. She could quit her job and use the twenty seven hundred dollars to pay for five classes at once. Or she could keep her job and take three classes next session, and probably save enough to take three more the following session. For sure, she'd take her mom for a weekend at the beach and pay a pest control company to spray her mom's apartment for six months.

The voice on Flick's walky-talky a few feet away startled her. "We're here. Looks clear."

Molli recognized the movement as the big delivery truck, stolen from a furniture store, made a slow turn. She helped Flick and another man whose name she had forgotten slide out a ramp until it protruded from the truck's bay like a tongue.

"Dig the Mustang," Flick said to the other man as they ran the first of the motorcycles up the ramp. As soon as it was in the truck, Molli rolled it forward to the specially constructed rack and secured it in place. She worked hard maneuvering the heavy Harleys, taking care not to scratch them on the walls or on each other. Flick growled threateningly when he had to wait at the top of the ramp with one of the machines. Molli pushed herself and the machines faster, banging her shins on shift levers and her hips on handlebars. A mirror jabbed her in the abdomen and she sucked for air, wrestling the next bike like a wayward heifer. Flick, breathing hard, thrust the last bike into its place.

"The ramp. Along that wall. Hurry," he whispered.

Come on you mother, Molli muttered as she heaved the ramp upward as the men lifted and twisted the ramp onto its side. Grunting like a weightlifter Molli tugged the rough lumber as they pushed it into place. The man ran for the passenger door. Flick pounded once on the steel side and rolled into the truck at Molli's feet. Her knees buckled as the truck bucked forward. She grabbed at his back for support.

"The door," he said.

Each yanked on a loop, bringing the sliding door down like a window shade on the man in the Bermuda shorts with a cigarette in his mouth standing in the light of the church doorway flapping his arms indignantly.

"Watch the mirror, Flea," Flick said over the radio to the driver. "Guy at the church door saw us." He put a small flashlight on Molli's face. "You don't look too good."

"Neither do you," she said to him. Sweat dripped from his long hair onto his face and collected in his beard like dew.

"License plates," he said, giving her another flashlight, a screwdriver, and a small plastic bag.

"Why don't we turn on the truck light?" she said.

"It's broken," Flick said.

"Oh." Molli played her light across the Harleys, creating ominous shadows like futuristic carnivores tethered for the night. They do have a certain beauty, she thought.

"Dream on your own time," Flick said, roughly shaking her arm.

She plopped down behind one of the bikes. Holding the flashlight in her left hand, she attempted to stick the screwdriver in the slot. The shaking of her body and the vibration of the truck made it a two-handed job. She saw that Flick held his light in his mouth. Molli felt the metal fill her mouth, cold on her tongue and the inside of her lips. She scooted on her butt from bike to bike, tossing the plates in the bag, as if harvesting some strange vegetable.

"Someone's coming. Fast," the driver said.

"Stay cool. Don't speed. No cops. See if it's a sixties Mustang," Flick replied.

"I can't tell. Shit, Flick. What if it's the cops? We're fucked."

"Stay cool. Tell what it is yet?"

"No. Headlights," the driver said.

"Slow way down. See if it'll try to pass. But don't let it get by, dig?" Flick said.

Still sitting, Molli wondered if she could take acting classes in prison and who would take care of Meryl. That's not going to happen. We'll get away and live happily ever after, she thought. The truck swerved suddenly to the left. The metal of a gas tank cooled her cheek.

"Woman in some foreign job," the driver said. "What should I do?"

"Let her by," Flick said. "Keep watching."

"I knew we'd be all right," Molli said.

"You know everything, right?" Flick said. "Ah, forget it. Let's get the rest of the plates."

As soon as they finished unloading the motorcycles, Flea and the man whose name Molli couldn't remember left for Kentucky to get rid of the truck. While Flick was on the phone, Molli stripped each cycle of anything personal — a couple of raccoon tails, a pair of baby shoes, small plastic crosses. The decals took longer. "Wheelmen are Real Men" joined certain ads and her father's trite phrases on her most forgettable list. She was working on the last bike when the semi arrived. A very small man in a dark suit and sunglasses holding a brief case nodded at her. He looks the part, Molli thought.

"She's cool," Flick said.

A second man, beefy and wearing a purple tank top and black sportcoat, placed himself where he could watch Flick and Molli. He stood with his legs spread and his hands cupped over his groin. The truck driver and his helper leaned against the wall by the door. Two of Flick's friends from the shop roamed among the stolen cycles, their eyes on the man in the purple top.

Molli remained hunkered down behind the bike, watching what happened over the front fender. She couldn't hear the conversation until Flick raised his voice.

"You're jamming me. We agreed on five grand per. Now you're telling me four. What are you doing?"

"Things change. You said there'd be at least fifteen, all you have are twelve. Some of them don't look so hot," the man in the suit said.

"That's crap. Adjust the odometer on any of these and you got a new bike. You'll get fifteen to twenty grand apiece, easy. You probably already have them sold."

"Four grand per. You want it or not? You know you can't keep the bikes here."

"We agreed on five. Right? Say it, Sid."

The man nodded.

"Then why are you doing this to me?"

"Four. That's it."

Flick shrugged as if giving up. "I guess I don't have a choice."

Everyone relaxed. The man popped open the suitcase and began counting money. Flick walked slowly, hands spread, toward the man in the purple top. "Don't I know you from somewhere?" Flick said. As the man began his response, Flick hit him as hard as he could in the nose. The man dropped and curled on the floor coughing blood. Flick whirled and caught the small man in a bear hug, lifting him. His feet danced on the air like a marionette.

"We ain't a part of this," the truckers said, putting their hands up to allow Flick's friends to search them.

Flick slammed the little man into a chair causing his glasses and briefcase to fall. The man squinted like he just woke up.

"Dig this. Here's your choice. You can pay me fifty-five hundred dollars per and take the bikes. Or you can be our guests while we use your truck to get rid of the bikes and you can pay us five thousand dollars per for our aggravation." Flick took Sid's hands gently as if they were little kittens. He wrapped his fingers around the knuckles. "What will it be?"

"Flick, I can't. I don't know. I need to call."

Flick squeezed both hands, grinding the knuckles together. The man's head convulsed back and his knees snapped toward his chest like closing scissors. He was panting in pain when Flick released the pressure.

"No calls. Six seconds. One, two, three, four, five," Flick said.

"No. No. Okay. We'll take the bikes. No. No," the man said

"Smart man. Fifty five times twelve is sixty six thousand, right?

"Right. But, Flick, I don't know if we have that much. I mean, I don't know. I have to see."

"Of course you know." He tightened his grip until the little man gasped. "Molli. Get over here and count the money. You're looking for sixty-six thousand dollars."

Molli enjoyed the spotlight. As everyone watched she strutted to the bundles scattered from the fallen briefcase. Deliberately, she picked a bundle, wet her thumb with a flourish and counted it so quickly that the paper crackled, like it was the till at the sports bar. There were fifty one hundred dollar bills. On Flick's orders, she counted half of the remaining twelve bundles and there were fifty in each. She capped two stacks of six with the odd packet.

"A grand short," Flick said.

"That's all there is, honest," Sid said.

"That's just the company money. Where do you keep your billfold?" Flick said, tightening his forearms as if to squeeze.

"Jacket, but I don't have it."

"Molli. Inside pocket. How much?" Flick said.

She found seven hundred fifty dollars. On her own, Molli rolled back the sportcoat of the man in the purple shirt, ignoring his broken-nosed whimper, and extracted his billfold. She stood quickly to escape the smell of blood and found four hundred dollars.

"I'll leave you the rest for ice and tolls," Flick said. "Dig this. You tell your boss that Flick always keeps his word. Tell him we're done doing business, and if he screws with me over this, I'll hurt him bad." He waved at his friends. "Help get the bikes in the truck and these useless fools in their car."

The man in the purple top could do no more than sprawl in the backseat. Molli found an old soiled pillow for the small man to sit on so he could see to drive back to New York.

"He's a tough little guy," Flick said as the car followed the truck out of the parking lot. "He'll make it."

"Now I can go, right?" Molli said, shaky from exhilaration and fatigue.

"This looks like a lot, but there's expenses and overhead. And risk. There's got to be a better way." Flick said, poking the stacks of bills with his toe causing them to tumble. "You have kids?"

"What? Kids? Not me. I got to go." She paused. "Why'd you ask?"

"This is heavy. My youngest is doing one of those drug rehab programs. Gets out next week. He'll come back here. Dig this, some animals let their runts go. Nature's law and survival of the fittest. I appreciate it, but can't do it. You know Hamlet?"

"Of course."

"It's like I'm at that same place of making a mind-bending choice. I can stay and do what I know, like tonight, to hustle money for the film. I know it'll kill him because he can't say no.

Drugs everywhere, like candy at Christmas. Or I can split and take him along. Saves his life, maybe —but I'd have to give up on the film," Flick said.

"Got to be other choices. What about his mom?" Molli said.

"A good woman. She'd take him in. But Cheyenne only wanted to be a biker like his daddy. Drugs have taken his mind and he's, like, welded to me. He wouldn't go without me." He picked up a bundle of bills. "Not your problem. Here's the rest of your bread. Like I said, Flick always keeps his word. Do you want to catch a flick? I've got a great collection of classics."

"I'm out of here. It's been, I don't know, interesting," Molli said.

"Sure?" Flick said.

"Sure."

"I dig it. See you around."

"Right."

Too revved up to sleep, Molli scattered the money on the ceiling to have it float down, like long pine needles, around her. She posed, strutted, pantomimed audition routines. It was kind of a kick actually. That's the way to move ahead.

CHAPTER SIX

Thirty years ago, Flick had known he had to leave town when he saw his picture in the paper.

"Got to go, momma," he said and kissed her on the throat. He put his hand on the baby Cheyenne who was sleeping at Sue's breast and placed the newspaper, folded open to the article naming those wanted for questioning, next to her. "I'll stay in touch."

He rode north, crossing into Canada near Vancouver where his gang had connections. A warrant was issued to detain him as a material witness which prevented his return because he did not want to be interrogated. Flick watched the televised reports showing his friends chained together in the courtroom in Oakland and heard the boasts that their convictions eliminated a major source of drugs in the Bay Area.

Realizing what was required, he promoted himself from part time salesman to full time regional manager of the gang's drug business. He worked hard to satisfy the growing demands of the flower-waving, pot-smoking, peace-loving members of his generation. A large part of the profits went to pay the legal costs of members and to provide for their families. Flick sent his share home. With his approval, Sue used some as seed money for a landscape business and invested the remainder in stocks which, years later, sent the kids through college.

For a quarter of a century, Flick lived as a migratory animal following weather warm enough to ride, unaware that the warrant for his arrest, forgotten by all except himself, had been buried by the events of the 1970's. Under clandestine circumstances, he met his children frequently and saw the three together for the last time when Sue married the carpenter who finished her shop. He kept riding as his comrades died, dropped out, or settled down. For the next generation of bikers, he was a legend entitled to an upwind chair by the campfire. Flick had always enthusiastically enjoyed movies. He used his years of riding alone to cultivate this interest by seeing virtually every film released and became a serious film student and critic.

Five springs ago, Flick busted his leg in Carolina when he laid his bike down to miss a horse that wandered onto the highway. He recuperated at the home and small studio of a friend of a friend who was an aspiring film director with more knowledge and equipment than common sense. As he recovered, Flick asked questions which the lonely director was glad to answer. That summer he limped with the director over grassy hills to reenactments of Civil War battles. The director wanted to make a documentary, but was having difficulty distinguishing one battle from another. He allowed Flick to run the camera. Flick didn't see columns of soldiers through the lens, he saw masses of bikers, and, he thought, the opportunity to record history.

He embraced his idea with the smug fervor of a man needing a major life change. The director became expendable after he said Flick's idea to film the history of bikers was an excellent example of autobiographical preening. Heavy-handedly encouraged by Flick, the director took a job in television and handed Flick the keys to his place, all equipment included, for a fair price to be paid over a long time. Flick converted the hair salon into a motorcycle repair shop and settled in for the first time in almost thirty years.

Cheyenne joined his father permanently the next summer. Cheyenne had Harley grease under his nails before he could reach the foot pegs. His mechanical skills quickly impressed the bikers who gathered at the shop. He rapidly fought, drank, smoked, and rode his way into acceptance.

Flick did not know the depth of his son's cocaine dependency until he caught Cheyenne stealing from him. Trapped by his past, Flick could condemn the theft, but not the use of drugs. Cheyenne expressed no remorse and no desire to quit. Unable to think of another solution, Flick agreed to give him money for drugs if he did not steal.

Cheyenne's self-directed downward spiral continued. Three times he checked into rehab programs after an overdose put him in the hospital. Each stay was like a pit stop. He rejected the programs' attempts to cure him by obliterating his life as a biker. He regained full speed within days of his release.

"This can't go on," Flick said as he sat one day on the corner of his son's hospital bed.

"Why not? Your life style is my life style. We're bikers," Cheyenne said. " I have everything I want right here."

CHAPTER SEVEN

She trembled as he drew the rose across her breast and belly to her inner thigh. The thorn's hooked blade skipped across her skin lightly, leaving the faintest white lines which quickly blushed red. A crimson petal dropped between her legs, vivid as blood on the sky-blue silk sheet. Watching her watch him with eyes on fire, he followed the rose's trail with his tongue and captured the petal between his teeth. Gently stroking her sides as he climbed upward, he tantalizingly divided her golden triangle with the tip of his nose and the flower's delicate edge. She raised her hips and said something prehistoric. Slowly, he dragged the petal through the valley between her breasts and slipped it into her half open mouth. Their lips locked. They sucked on the petal. Its fragile membranes parted and dissolved as their tongues wrestled playfully in the dark cavern of their passion.

The slow spin of the ceiling fan mixed the subdued light from the sconce with the insistent strumming of the classical guitar. The scent of the two dozen roses absorbed this mixture and delivered it to the jasmine oil Gant drizzled up the length of her body. The cool oil, charged with sensory electrons, danced on their hot bodies. They undulated against each other in long, languid strokes and swept the sweet substance into cracks and crevices with great circular motions of their hands.

"You feel so wonderful, Rebecca. It's been such a long time." Gant panted. He shoved both breasts upward and nibbled on the nipples rapidly, like a feeding piranha. She kneaded his buttocks, pulling him close, and laid a wreath of moist kisses on the top of his head.

He rolled on his back, taking her along. "Now, Rebecca, now."

Straddling him, she pleasurably impaled herself. Gant pushed up against her weight and rested his hands on her hips as she moved up and down in time to the guitar. He closed his eyes and marveled at her black hair swinging against her cheeks, her eyes full of love and her lips glistening.

"Gant, Gant, Gant," she chanted in response to his thrusts which became more defined and urgent. Without opening his eyes, he rolled her over without missing a stroke. Hooking his arms behind her knees, he stretched her legs up and went at her faster and faster, gasping her name, until he came in a short, hot burst.

"You were right. I was wrong. Please forgive me," she said moments later. "You were fantastic." His head rested on her shoulder. She stroked the arm that formed a ninety degree angle across her body.

"You did a pretty good job tonight yourself," Gant replied without warmth. The oil smelled rancid and his mouth tasted brackish. He brushed a strand of blonde hair from his nose.

"Did I say everything right, the way you wanted me to?"

"You did fine."

"I know it's almost time for me to go. I don't mind that you call me Rebecca while we do it," Lola said. "As long as I can be with you, Mr. Gant."

"Okay, I'll see you later."

"Ten more minutes, please."

"No, go. Now. Money's on the dresser."

As Lola got dressed, he closed his eyes and watched Rebecca disappear in a black velvet robe.

Not unexpectedly, Gant couldn't sleep. Next week he would try the Rotten case. The following week the reunion would begin. He was kept awake by shadowy questions about the wisdom of this masquerade which merged with the panicky desire for a continuance common to every trial lawyer, no matter how well prepared. He was satisfied he'd be ready for court. Gant had plotted the only possible route, as the successful whitewater canoeist charted a trip through stage four rapids. As always, he would do what was required to win.

The plans for the reunion were less settled. Mouse had said he thought he had it worked out. But Gant knew, with bikers, nothing was certain until it happened.

He splashed vodka with tonic and took his cigarette to the balcony.

"We should be doing this together, Rebecca," he said out loud as if she were standing with him. "You should be the one riding on the back of my bike like we drove through the gates to my parents' new pink house. You went for me, even though you hated Florida. You gave them each a clammy hug, not knowing they hated to be touched by strangers. They blamed you for the beer on our breaths and banished you to the first floor guest room, despite the fact that they knew we lived together. When dad caught me going down the stairs at three a.m., he made me wake you. Remember, he and mom looked like Puritan elders when they ordered you to leave. We both went. Took about two minutes to pack. We laughed all the way to Atlanta."

His parents never had allowed themselves, or him, to forget that this was the first time he defied them. When Gant broke up with Rebecca, they Fedexed him first class tickets home for a weekend of chaperoned activities with the long-legged daughter of a police captain. Gant ended that stay with a colder relationship with his parents. He promised only to send clippings of his successes for their scrapbook and to visit at Christmas.

Gant finished his drink. The consolation of having had the last word years ago meant nothing. He had more to say. Once again, he called the information operator to get Rebecca's home number.

"I'm sorry, sir, she has requested that the number not be given out," the operator said.

"Couldn't you? I'm a friend from out of town. Sure she wouldn't mind," Gant said.

"Sorry, sir."

"Are you actually looking at the number? Read it out loud. I'd never tell."

"Sorry, sir. Do you want to speak to my supervisor?"

He napped with the phone on his lap until the morning chill woke him.

*

Gant had left last night's reminiscences of Rebecca at his condo. He instructed Joan to track down the elusive Mouse and to hold all calls. Gant concentrated on formulating the questions he would ask prospective jurors. Language and cadence were as important as the question itself. Gant worked hard, seeking that smooth rail of confidence and persuasiveness that he could ride straight through the trial. He did not notice Larry until he coughed.

"What?' Gant said sharply.

"Finished the briefs, sir," Larry said.

"Good. I'll read them in a minute. Stick around," Gant said.

"Sir, excuse me, about this weekend. I was wondering if you really need me because —"

"Trial starts Monday. Means we work Saturday and Sunday. You want the weekend off, don't come back. Get a job where everybody works when they want and nobody cares what gets done. Your choice," Gant said. "Go see if Joan has something for you to do."

Rich and Jeb swept around Larry like New Yorkers around a lost tourist. More surprised than upset by this unexpected invasion of his space, Gant greeted his partners cautiously.

"Morning. What's up? My trial starts Monday," Gant said.

"Won't wait," Rich said. "I need to talk to you."

"Quit bullshitting me. Of course it will wait," Gant said.

"Not this time," Rich said.

"Have to. I'm busy," Gant said.

"Too bad. You're going to listen," Rich said.

"Hey, guys," Jeb said. "Wasting time. Let him talk, Jake, and be done with it."

"Talk, talk, talk," Jake said. "You two get paid for talking. I'm a trial lawyer. My clients expect action. And that's what I give them." He slammed a book down on his desk.

"Save the theatrics," Rich said. "I have a new case. Great injuries. Could make us a lot of money."

"Certainly. Sit," Gant said.

"You remember the day care fire last month?" Rich said.

"Vaguely," Gant said.

Rich explained that the sister of one of his clients called him at home last night and that he met her for breakfast.

"All the parents want the same lawyer. She's the spokesperson for the group. Her son was horribly burned," Rich said.

"Weren't there a number of kids hurt?" Gant said.

"Two died," Rich said. "Ten total with third degree burns. Several others with lesser injuries. One of the American Methodist Episcopal churches sponsored the pre-school. Building was owned by some corporation. Has buildings throughout the Midwest. Deep, deep pockets. She said the fire marshal investigated and seemed sympathetic, whatever that means."

"You sign her up?" Gant said.

"Not until she meets you, which she is willing to do," Rich said. "I say willing because she has no use for whites. But she knows she needs a trial lawyer and she knows I don't do your kind of trial work, although I could if I had to. She couldn't find a black trial lawyer with your track record. You would be flattered if you heard what I told her about you. You and I would work her together. I'll do the hand-holding. You would be her tool. The means to an end, like a sharecropper might use a hoe to chop cotton. You tolerate that?"

Gant snorted. "Clients have worn my handle shiny smooth by using me as a tool. Don't kid yourself, that's all we are. Tools."

"I disagree with that," Jeb said indignantly. "I have truly meaningful, mutually respectful relationships with my clients."

"Wonderful. I'm happy for you. I have respectful relationships with my clients, also. They do what I say and I make us both money. When can she come in? I'll make room this afternoon. Call her now," Gant said, pointing at his phone. "Get her signed up before some other eagle carries her away."

We're all each other's tools, Gant thought as Rich dialed. The heart of every relationship beats with the rhythm of the falling hoe. Kids use their parents. Lovers use each other. Mutual respect means what each got. Some people understand this instinctively. Others never learn.

"Four thirty today," Rich said.

"Got it. Now, tough as it may be for you two to imagine, I've got to get back to work," Gant said.

"More to the deal," Rich said.

"Christ," Gant said. "Okay, but not if it has to do with hiring your nephew."

As he outlined his political opportunity, Gant saw the hunger in his eyes and wondered how close to the edge Rich was.

"I need out," Rich said. "Not only for this, but my family. Cash me out. A quarter of a million for everything, including my share of this case. One hundred thousand now and a note for the rest. I'd wait for all of it except for Keesha. Checked with the bank. They'll give you two a loan. Let's call it quits, Jake, please."

Gant smiled. "Not even for a pretty please. You want out, walk away from everything. You want money, start a lawsuit. Otherwise nothing changes."

"Jake," Jeb said. "Think it through. It's a good deal for us. I'll even go along with the loan if we keep it small. I think we could get close if we used the cash in the various accounts. How much is in that account you use to pay experts?"

"I said I wasn't paying anything," Gant said.

"How much is there?" Jeb said. "Don't screw around."

"Almost ninety thousand the last I looked. Most of it is allocated, though," Gant said. "It doesn't matter. If he goes, it's more work and less money for us. He wants out, he can take his personal stuff and go. That's it."

"You're messing with my daughter, man," Rich said coldly.

"Guilt won't work," Gant said. "You think I'm making this personal, you're correct. I thought I was doing right including you in this firm. Then you decided you were a black before you were our partner. Screw that. You want to be the black political messiah, go for it. But I'm not paying a penny in tribute."

"Jake, you're wrong on this one," Jeb said.

"Don't do this," Rich said. "You've gone crazy."

"No, I'm just getting even. And what I love the most is that you can't do anything about it. Like this day care case. If you send it to another firm, you'll lose the money that might let you leave. Someday."

Rich came at him with the quickness of a basketball player. Gant slid his swivel chair at his partner and painfully banged his thigh on a desk corner as he escaped. Rich almost caught Gant, but he stumbled over a pile of law books Gant had swept to the floor. The third time around Rich jammed his hands in his pockets and walked away.

"Christ," Jeb said. "What will the staff think?"

"Sorry. Lost it," Rich said to Jeb. "He's disgusting."

Gant smiled. "I have work to do," he said. "Either you leave my office or I'll use yours."

"I'm not done with this," Rich said.

"Okay, Rich, you can have the last word," Gant said mockingly as his partners left.

"Mr. Mouse on the phone," Joan said from the doorway. "Are you all right?"

"Why wouldn't I be all right?' Gant said. "What kind of dumb question is that?"

"Never mind. I'm going to lunch. Want me to bring you something?" she said.

"No, coming from you, it would be too boring. Just kidding. Sure. You decide. Cheese. Meat. Light rye. Whatever. Thanks," he said.

CHAPTER EIGHT

Mouse had known no one in North Carolina. He did know Fang, the president of the Vipers affiliate in Kankakee, Illinois. Fang's cousin Big Sam held office in the Atlanta gang, which did business with Flick. Mouse discovered this connection during a business lunch of bratwursts with Fang at a truck stop with a telephone in every booth. In passing, Mouse had mentioned the unpaid fees and Gant's unusual request. Fang hit on the idea like a striking snake and called Big Sam between bites. When Big Sam called back, he said Flick would listen to any proposals but that he wasn't in the business of doing favors. Mouse caught the sequence. He would have preferred to deal directly, but understood that Fang and his contact wanted their piece.

Fang told Mouse he wanted a state of the art multi-media sound system installed in his clubhouse. Mouse said okay because VD could obtain this item on excellent terms from the mega appliance store where he worked. VD would install it in sixty days if Fang provided the grunt labor. Fang agreed on the labor, but insisted it be ready for the Labor Day party, and he wanted one kilo of high quality marijuana. Mouse agreed with getting it in for the party and a quarter kilo, but that was it.

"Make it a half kilo and we're done," said Fang.

"Okay," Mouse said. "Usual terms. Our personal bikes as security. Ownership transfers upon delivery, and risks and liabilities remain with seller until transfer. No guarantees, surcharges or handling fees. The customary full disclaimer for responsibilities not agreed to and for failures of upstream participants."

"Agreed. If this lawyer doesn't go south, that is, he doesn't get on the plane for NC, you pay ten cases of beer to me for my grief," Fang said.

"Yeah," Mouse said, "and you understand Gant comes "as is," without any warranty or representation of fitness."

Fang expressed mild curiosity about Gant. Mouse described him as a wealthy lawyer with a weird taste in entertainment.

Big Sam insisted that Fang agree to act as a much-needed distribution center for an overstock of stolen bikes. They haggled for three phone calls over division of the profit, costs of transportation, and assumption of the risk. They resolved their differences when Fang said he'd toss in a quarter kilo of marijuana and more information on Gant, and Big Sam agreed to pass on Fang's demand for two percent of anything made off the lawyer. This meant nothing to Big Sam except that he should consider the lawyer a viable speculative investment.

Flick's interest, of course, was financing. He scorned Big Sam's offer of immunity from the group in New York which demanded Flick return the extra money he took in payment for stolen bikes. Financing, he repeated.

Big Sam became creative. To Flick, he portrayed Gant as 186 pounds of gold bullion, a man who lit two hundred dollar cigars with one hundred dollar bills, generously subscribed to the arts, and invested regularly in new businesses. Truly a philanthropist, a rock-solid American moneyed man with a kinky interest in bikers. Financing? He might give an unlimited loan at no interest.

Running a biker training program for a lawyer sounded as blasphemous to Flick as he knew it would to the traditionalists among his biker friends. He agreed out of his desperate need, like the gambler who borrows at a usurious rate. He told Big Sam to get the lawyer's sponsor to provide the clothing, including the boots.

"That's personal," he said. "We're doing business."

"Certainly agree, man," Big Sam said.

A prepackaged Gant would be shipped up the stream of commerce like a mail order bride. He would never learn the conditions and expectations of the multiple transactions which bought him his ticket to ride for the reunion weekend.

*

"It was a bitch to put together," Mouse said, "but you're set."

"Great." Gant wedged the phone between ear and shoulder and picked up the books from the floor. He grimaced at the mess on his desk.

"I found everything you need to be a righteous biker. Bike, broad, and accessories. You'll be a real weekend warrior," Mouse said.

"You being sarcastic? You don't think much of the idea, do you?" Gant said.

"Your life, man. I wouldn't want to play lawyer for a week. I think it's hard to step into somebody else's boots. But," Mouse said encouragingly, "if anybody can pull it off, you're the one."

"That would be different - playing a lawyer," Gant said.

Mouse snorted. "You got that right. I can't imagine why anyone would want to. Anyway, man, I need a commitment from you.

"Let me think for a second," Gant said. He again pictured himself and the babe whose name was something like Candy getting off the bike in front of the hotel. Classmates gawked at the couple like they were film stars. Conversation dribbles into the silence of an empty bottle. As they stand at the registration desk, Candy flattens her left breast against the back of his arm. The closing elevator doors, like scissors, snip the amazed stares of his peers. Inside the room Candy comes into his arms while, in the no-parking zone outside, a few bold men admire from an awe-mandated distance the black and chrome machine still shimmering with heat.

Worst case, Gant thought, it goes flat, a possibility with any vacation.

"Let's do it," he said.

"You're sure? Like I said, I need a commitment," Mouse said.

"You got it."

"You get your weekend and we're even on Rotten, right?"

"You said you have no more money out there for fees, right? Gant said.

"Yeah, tapped out."

"Then we're even. It's better than an IOU."

"Your partners won't come after us?" Mouse said.

"I'll take care of that. But, Chrissakes, don't advertise it around town. It's a one-time thing."

"Of course," Mouse said. "All right, the specifics. A week from Tuesday you'll meet a man named Flick."

"Flick? You know him?"

"No, but I hear he's a real biker."

"Better be. You say Tuesday?"

"You have to be there four days before you expect to ride the bike to your reunion," Mouse said.

"Four days! No way," Gant said.

"Four days or no deal. Flick says no compromises."

"Why? What's the big deal that he needs four days?"

"Shit, Jake. A leather jacket and a Harley don't make you a biker. Look, if you don't care if people know you're not real, go rent a super hero costume. But if you want people to believe you're a biker, well, you ain't got enough time. In four days, maybe you learn enough to fool them for a weekend. Be thankful Flick's willing to give you four days. You have to have the walk and know how to talk about certain things." Mouse hesitated, then added in a voice tinged with disgust, "if you don't want to do it right, fucking don't do it, man."

"How about two days? That should be enough."

"No compromises, I said. Four days. You gave me your commitment, Jake. You going back on that?"

Over the amaryllis, Gant watched a plane climb out above the buildings across the square. He recalled Rebecca's brother, a pilot, explaining how much quicker he found reasonable doubt in the air. No doubt about it, he thought, something about this biker/reunion thing gives me pause. But does it create reasonable doubt? He wasn't sure.

"Jake? Hello. You there?" Mouse said.

It'll be an experience, Gant decided. If it doesn't work, I'll leave.

"I'm in," Gant said.

"You sure, because —"

"God damn it! How many times do I have to say it. You want it in blood?" Gant said.

"Okay, you're in. Relax," Mouse said. "You'll need clothes — leathers, chains, boots. You know, like what the Vipers wear?"

"Yeah, you've got stuff I can borrow, right?"

"You could if we had it, you know that. But we don't," Mouse said.

"Nothing? I don't believe it," Gant said.

"True. I asked. No one has anything to loan you. Have to buy it. I'll give you names of stores."

"I hate to spend money on stuff I'll wear one time."

"That's the way it is. You can afford it. Probably won't set you back more than one of your beautiful suits."

"Thanks for being no help," Gant said.

"I can be no help, or I can give you some names," Mouse said.

"This conversation's getting old. I've got work to do on this deadbeat biker's trial I have Monday," Gant said.

"I wouldn't go shopping in your suit," Mouse said, and gave Gant a short list of biker stores.

*

"Great sandwich," Gant said to Joan when she brought the mail to him, "even though you forgot the dark mustard."

"You didn't ask for dark mustard," she said.

"The good news is, Mouse set me up for the reunion. The bad news is, four days of basic training. Four days, can you believe that? Should I grow a beard? What do you think?"

"What dates? You check your calendar?" Joan said. "What exactly will you do for four days?"

"Learn to act like a biker. How to stand. What's the word Mouse used? Righteous, that's it. The essence of bikerdom, if you will," Gant said.

"And you think they can teach that?"

"Why not? All attitude and ad lib. How hard can that be? The reunionists won't know I'm not real. It will be great."

Joan unconsciously smoothed the stack of opened correspondence she held and opened her mouth as if to introduce speech, but no words followed.

"What?" Gant said sharply.

"Nothing." Her face showed a brief, false smile. "Sounds like an interesting vacation."

"You think I'm missing something?"

"Not for me to say. Here's your mail."

"Yeah, thanks for sharing my excitement," Gant said.

Gant irritably flipped through the pile of letters, notices and advertisements. Her idea of an exciting vacation is a bus tour of the suburbs with her mother, he thought.

CHAPTER NINE

The oily fingerprints on the shatterproof Plexiglas made the woman's face blotchy and dulled the brightness of her green dress.

"Yes?" she said.

"I have an appointment with Rebecca Varner at four," Rich said.

"Speak up," the woman said, tapping the glass.

"Rebecca Varner at four," Rich said, aware that his words echoed off the glass, guaranteeing that no private business was conducted in the district attorney's waiting room.

"Name?"

"Richard Johnson."

"No, not on the schedule," she said.

"I called earlier this afternoon," Rich said.

"Sorry. Perhaps she can see you next week."

"I talked to her secretary. She said four o'clock today."

"Nothing written down," the woman said.

"Look. Maybe she forgot to write it down," Rich said patiently. "Please check with her. It's very important."

The woman sighed and stood. "Take a seat," she said.

"Hot in here," Rich said as he turned. He unbuttoned his suit coat, loosened his tie and ran a white, linen handkerchief across his forehead.

Rich had not been in this office since he delivered legal papers as a law student working part time at the Attorney General's office. Except for the enclosure of the receptionist, little had changed. It continued to be an untended garden of humanity grown in undernourished soil. A tearful woman, her face raw with scrapes and bruises, tried futilely to keep her child from drumming his foot on the metal leg of the chair. A old man, shaking from withdrawal, stared emptily in the direction of travel posters, hanging faded in their frames. Two black teenagers glared at Rich like he had turned them in. Carelessly dressed public defenders in cords and poorly dressed shysters in polyester curiously watched him.

Defensively, he fanned through the pages of a ragged magazine and reflected on the decisions which had lead him back to this room.

Upon graduating from law school, despite the urging of his family, he declined all jobs offered to him because he was black.

He didn't want to defend criminals nor to advocate for the rights of the poor. He had political ambitions which he knew meant access to white money and votes. Rich went to work in the legal department of a land development company owned by the friend of the father of a former roommate. He learned to maneuver comfortably in the white corporate world.

Preparation, not luck, Rich believed, brought a person to the right place at the right time. He married right, joined a church, and built strong bridges to all parts of the community without being tainted by partisan politics. He selected partnership with Gant and Jeb because he wanted be his own boss, correctly perceiving that Gant's drive matched his own and that they would be successful. He had positioned himself perfectly to answer the party's inevitable call for a strong, untarnished candidate.

Rich had not anticipated Gant's unyielding animosity toward him. The day's confrontation made him seek out Rebecca. Somehow, he had to turn Gant around.

"Mr. Johnson," the woman said loudly through the small opening at the bottom of the glass. "You'll have to call for an appointment next week."

"But —" Rich said.

"Ms. Varner is in conference and can't be disturbed. Her secretary left for the day. There's no record of the appointment. I'm sorry."

"Talk to your supervisor," Rich said, "or the district attorney. I'm an attorney."

"Of course you are," she said. "Our rules apply to everyone, even attorneys. No one gets through that door without an appointment made by phone. Call next week."

"Hot in here," one of the teenagers said as Rich left. His friend laughed.

*

"Couldn't you settle it, boss?" Rebecca said.

Bartley Suss' office was at the opposite end of the hall from hers. She had stopped on Friday afternoon on the way to her car. The district attorney removed his thick, wire-rimmed glasses and leaned his head back. His jowls slid toward his ears and the thick skin behind his neck bunched into a pile of sausages. The small work table contained the crusts of a fast food lunch, the scattered guts of a file, and a smiling full length photograph of his wife standing in front of their house.

"Gant wanted drunk driving. I couldn't do that. Not with that test," Bartley said. He slowly massaged his face with his swollen hands. "Gant and the bikers would think they owned this office."

"You go on Monday?"

"Yeah, we're number one on the judge's calendar. Draw the jury and go."

"You ready?" she said.

"I will be after this weekend," he said. "You'd think after thirty five years, it would get easier."

"It's pretty straightforward, isn't it? Have the officers testify and introduce the test results and the photographs. What else is there?"

"Gant. He's a snake." Bartley walked his haunches to the edge of the seat of the chair, planted his feet and pushed with his hands. He rose with a quick gasp, as if his success startled him. "Come to the house next Saturday. Our youngest grandchild turns ten Tuesday. Carol wanted the party this weekend, but something rotten came up. Pun intended."

Rebecca gave him an obligatory roll of her brown eyes.

"Seriously," he said, "come. Carol and the kids want to see you."

"I'll be there. Promise."

"And what great adventure do you have planned this weekend? Where can I picture you when I need to escape from Willie Rotten and Jake Gant?"

Rebecca laughed. "Up north. Camping with some friends." She squeezed his meaty arm with both hands. "I'm sorry. Damn it. Next time Gant's mine."

"No matter. Have fun. Watch for snakes." He waved her out the door.

"Monday," she said.

The last shot of Bartley's brave, tired face came with her to the stairway only to be replaced by the red, angry face of Jake Gant on their last night together. Because it seemed important, she confronted the face and remembered the events leading up to that night. They had spent the previous weekend camped in a snow bank as part of a bizarre and private game they were playing their first and only winter together. Previous weekends they had challenged each other with extreme cold weather activities. Next weekend was her turn and she had signed them up for the annual polar bear swim in Lake Michigan. Each Monday night, she brought home pizza and a bottle of red wine.

For the first time, she liked living with a man. She thought their lives were set on cruise control until that Monday when she saw her stuff piled in the hall outside Gant's apartment. She knew what it meant, but was clueless as to why.

"Early Spring cleaning?" she said

He ignored her. "You gave information to the enemy."

"You're joking."

"Told your buddy Finkelstein about the other gun in the Shapiro case"

Rebecca dropped the wine and the pizza. She screamed her denials and offered up her soul in sacrifice if she was lying.

Gant was judge, jury and executioner.

"My place. You're gone," he said.

She spent a month trying to figure out what she'd done wrong, then said to hell with that and easily regained her past friends and activities. Rebecca worked hard and she knew she was widely accepted as Bartley's successor when he retired next year. She could not totally avoid Gant. Four times she had sat across the table from him to work out a plea bargain on cases neither wanted to go to trial. Nor could she completely forget that night. Each time she saw him she wanted to lock him in a room and question him until he explained what happened or confessed to schizophrenia. She monitored detachedly the growth of Gant's reputation and concluded that he sought to break Icarus' record and fly into the sun.

Poor Bartley, she thought. I should have agreed to try the Rotten case when he asked me to. Not afraid of Gant any more.

Rebecca tripped on a broken piece of sidewalk and blended her stumble into an impromptu dance step. A horn honked. The late afternoon sun changed a glass office building into a golden temple.

She veered into the lot. A big black man came at her fast. Rebecca hesitated. Convinced of his intent, she hurried toward her car. The tight skirt bound her legs. He was beside her. As she rummaged in her purse for the pepper spray, she turned to face him.

"Rich Johnson. Remember?" he said. "Been awhile."

"Yes. Sorry." She laughed nervously. "Surprised me."

"I apologize. Buy you a drink? It's important. Gant."

"Ah," she said.

They sat outside. A waitress in shorts brought beer. They clinked their glasses together.

"To the unexpected," Rebecca said.

"Need your help," Rich said.

He told her about his political opportunity and about Gant's refusal to buy him out. He explained he did not have time to force the issue in court and that his campaign would not survive the publicity from a public brawl.

"Need to pressure Gant. You must know a soft spot." Rich said hopefully.

"Haven't talked to him - really - since he threw me out."

"Must know something. Some dark secret. I admit it, I'm one desperate dude."

"Like whether he cheated on his taxes?" Rebecca said. "Can't help you that way. Wouldn't if I could. What about Jeb? Rich used to listen to him."

"Gant listens only to Gant," Rich said.

"What's he like now?" Rebecca faked nonchalance.

"Arrogant. Belligerent. Consumed. Driven."

"A good trial lawyer."

"He is that," Rich said.

"Driven always, but with potential. He's drifted, you know? What happened?" Rebecca said.

"Don't know. We don't talk. If I had to, I'd guess success made him think he was something special. Real asshole. Excuse me."

"Sad somehow," she said.

"Maybe. His life. That's cool. But he's messing with mine. Got to find a way," he said.

"I don't know. It doesn't seem right." Rebecca touched his forearm. "Sorry about your daughter."

CHAPTER TEN

"Excuse me, your honor," Gant said. "Where's Bartley, I mean Mr. Suss? This is his case."

"Mr. Gant," Judge Harris said, "don't you watch the news?" She surveyed those sitting in her chambers for the Monday morning, pre-trial meeting. Gant, Willie, Larry the Law Clerk, and Rebecca Varner. Off to the side were her court reporter and clerk. Behind them, the bailiff was sipping coffee from a Styrofoam cup.

"Not when I'm preparing for trial," Gant said. "Why? What happened?"

"Bartley had a heart attack," Rebecca said, slipping on the words. "Yesterday in his office. Critical condition."

"Too bad. Always liked him. Which hospital?" This screws up my schedule, Gant thought. Rebecca looks deliciously vulnerable.

"Methodist." Rebecca paged aimlessly through Bartley's case file.

"Do you know to whom the case will be assigned?" Judge Harris said gently.

"I've assigned it to myself," Rebecca said.

"Very well. I suppose you'll need time. Mr. Gant?"

"No objection, your honor, given the circumstances. Unfortunate. Mr. Rotten and I are ready to go," Gant said.

Gant kept Willie silent with a shake of his daybook as Harris and her clerk held an animated discussion concerning the notations in the scheduling book.

"We will try this case three weeks from today," the judge said.

"Fine, your honor," Rebecca said.

"I do have a hearing that day in another case," Gant said. "I'll get someone in my office to take it. Mr. Rotten and I want this matter tried as soon as possible. And while we're on this subject, your honor. I understand this delay not the DA's fault, but they've got his motorcycle. It's a hardship for him. Needs it to get to work. I'm asking for an order releasing it immediately. We agree to produce it at trial, if they want it."

"No," Rebecca said. "Critical evidence. The vehicle Mr. Rotten was driving at the time of the victim's death. It's important to maintain the chain of custody so that it can be used as evidence at trial. Mr. Gant's experts have examined it. Can't believe this request. He knows better."

"We've heard enough. The motorcycle will not be released at this time," Harris said. "Okay. The question of greater import this morning is whether we can resolve this case. Have you discussed this?"

"We have, your honor, their plea bargain was not —"

"That offer expired." Rebecca said. "Mr. Rotten can plead to the charge. We'll agree to seven years in prison if it's done today. After he's convicted, I'll ask for all ten years."

Before she finished, Gant stood, manufacturing the maximum amount of disgust and stacking it around Varner's chair. "Let's go, Willie. Excuse me, your honor. Anything else?"

"No. That's it. We want you ready to draw the jury in three weeks," Harris said.

"Thank you, your honor," the lawyers said together.

In the hallway, Larry gawked at Gant wide-eyed and slack-jawed like a kid on his first visit to a theme park. Gant recalled the first time he attended a trial in his second year of law school. To Gant's delight, his mentor and opposing counsel went at each other with the unbridled ferocity of barroom brawlers. Gant innately knew his own qualities of strength and cunning would flourish in the wide open arena of the courtroom. The experience gave him some badly needed direction. Gant tried to provide the same for his law clerks. To make him feel useful, Gant sent Larry for coffee.

"Seven or ten years, man. Did you hear that? What's her problem?" Willie said.

"I'm not surprised. Let me tell you a story about her," Gant said. "Man arrested for selling half a kilo of coke to an undercover cop. Kind of a setup, but he knew what he was doing. He'd lost his job and needed money for his family. Normally, a guy like that, with no priors, he's looking at a couple of years, maybe straight probation if he catches a break. Varner argued for the max — twenty years. She told the judge he had an obligation to make an example. Used all the 'war-on-drugs' language. Judge bought it. Gave him the whole package. Guess everyone in the courtroom was crying when they led him away except the judge and Varner. "

"What should I do?" Willie said.

"You want to do seven years?"

"No way."

"Then trial is your only choice."

Larry marched down the hall, carefully holding a triangle of three coffees. The brown stain on his blue shirt looked like a continent surrounded by ocean.

"Jesus! What happened?" Gant said.

"I can't explain it, sir. I was putting the lid on and the cup tipped and like the coffee jumped out at me."

"You're no good to me looking like that. What would the clients think? Get changed and get back to the office. Go," Gant said.

Christ, what a morning, Gant thought. Too bad about old Bartley. I felt like a fool, not knowing. How come no one told me? I have to get fired up for this trial again. And against Rebecca. I wasn't ready for that.

"The DA, man. Can we ask for a different one?" Willie said.

"You don't get to pick the DA," Gant said. "She's good. But she doesn't change our case. We'll spend whatever time we need. You'll be ready for her."

"You sure?"

"Yeah. Don't worry about it. I'll take care of her."

"What about my bike?"

"You heard the judge. They keep it until trial."

"That's the shits," Willie said.

"Take a cab. What can I say. I'll call you before trial. I'm out of town next week," Gant said.

"I heard about that," Willie said. "Sounds fucking weird. You trying to change your life or what?"

Gant went directly to his office. Flushed and puffing softly, he startled Joan by bursting through the waiting room door into her space.

"How come you didn't tell me about Bartley's heart attack?" he said.

"Pardon," Joan said.

"I felt like a dumb ass."

"I assumed you knew. It was everywhere."

"I'm not paying you to assume. Don't let it happen again," Gant said. "Varner's trying the case."

"That's interesting," Joan said noncommittally.

"I think she still hates me."

"It's possible."

"Nine years it's been. You'd think she'd move on. I have.

Whatever. Makes the trial a heck of a lot tougher. She's good."

"You have a good case," Joan said earnestly. "Don't let her distract you."

"I know that. Have you seen Larry ?"

"He called. Said he had to wait until his roommate got home from class so he could borrow some money to get another shirt. What happened?" Joan said.

"He slopped coffee on himself. Everybody's useless," Gant said, disappearing into his office. "When he comes in, tell him to get some motorcycle magazines. He and I need to go shopping."

*

The Bikers Boutique was in a low-rent strip mall on the east side of town, down wind from the mill. Early Tuesday afternoon Gant and Larry had both sales people to themselves, except neither did more than glance up when the men entered the store. Larry wore his new button down court shirt with creased chinos and brown wingtips. Gant had chosen black tasseled loafers, jeans and a monogrammed blue sport shirt with the top two buttons undone.

They moved through the store cautiously, suburban explorers in a jungle of black leather. Larry went to the left, pawing his way along racks of fringed vests and jackets beaded with chrome. Gant circled to the right, wondering if he should buy a pair of undies or a nightie labeled "I belong to a biker" for his companion. Gant had found the look he wanted in one of the magazines.

"Excuse me," he said to the man and woman behind the counter in his most honeyed courtroom voice. The two contemplated him with rank indifference. The man tossed his head at the woman and returned to his book. She sighed and stood with the speed and desire of a person condemned.

"I need," Gant said, forcing calmness into his voice, "boots, a vest, leathers, some shirts, and some smaller items."

"Change over there," she said, gesturing at a closet door. "Pay over here. Like any other store." She sat back down.

"My question, young lady, is whether you have anything pre-owned?"

"Come again?"

"Pre-owned. Used. Worn. Not brand new. You know what I mean. Don't be obtuse."

"Wait a minute here," she said. "Who are you calling obtuse?

Talk like that will get you an obese lip."

"I know, you're a doctoral candidate in linguistics and work here for kicks. It's a simple question, used clothes. You have them or not?" Gant said.

"Do you have a bike?" she said.

"Not exactly."

"What was that word you used? Ob something. Obtuse, it was. Either you have a bike or you don't."

"I don't. And you either have used clothes or you don't."

"Wrong, baby biker. Our things look new. But, as you know, things aren't always as they appear. Something can be used, but look new. And something can be unused, yet look totally beat to shit. Deception or perception. For people like you who need a costume for whatever reason. You want to look like a real biker, not like some urban cowboy at a rodeo dance, is that right?"

"It's not a costume exactly," he said.

"Oh yeah, of course, not exactly a costume. Whatever. Here's how it works. You assemble your not-exactly-a-costume. For an extra fee, we apply American ingenuity and technology and, voila, you leave with a righteous outfit."

"Very clever," Gant said, genuinely impressed. "A niche within a niche."

"Within a niche," she said. "Get it right."

*

The day before his flight to North Carolina, as he surveyed his biker outfits, Gant was uncustomarily unsettled about two matters. He didn't have enough clothes for four days of training and three days at the reunion. He assumed, aware of his reluctance to assume anything, that he would be able to get them washed before the reunion.

The second was more troubling. With acid, oil, and a wire brush, the store transformed the clothes from new looking to old looking before the price tag came off. However, a relentless succession of uncertainties about their suitability beat on Gant like waves on a beach. He knew the difference between a costume and a uniform. A costume is a sly wink at reality, like the Halloween skeleton and the fairy princess. The uniform means clannish acceptance, like his suits and Highland kilts. Beneath the uncertainties subtle distinctions and tricky ambiguities existed distinct from those in the courtroom.

To lessen these mysteries through possession, Gant had worn the clothes several evenings in the privacy of his condo. Now, he neatly packed them, placing the obligatory black wallet with chrome chain on top, and zipped the blue nylon flight bag. He would see how they played at the office.

*

Mid-afternoon that day Gant leaned back in his chair, fully attired, with his boots on the desk. Joan purposefully strode his direction flapping a single sheet of paper at him.

"How do I look?" he said.

"Summons and complaint," she said.

"What? Who?"

"Small claims. Joy Friendly."

"Joy Friendly? Who is she?"

"The woman who says you should pay her ticket. The one you wouldn't talk to."

"Now she's suing me? Christ. People," Gant said disgustedly. "Give it to the new associate, what's her name, you know, the young barracuda. Tell her to chew all the joy out of Ms. Friendly."

"You sure, Jake? I read the complaint. Bad press if you did steal her parking place," Joan said.

"You know, you worry like a mother. The press will never touch it. They love me too much." He stepped from behind the desk doing a burlesque of a model on a catwalk. "Now, what do you think?"

"I think it's fine," she said diplomatically.

"It's terrific," Gant said. "All genuine. Steel toes in these boots. These are called leathers. Supposed to protect you if you fall. Not cheap. My jeans could be dirtier. Look at the Harley eagle stamped on this wallet. Chained right to the belt. Takes some getting used to. Vest should have a gang name on the back, I think. None like that at the store. Mouse was no help, of course. Let me tell you, I'm going to drive them crazy at the reunion."

"You're not seeing clients like that, I hope," Jeb said rapping on the office door.

"All day. I'm going to blow them away," Gant said with a grin. "How can I help you two today? Other than by giving it all up and joining a monastery."

"Don't think they'd take you," Rich said flatly. "Bring us up to speed on our case."

"Our case. The one that binds us together. Sure. Bring us coffee, Joan," Gant said.

Sitting beside each other in the leather side chairs like old buddies, the men disregarded Gant's appearance. He told his partners he had signed contracts of representation with all the parents. A professional had photographed all the injured kids, including color close-ups of each injury. The doctors promised preliminary medical reports at the end of next week.

"I talked to the fire marshal," Gant said. "He found numerous building code violations including improperly maintained smoke detectors and blocked emergency exits. He hopes to have his report done in two weeks. Very helpful. Promised complete access to his findings once he's finished. Off the record, he said the kids wouldn't have been hurt if the owners had followed code. Real straightforward about it.'

"What's next?" Jeb said.

"Nail down liability. As soon as I get back, I'll get the experts on board. We've got the money for it," Gant said. "Need to follow the medical progress of each kid. Joan and a paralegal are setting up a system. It's a huge case. Millions, maybe."

"What about insurance?" Jeb said.

"Don't know yet. Can't get that information yet unless they volunteer. But I got a very interesting call from a Chicago lawyer purporting to represent the insurance carrier. All warm and gooey. Wants copies of what we get. He said if evidence shows liability, they want to try to settle it. Could be all smoke. I'm checking him out."

"When?" Rich said.

"No way to settle until we get final medical reports. Could be a year, maybe more, for some kids," Gant said. "Best thing we can do is get liability cold."

"You know we're getting big money," Rich said. "Cut a deal and let me out. Now."

"Let's try to work that out," Jeb said earnestly.

"Can't. Won't. Anything else?" Gant said.

He met Larry on his way to change.

"Awesome, Mr. Gant," the young man said.

CHAPTER ELEVEN

The inside of the taxi smelled faintly of curry. Gant cracked the window. Immediately the driver's brown eyes found Gant's face in the rear view mirror.

"Window closed please. AC," the driver said, his eyes flicking from road to mirror until Gant complied. The car phone had rung at least three times since they left the airport. Each time, the driver babbled rapidly in what Gant assumed was something like Hindi and hung up in what sounded like mid sentence. Sitar music, discordant to Gant's ear, droned on the radio. Despite the air conditioning, the humidity glued his bare arms to the plastic seat covers. To Gant's dismay, he maintained the speed limit like a religious vow, despite the parade of cars passing on both sides.

"Yes, no problem, I know where that is," the man had repeated as he studied the address on the paper Gant gave him at the airport. "No problem. No problem."

They crossed the Cape Fear and twisted past suburban developments to the fringe of the Green Swamp. The phone rang again. The driver chattered at a faster rate, slowed down when he read Gant's directions to the person on the other end, then ended the conversation. Abruptly, he veered into a service station parking lot.

"You must here get out. I cannot further go. It is out of my delegated area," the driver said. He reacted inanimately to Gant's profane protestations. However, he made it clear that he wouldn't retrieve Gant's bags from the trunk until he was paid.

Gant's mood continued to rot during the hour he waited for the local cab. The sun pushed him into the small waiting area where the still air tasted of used motor oil and clung like grease. The only fan whirred in the service bay protected by a dirty "Employees Only" sign.

Gant nearly lost all control when he got in the dilapidated station wagon. Both cab and driver had been ravaged by life, making it impossible to determine the age of either. The cab's speed was made life threatening by the driver's arm motions mimicking a drowning man which accompanied the monologue. The hot wind stormed through the open windows. Gant squinted to save his eyes from assorted particles which stuck to his clammy skin like flies on flypaper. The wagon's brakes and tires squealed as it slid to a halt a respectful distance from the motorcycles.

"Thank you," the driver said, signing out by leaving three feet of rubber on the asphalt.

Gant composed himself as he listened to birds sing in the woods across the road. Clearly, this vacation is closer to Outward Bound than to Club Med, he thought. It was hot and quiet. He walked toward the faint sound of music from inside the motorcycle shop.

"You're late," the man said, opening the door in Gant's face. He wore his full outlaw biker regalia including a Bowie knife sheathed at his left hip.

"I'm Gant. Who the fuck are you?"

"I'm not who the fuck anyone. I'm Flick and you're late. Dig?"

Gant heard a snicker from the room behind Flick. He didn't flinch and locked his eyes onto Flick's. Perhaps a minute passed, the two men staring a each other.

"We'll just have to work a little faster," Gant said coolly. "Where can I change?"

"Follow me." Flick led Gant to a large room in the studio.

Gant made note to ask where he could get the design on the back of Flick's jean vest. Before entering the dressing room, Gant gave Flick a piece of paper.

"My outline of what I think I need to learn. Look it over and let me know if I missed anything," he said.

More apprehensive about his outfit than he had been during the office show and tell, Gant found himself fussing over ridiculous details, like how far down to unbutton his shirt.

The bikers waited for him spread along the walls of the large room like Old West gunfighters around a corral fence. A few whistled or said "oh, baby." Flick stood in the far corner. He didn't speak until Gant stopped in front of him palms up as if to ask "so?" Flick circled Gant slowly.

"Boots too clean. Designer jeans a waste. Get some at the co-op. Leathers need some wear, otherwise, they're cool. Vest actually pretty far out. Shirt marginal. Watch goes. Same with the ring. And the handkerchief headband who do you think you are, Willie Nelson? And you need an earring. Better do that first," Flick said.

Gant relaxed. Watch and ring, no problem.

"Right, left, or both?" one of the bikers said, holding a tray of ice and an icepick.

"What's this?" Gant said sharply.

"Which ear?" Flick held the pick in one hand and an ice cube in the other.

Gant didn't blink. "You serious? No way. It's not happening."

"Pain's nothing. Little girls get it done," Flick said.

"Nobody's touching my ear."

"Never seen a biker without a pierced ear," Flick said.

"You've seen your first," Gant said, increasingly irritated.

"Yeah, that, or you're not a biker."

"Let's quit screwing around and get started," Gant said. "Did you look at my outline?"

"I filed it." Flick nodded at the wastebasket. "Dig this. This is my show. I make the rules. Tell people what to do. My word is my bond and I expect that from everyone. Here, you're just a man off the street. You handle that, man?"

"It works if we get started," Gant said.

The other bikers drifted away when Flick began his well-worn story of his thirty years as a biker, punctuating it with displays of tattoos and scars. Credentials he openly presented to impress the lawyer, just as Gant detailed his successes to prospective clients.

Flick alluded to a film about a Taiwanese chef.

"Who knows if, in real life, he could boil rice," he said. "It doesn't matter, Because, in the film, he convinced me he could cook like a master. At the end of these four days, you won't be an outlaw biker with thirty years experience, but you'll be able to act like one."

He framed Gant's face in the rectangle formed by his hands.

"I'm the director, you're the actor," Flick said, swinging his hands around like a camera to the front door. "Your bike is the burgundy and black Lowrider. That's where it all begins. Go get acquainted. I expect you to know the name and purpose of every visible part, or to ask questions. We ride in a half hour."

"Asshole," the biker who brought the ice pick said contemptuously. He and Flick watched Gant take notes about his bike.

"Maybe not," Flick said. "He's not used to taking orders. I dig that."

Information and preparation are the lawyer's life jackets. Gant lost himself in the bike's mechanics in the same absolute way that he prepared for trial. For him, the Harley's parts fit together as logically as the female reproductive organs in a medical malpractice case — small bits of random information to be borrowed, used and released. Give the jury a chance to find passionate belief in the wonder of ovaries and the old shovelhead engine.

*

Over the next two days, Gant did everything Flick asked of him. When Flick topped one hundred, Gant casually stayed right with him as if he did it daily. If he had to polish the bikes, Gant made them gleam like pieces of jewelry. He copied Flick's gestures with such seriousness and accuracy as to provoke laughter from the bikers and pretended dismay from his mentor.

Like the fingers of sound from a blues guitar, the rumble of his Harley wrapped around Gant's guts and twisted him into a state of reverie. If he could have figured a way to get it into bed, Gant would have slept with his bike.

At the close of the second day, they traveled on a straight country road leading toward the city. Behind them the sun sat directly over the highway glowing like the red-hot headlight on the train from hell. Flick rode nearest the dashed centerline. Gant was forty five degrees and fifteen feet behind him. A dark-colored pickup, three men crowded into the cab, crossed momentarily into their lane, barely missing Flick who swerved to the right and did a tightrope act on the edge of the pavement until he could slow his cycle down and slide it into a U turn.

Gant saw the truck driver toss his head back in laughter as he sped by. He stopped, expecting Flick to join him. Gant saw the back end of Flick's Harley twitch as if goosed as Flick gave it full throttle coming out of the U-turn. The biker hit second as he raced by Gant without looking in pursuit of the pickup.

Gant found Flick at work in the tavern parking lot a few miles up the road. He had smashed the pickup's windshield and dented both doors and the hood into crooked V's. Flick hammered the outside mirror like it was a fast ball down the middle and tossed the tire iron into the truck bed.

"Put your bike around the side by mine and let's get a drink." Flick's tone gave Gant no choice.

The three men sat laughing in a booth with a half pitcher of beer. Construction workers, Gant guessed. He followed Flick to the bar and said "make it two" when Flick ordered a Jack Daniels and water. Before they finished their drink, two more men came in fast.

"Clete," one of them said, "what the hell happened to your truck?"

"What'd you say?" said the man in the maroon blue Panthers cap.

"Your truck. Looks like it went off the cliff," the second man said.

As Clete ran by swearing, Flick bought two bottles of beer. He swiveled the barstool for a one eighty view from door to booth and planted his feet spread apart as if he planned on splitting wood or lifting weights. Arms double wide along the bar, Flick waited.

Gant did a pale imitation. He knew no other way to prepare. He hadn't fought since Robby Ashbaugh pulled his pants down during sixth grade recess. Caught up in the unfolding of events in a life no longer his own, Gant realized only that escape and reason weren't possibilities.

Time temporarily disconnected itself. The ceiling fan squeaked. The ice machine droned. The men stared.

Clete returned hot and wild as a forest fire. "Some motherfucker...." Flick stood, demanding and getting comprehension from Clete. "Biker," he said, surprising Flick with his speed, getting inside, and splitting Flick's lip with a sharp right an instant before Flick busted the full bottle of beer against the side of Clete's head.

The bartender's belated "Take it outside" went unheard as the four other men rushed Flick. He punted one in the crotch with his boot and dropped a second with a vicious shot to the windpipe. The third attacked Flick's back, applying a choke hold with his arm and biting his ear. The fourth, finding Gant in his way, grabbed the lawyer's blond air, and like a discus thrower, hurled him across the barroom nose first onto a pool table. He glanced a wild blow off Flick's forehead and aimed a kick at his groin. Flick twisted, catching the boot on his hip, and kicked the man in the shin. The man shrieked in pain and hopped like a one-legged rooster.

Gagging, Flick groped the head of the man who clung to him until his thumb found an eyeball. He gouged until the man let go with a scream.

Savoring the taste of his own blood, Gant flailed with a pool cue at the man who held his crotch with one hand and an open knife with the other. The man turned as if under attack by bees, undecided whether Gant was worth any additional stress to his throbbing crotch.

"We're quits, right." Flick held his drawn Bowie knife. His voice caused the bar's walls to bulge. It was not a question, but a statement of fact.

No one moved. Flick squatted and wound Clete's beery and bloody hair around his fingers. "I'll cut off your ears, boy, if I ever hear of you messing with bikers." Flick dropped money on the bar to pay for cleanup.

"I appreciate you wanting to help, counselor. Far out," he said to Gant as they walked to their bikes, "but I had it under control. What if that guy had come after you with the knife? What would you have done? I'd have had to save your ass. Can't have a famous lawyer getting hurt while he's under my command. Don't be pissed. I know you wanted to help." He staggered the lawyer with a shoulder slap. "But dig this, next time, turn the cue around. It works better."

The bikers examined with approval Flick's split lip and the teeth marks on his ear and the crusted blood around Gant's nose. They listened to Flick tell the story with the rapt attention given to news of new women or dope buys. When he described Gant's part, Flick altered the spin to give him credit, but certainly not equal billing. Several nodded at Gant, for the first time acknowledging his existence, but not his acceptance.

"You haven't fought much," Flick said. The two men stood next to each other over sinks, cleaning up.

"Never had to."

"Bikers assume they'll be fighting. Wiseguys, like today. Other bikers. Each other. We never back down. No matter what the odds. Rather get our ass kicked. We back down, we're off the road. Dig?"

A neglected part of Gant prodded him to continue the conversation. "I'm concerned about the potential consequences. I punch somebody in a bar. He falls the wrong way and dies. I lose my license and maybe go to prison. Not worth it. That guy you hit today with the bottle, he could have died."

"But he didn't. Can't worry about it. Not a problem until it happens," Flick said.

"Or say he had a gun. Shoots you dead." Gant said.

"Possible," Flick said. "Could have killed me with his truck, too. Not to be melodramatic, but each time we ride we could die. That kind of death, it's not so bad."

"I agree about the bikes. I accept that. But the other, it seems unnecessary."

"You were never in the service."

"True."

"Me neither. I never understood putting it on the line because somebody I don't know orders me to. But I'll tell you what's cool. The guy who does and dies because he stands up for what he believes. The soldier, the biker, the cop. Die in the saddle."

"Like the stressed-out lawyer who dies in the courtroom from a heart attack?"

"Man, I don't know about that."

"What, not Marlboro-man macho enough for you?" Gant said, thickly sarcastic.

"I'm hungry. Let's go eat. You'll meet Molli tomorrow. She's a far-out righteous woman, and that's all I'm going to say about her, so save your breath on the questions."

Gant didn't figure it out until well after Flick finished his dessert. The biker had chosen a family restaurant and firmly requested a table in the corner far from the few other mid week diners. He fervently detailed his documentary film, emphasizing his studio and equipment and his perception of the project's historical value. He eloquently praised the great philanthropists and called those who financially support the arts visionaries. Flick said Gant had the soul of a biker. He would be the perfect financial underwriter for the project. He'd be revered by both bikers and film lovers. It was a true once-in-a-lifetime opportunity. Fate, Flick said, had brought them together.

"You want me to put up money for this biker film of yours, is that it?" Gant said, haughtily incredulous.

"Yeah, that's it. After that, corporate sponsors. I can show you a business plan."

Gant marveled at Flick's diminished size and spoke down to him, delighted to be back in control.

"Are you kidding, Flick? No, I can tell you're actually serious, aren't you?" Gant shook his head in disbelief. "I don't know what you heard about me, but I'm not giving you any money."

"Wait, man. I thought — "

"My deal is that you get me ready for the reunion. That's it. No money exchanges hands. If you got other information, it's wrong and you'll have to deal with it. I'm not involved."

"No financing?"

"Not from me. Flick, think about it. Why would I want to be involved with you? You're a biker. What do you know about the business of making movies?"

Flick cleared his throat. "I see," he said calmly with a quivering undertone of tension. "It's true I haven't made a full-length film. But I am a good businessman. I've built several successful businesses." He sent his forefingers at Gant like attack airplanes. "I wouldn't trade with you or any lawyer. Money and yourself. That's your whole agenda. At least my film will mean something for a lot of people. I'll find the financing somehow. Bet on it."

Gant watched Flick as he had watched many clients. He understood the phases — rejection, anger, comprehension, acceptance, revival, rejection. This unbroken spiral of disappointment was a dark-colored strand coiled around the linear heartbeat of life, like on an old-time barber's pole.

"I want you to know I appreciate all you're doing for me. You're really a pro. I want you to know that," Gant said.

"Yeah, well, it's been different. Tomorrow, be here by eleven."

*

Molli's horoscope said fun and financial opportunity ahead which made her laugh because lawyers had been the predators of her life with her parents' divorce and then the fight over her father's estate. She didn't comprehend Flick's explanation except for the one thousand dollar fee. Be a biker chick to some lawyer for his fantasy high school reunion, he'd said. Bizarre. Far out, as Flick would say. I won't tell mom about this one.

She parked Ingrid under the magnolia. Flick met her halfway to the shop. He looked agitated, as if his emotions were jumping around like popping corn. Right away she got nervous. In the large room he paced, and Molli decided not to ask for the money first thing.

"So, how you been?" she said to get it started.

"Financing. This lawyer won't do squat. He's a taker. I figured he'd be some biker groupie who'd be honored to give. He blew me off like I was lint."

Caution flags came out for Molli. She didn't want a lawyer breathing on her unless she got her money up front.

"So what does that mean for me. Should I go home?" Molli said.

"Financing."

"Yeah, that's what I'm asking. Is there money for me, up front, or should I go?"

"Financing for you? Of course."

Molli shoved his hand away from her breast pocket.

"Do you think that's the night depository slot? Give it here. Thank you. What do I do for it? I can give it back, you know."

"There's got to be a way to get some money out of this guy," Flick said.

"Flick, look, I mean listen — I can't help unless I know what's going on. Tell me everything," Molli said.

Flick replayed the entire experience histrionically and loudly. Flick understood he could lose when he took the risk, the same as if he had bet on a horse to win. But that made it no less grim that he would make the guy's fantasy a reality, and not get paid, he said.

"I wanted to truss him like a turkey and drag him behind the bike until only the rope remained," Flick said.

"And he's got money?" Molli said.

"So Big Sam said. He's a successful lawyer. That I checked."

A fool and his money are soon parted, Molli thought. That old line that leads to the room with the star on the door. I'll bet my body on it.

"I have a spark, a glimmer of an idea," she said. "But you and I have to agree. We split anything we can squeeze from him."

"Seventy-thirty," he said.

"Nope."

"Sixty-forty."

"Half to each, Flick, that's what's fair." As they shook hands Molli said, "nothing crossed?"

"Not me," Flick said, looking up at her from his chair.

Molli sat on his desktop and uncrossed her long legs. The toe of her right foot dangled less than an inch from his left calf. She leaned forward, looked him in the eyes, smiled, and lightly rested her hand on his shoulder.

"Now that I have your attention. Let's do this," she said, and explained her idea.

"Far out," he said at the end, and told Molli it was technically no problem.

"When we're finished with him, he must believe that he's a genuine biker, only genuine is not it exactly," she said.

"Righteous," Flick said with a rare smile.

"That's it. Righteous. You must support everything I say. He'll look to you, man to man, as the authority," Molli said.

"That's cool." He listened to a bike shut down outside. "That's his. Let's do it."

At least he's not a fat pig or scrawny nerd, Molli thought as Gant entered with an awkward swagger. He was the average garden variety, not-bad-looking white American male who expects women to flop, legs apart, like penitents at his feet. She hitched up her tight black leather pants and tossed her black wig as if it were real.

"Sorry about last night, man," Flick said. "Didn't mean any offense."

"Oh, none taken," Gant said, distracted by Molli. "Don't worry about it."

"Take me for a ride," Molli said. They got on his bike and rode away.

"Turn around and stop there," Molli said, pointing toward an empty wayside.

Gant muscled the Harley around and stopped. He swung off the cycle and came at her as if she were in heat.

"Forget it," she said sharply. "You need work on your mounting and dismounting," Molli glared, daring him to make the obvious retort, "and I wanted to save you the embarrassment of doing it at the shop. That's a tough crowd, believe me, I know."

"What's wrong with how I get on and off? The bike, I mean," Gant said.

"You act like you want to kiss its feet. Instead, think of it as your girlfriend. You have one, right?" Molli said.

"No."

Molli put on her surprised face. "Let me tell you, I want a man to respect me, sure. But I don't want him mousing around, feeling like he has to ask if it's okay before he gives me a hug. Bike's the same. Treat it with respect, but just get on it. Understand?"

"Are you serious?"

"It's not a question of whether I'm serious. It's a question of whether you're serious. Now, we're going to this reunion, right?"

"Yeah, sure," Gant said.

"I'm going as the biker girl?"

Gant didn't speak.

"Come on, answer the question," she said.

"Yeah, of course"

"And you want them to believe that I am?"

"Sorry. Am what?"

"A biker chick. You want them to believe I'm a biker chick."

"Oh, I think they will."

"You expect I'll do what's necessary to convince them, correct?" Molli said.

"I'm sure you'll convince them, don't worry about it," Gant said.

"And you expect me to convince them?"

"Yes. But don't worry about it. You'll be fine."

This is fun, Molli thought. Dad's attorney taught me that a lawyer may be the easiest part for an actor to play. "Isn't it true that and isn't it true this?" he kept demanding of me. The question controls. The answer is a small dog jumping through a hoop at the circus. It takes acting skills straight from my classes, as familiar as driving a car.

"And you want them to believe that you're a biker?" she said.

"Yeah. That is what this is about," Gant said.

"You'll do what's necessary to convince them?"

"Best I can."

"You want Flick and I to teach you what's necessary?" Molli said.

"He's done a good job, so far," Gant said.

"You don't know much about being a biker, that's what you expect us to teach you?"

"Right. You playing lawyer or what?' Gant said.

"No, you're the lawyer. Flick and I are the bikers. If the script called for lawyers, I'd be listening to you. Since it calls for bikers, you listen to us."

Gant nodded impatiently.

"So you'll listen to what we tell you?"

"Sure, yeah," he said.

"And do it?"

"Well —"

"No, 'well' isn't an acceptable answer. You either say yes or I'm gone."

"Wait a minute."

"Listen," Molli said, "if you're not committed to being the best biker you can be, then forget it. I'm not spending the weekend in a hotel with a fool."

"No, no. Yeah, yeah. I'm with you all the way. Let's do it right." He laughed. "Just don't be too hard on me."

"Do I look like someone who would be hard on you?"

He stood silent.

"Go get on that bike like she was your woman," she directed with a wink. "You seem to know what that's about."

Gant laughed. He wiped his palms on the front of his shirt and climbed aboard, looking at Molli for approval.

This guy, Molli thought, is high maintenance. He shouldn't be doing this. I could spend a lot of time trying to convince him to go home. Focus on what's best for Molli — my future, my mom, my car, my cat, and myself. Keep your eye on the dressing room star.

"Better," she said. "You know what you need? An earring."

"No earring. I've been through that already," Gant said.

Molli shrugged. "You don't quite have the walk. Flick will help. I do know you have to puff up. Because I'm a woman, I really have to puff when I ride. A small woman, she'd have to puff even more. You're a big, good-looking man, naturally puffed. Stick your chest out and act like this part of the world belongs to you. Know what I mean?"

"Actually, I do. The courtroom."

"Of course. Only don't be polite. There's no judge. You're a biker. You don't ask anyone for permission for anything. 'May I,' ' please,' and 'thank you,' they're out of your vocabulary. Mostly you don't say anything, you just do and take. Now, big boy, take me home."

"Let's ride, woman," Gant said, his voice deep and phony.

Oh, brother, Molli said to herself.

CHAPTER TWELVE

Gant bought the Jack Daniels for general consumption, one quart for the bikers in the shop, the second for Flick, Molli and himself, in appreciation for the good reviews. His performances on the stage of the biker theater were filled with nerveless presence he piped directly from his courtroom experience. Gant's increased confidence chased away his uneasiness. His triumphant vision of the reunion returned, more splendid than ever. He and Molli would be the stars, Gant was certain.

Flick kept him away from the other bikers. One of them called him an ass pretending to be a quarter horse. The bikers laughed about that as they sipped his Jack.

Flick and Molli praised Gant's progress, real and imaginary, as they drank in the large room of the studio. Flick rolled two joints. Gant took a hit, coughed, and apologetically explained that it had been since college. He passed next time and the others nodded knowingly. Molli wanted biker pictures. Flick loaded his camera and checked the flash.

"You two first," she said. They posed, toasting each other, arm wrestling with Gant winning, and trying to imitate Butch and Sundance.

"Terrific," Molli said, giving Gant the camera. She called the shots — the compulsory toast, Molli, her mouth an amazed circle, squeezing Flick's bicep. Molli, standing in front of Flick and clutching his cupped hands to her breasts, both sternly defiant as prairie farmers, Molli sitting on Flick's lap French kissing as if they meant it.

"One more," Flick said, handing her the matches. "Don't actually light it." He put the fresh joint in his mouth and leaned toward her.

"Our turn, Jake," Molli said gleefully. They repeated the sequence. Gant did fine with the toast and bicep squeeze.

"God, will you relax? Your hands feel like saucepans," she said, glowering at him over her shoulder and holding his hands on her breasts. "It doesn't mean anything. Just photos for fun."

"Nor does that, although it was very nice," Molli said after the kiss scene, straightening his hair with her fingers. "Now, put the joint in your mouth."

"No. Sorry. That I won't do," Gant said too loudly.

"Oh, okay. Whatever. Like I said, we're just having fun," Molli said.

"Biker shots, man," Flick said. "Nobody's going to know."

"I can't do it," Gant said.

"Okay, a family shot. You be in the middle, Jake." Molli threw her right arm over Gant's shoulder, still holding the joint.

Molli's right, Gant thought. What's a vacation without photos.

"Hey, Flick," he said full of himself and the Jack Daniels, "get a shot of me and Molli on the bike. Do I look all right now? Notice, new jeans. Got them at the co-op today."

"Cool. That's right," Flick said. "It went all right?"

"Fantastic. Tell you in a minute. But, I need a jacket like yours with that design on it."

"Design?" Flick said.

"The skull. It's the only design on your jacket."

Flick's laugh erupted from some hidden place like an undiscovered undersea volcano. It filled the room and brought in the other bikers, most of whom had never heard their leader laugh.

Molli waved them away. "Get it together, Flick," she said sharp as a slap. "So you call the design your colors. Big deal. Jake didn't know."

"Design. Far out." Flick brushed at his eyes. "I know. Not laughing at you, Jake. Can't do it, man. Have to be in the gang to wear colors." His chuckles continued like aftershocks.

"Gang colors. I knew that. What about the ones hanging up side down on the wall in the other room?" Gant said.

"They belonged to gangs we took off the road," Flick said.

"Which means?"

"Years ago, a couple of gangs tried to establish themselves in our territory. We took them off the road. Put them out of business. Dig?" He paused. "You could wear one of those. Been so long, nobody would know. Nobody would care." He chuckled again. "Tell us about the co-op."

"I parked right in front of the co-op like you said," Gant said as Flick popped the roll of film from the camera.

Molli intercepted the roll on its way to Flick's pocket. "I'll take it."

"The five or six people by the door seemed to freeze when I

pulled up," Gant said. "They stayed that way until I was in the store. I have to tell you, it was the damnedest feeling. Made me smile." He held up his hand. "Don't get me wrong. I'm not saying I think I'm a biker. I know I'm not. But they thought I was a biker. That's the important part. It was cool."

"Did you say you smiled?" Flick said.

"Yeah, why?" Gant said defensively.

"Except when he's with his own, an outlaw biker never smiles at strangers. That's number one. Number two, always challenge people by looking them right in the eyes. Three, don't give ground to anyone, unless they're using a walker. Dig?"

"No smiles. Look them in the eye. Don't give ground. I got it," Gant said.

"It has to do with perception, not reality. All those good citizens out there expect bikers to be rude and crude and scary. They see a cement block on every biker's shoulder. They're conditioned to believe this means 'don't even look funny at me or I'll bust your head in.' You have to fit their image of you or they don't believe you're real. If you go to this reunion all happy and smiley, they'll think you made a wrong turn on your way to a costume party. You don't want that to happen, man. You've worked too hard," Flick said.

"And done an excellent job. You should be proud," Molli said. She looked at him. "I mean it. To Jake Gant, righteous biker." She toasted and drank her whiskey down.

"To great teachers," Gant said earnestly. He finished his drink and refilled the three tumblers. "What you say about the good citizens perception is true. I had this case. Biker accused of killing a girl. I made him shave his beard, lose the earrings, get regular clothes. Generally clean himself up. I wouldn't let any of his friends come to the trial, just his wife. Both small people. She looked like she worked at Awl-mart. He looked like he installed cable. DA was a real bitch. Kept going on about him being an outlaw biker. He's answering 'yes ma'am, no ma'am.' Hard to imagine him terrorizing anybody." Gant took a sip, enjoying their attention. "Jurors looked very surprised, shocked really, when they came back with their decision and found the courtroom full of bikers behaving as the DA had described. Of course, it didn't matter because they had made their decision. I really fooled them."

"Which was?" Molli said.

"Acquittal. The DA was extremely pissed," Gant said.

"Did he kill her?" Molli said.

"Don't know. Don't care. I never asked him."

"Man, you're too much," Flick said.

"As the saying goes," Molli said, "looks can be deceiving. Either of you been to Mardi Gras?"

Both men shook their heads.

"Now that's a party," she said. "People say what they want, do what they want. It's crazy. Lot's of costumes and masks. Some are beautiful. I mean really beautiful. I'm in this bar. Bikers. Students. Who knows? Someone has grass. I'm feeling no pain. It's so crowded that people press up against you, then move on. You've been there, right? You wait for the right fit. Suddenly, I had mine. Like Marlon Brando in "The Wild Ones," only taller. Pretty soon we're in his hotel room. He goes into the bathroom and I strip and hop in bed. I'm wondering what's taking so long when he calls out that he needs the light out. It seemed weird, but it's Mardi Gras, I'm high, and all I want is him in bed. So I turn out the light. I reach down to check the goods and my hand finds nothing but fur. I feel around, thinking it must be here somewhere. Then Marlene says in a throaty voice, 'honey, that feels wonderful.' I'm dressed before she takes her next breath. I just wasn't in the mood."

Gant lit a cigarette, and Flick drew on his joint, both waiting.

"What?" Molli said, wide eyes expressing mock surprise. "Some nights beef, some nights fish."

Gant and Flick exchanged the conspiratorial grins of boys outside the girls' shower.

"We had something like that out in Oakland," Flick said. "This undercover cop dressed as a she. Tough looking. Found out about it when we got drunk and decided to gang-bang her. Left him naked in the can of a mean gay bar on Saturday night. Bad scene. Never did see him again. But that was a while ago. You know, New Orleans used to be a major drug distribution center. Along came the feds and, boom, everything moved to Miami. And Houston. Caught a lot of lawyers, as I recall." He looked at Gant. "You remember that?"

"As a matter of fact, I know someone who defended one of them. Big money involved," Gant said.

"Money and drugs go together like," Flick slid his glass at Gant with a pot-induced grin, "Jack Daniels and water."

"Leather and lace," Molli said.

"French fries and ketchup," Gant said.

"You hungry?"

"No. Why? Are you?" Gant said.

They all laughed.

"What happened to the lawyer your friend defended?" Molli said.

"Not my friend. Plea bargain. Don't remember exactly. Some prison time, a fine. Main thing, he lost his license." Gant held the three-quarters empty bottle to the light and searched the whiskey for hidden truths before sloshing another three fingers into his glass. He knew that the whiskey lured him outside the safety of his walls into the general populace. Liars, manipulators and sweet talkers lurked everywhere, often disguised as the innocent, deserving and needy. Gant knew, but no longer cared. He rambled on.

"Lost his, or her, license. That's what we say, isn't it?" Gant said with a drunken politically correct acknowledgment to Molli. "Not careless-lost like a coat at the arena or a purse at the restaurant. Too precious for that. It's practically sewn into the skin for safekeeping in law school. More lost like a person in a crowd. The lawyer is seduced by some unexpected fireworks show of new experiences and neglects the indispensable for an instant. The license disappears like a small child momentarily released from the parent's hand.

"Mostly, lost kids turn up, but not lost licenses. His license got lost in big pile of money. Money, that's it almost always. I've been asked 'Jake, what would it take?' You know, with drugs, how much money to take the risk. Not serious, you understand, because it was other lawyers asking." He giggled. "Of course, other lawyers, they could have been serious, ha. I always said five, ten million. Today, somebody offered me that kind of money, I might risk it."

"No maybe for me," Flick said quickly.

"Me either. I'm there in a heartbeat." Molli focused through the fog from the evening of booze and grass. "But, then, bikers and drugs go together like, what did you say, French fries and —"

"French fries and ketchup."

"Right, Flick?" Molli said casually. "Tell him about your operation."

"No, Molli, I don't —"

"He's cool. Tell him," she said.

"A good business. I'm small time now. Regular customers. Regular orders. Need a dependable supplier. Mexicans now. Quality control. I buy from the same people. No way they'll screw with me. Cash, of course. Everyone thinks that bikers can get drugs. I generally keep a small amount for those emergencies, for friends. But, yeah, definitely bikers and drugs." He grabbed Gant's arm. "Of course, if anybody asked me about what I just said, I'd call them a liar."

"What did you say?" Gant said, cupping his ear and smiling stupidly.

"That's right," Flick said. "Drugs and bikes and women and money. That's what we know."

"And that's what they'll expect us to talk about," Molli said. "You okay with that?"

"Absolutely!" Gant leered crookedly. "And sex and rock and roll."

"Far fucking out," Flick said.

Molli engulfed Gant with a hug. "This is going to be so much fun."

CHAPTER THIRTEEN

The hotel was a tacky glass tribute to greed and expediency located near the airport. A smooth asphalt road, named after the hotel, tethered it to the rest of the world. Gant and Molli cruised up that road and stopped in a no parking zone under the wide, arched canopy outside the front entrance.

Molli noticed the nondescript tan van which Flick had parked as close to the hotel as possible earlier in the day. He had told her not to worry about what was in the van and that, as long as she didn't lose her watch, the operation would run as smooth as a Harley on the open road.

"Nobody touches the bike or I'll have your ass," Gant said to the startled doorman, looking him right in the eyes and not smiling. He stretched his body with a ripple, as if he had been riding for hours, as Molli brushed her hair.

For the benefit of whoever watched her, she bent over to replace her brush in her small overnight bag, stretching the skin-tight leather pants around her buttocks and legs. The knee-high slits along the side of her pants were stitched with black thongs. Her long sleeve shirt of pale blue fishnet complimented the white skin left exposed. The cleavage of the black leather vest plunged to the first silver snap several inches south of her breasts, which were highlighted by a large gold pendant and four gold chains. The chain of her maternal grandfather's watch looped from a vest pocket. On the sides, she cropped her hair close to emphasize the angles of her face. The two-inch flattop dropped like a waterfall down the back of her head to a point. Her earrings, clusters of dangling gold, captured the sunlight. She smiled savagely and came at Gant and the doorman like Mad Max's girlfriend in her deeply oiled, black, square-toed boots.

She squeezed Gant's hand with both of hers and nuzzled against him. "Let's go, big boy."

Hand in hand they sauntered through the automatic doors into a lobby with dozens of Gant's middle-aged classmates trying to catch up on twenty-five years by chattering excitedly about the middle class trinity — children, jobs, and houses. With each clomp of boots, creak of leather, and rattle of chains, another cluster stopped talking and stared, trying to fit Gant and Molli into the picture. By the time the couple reached the hotel registration counter, no one spoke except for a gossiping trio by the large fern who quit with red-faced chirps when they realized everyone was listening.

"Gant," he said loudly to the clerk. "Jake Gant. I want the best you've got. I'll be paying cash."

As he turned to face his audience, Molli pressed her left breast into Gant's arm. Cheap thrills for Jake and the men in the audience. Look at them, she thought, working hard to repress a grin. They're in a stunned state of absolute awe. Jake's acting like royalty of the dark side. Best of show at Halloween. And me? Queen of the biker's ball.

"Excuse me," a short, pear-shaped woman in a violent blue dress said pleasantly, interrupting their stroll to the elevator. "You need to come get your name tag. You too, Mrs. Gant. It is Mrs. Gant, isn't it?"

"Actually, no," Molli said.

Gant groped awkwardly for control by hooking his arm around Molli.

"Just put her down as my chick," he said dumbly.

"That wouldn't do for the name tag," the woman in blue said. She looked at Molli, pen poised. "And what should I put down as your name?"

"Molli. No 'e'," she said.

The woman repeated the letters silently as she neatly printed them in the first name side of the space. "And your last name?"

"None," Molli said.

"None?"

"None. Like Cher."

The woman considered Molli's suddenly lopsided name tag from an artistic standpoint, obviously displeased with its off center appearance. She sniffed as she put the paper into the plastic holder and held it at arms length to Molli.

"It must be worn at all times."

"Of course," Molli said. "I know you'd forget me without it." She stuck out her chest at Gant. "Here, dear, you can do me."

"Oh, my," the woman said, blinking rapidly and retreating.

The women and men in the crowd stirred reflexively for

different reasons as Gant unhooked the pin and shoved it into the leather of the vest.,

Gant maintained his biker decorum until Molli closed the door to the hotel room. He sprawled on a bed and laughed as he did when an opposing attorney disappeared irrevocably through a verbal trap door Gant had set.

"They were speechless. Dumbstruck. Completely baffled and amazed. Come here. Wasn't it perfect? Come here! I'll tell you what, they were completely fooled. Come lie down here," he said.

You knew it was coming, she thought. Put him off until you can trade it for what you want. Play him like a piano, using all the keys, she thought. "I never ball in the middle of a job," she said bluntly.

"Job?" he said.

"Yeah. Job. As your biker chick, remember?"

"But, I thought."

"I know. Because of how I come on to you. That's part of the role, understand? Let me sit and tell you something. Don't touch, now." Molli sat down beside him on the bed absently fondling her watch. "Being with you isn't a job. But down there is a job. We have two more days. I want to keep doing it perfect for you. I like you a lot. Truthfully, I think, once we get started, we may come up for air and that's all. It'll be that good. Be patient. Our time will come."

Gant resolutely put a hand on her thigh.

Molli froze. "Don't!"

His hand slowly inched upward. Molli stood quickly and frowned at him.

"Tonight, then," he said with impatient finality.

"We'll see," she said, rolling her hips. "Who were those people down there? Did you recognize them?"

"To tell the truth, I didn't pay attention to them," he said. "I was watching you."

She again deflected the conversation. "Am I going to hear wild stories tonight about your high school life? Chasing girls? Doing dope?"

Gant shook his head. "I never cared much for high school. It was something I did. That's all."

"Did you have a lot of friends?"

"No, not really," he said.

"I don't get it. Why did you come to the reunion?" she said.

"I wanted to fool them. Shock them. And see how they turned out so I could compare," Gant said.

"Comparing your lawyer life, not your biker life?" Molli said. Gant nodded.

"You're one of the smartest people I ever met, so if you say that works for you, I believe. I don't understand it, though."

"How about you? I suppose you loved high school?"

"I did, actually," Molli said. "Had a good time. Never have been to a reunion. Figured that was then, this is now. I never wanted to mix them together."

*

By definition, a reunion not only reunites the participants, but unites now with then. Blood brings families together to measure the children and honor the elders. A common event, often terrifying, causes participants to periodically gather to celebrate the wonder of their survival and commemorate the courage of the victims. High school classmates, randomly tossed together like a jury, assemble to weigh themselves on the scale of relativity. Their incestuous judging of each other continues until the last triumphant cackle of the sole survivor.

Gant was ambivalent about attending a sit down meal followed by a program of unspecified length. But Molli looked so stunning in a new sheer white shirt with black sequins that he was willing to follow her anywhere. On the way to the banquet room, the elevator door opened on a couple obviously anxious about riding with bikers, which added to Gant's pleasure.

They entered the hall like they knew important secrets and sat by themselves at the end of one of the long tables. Gant tersely returned a nod from someone who looked barely familiar and ignored a friendly, anonymous yell of "she's looking good, Jake." A woman in a high-cut evening dress and diamond cross sat next to Molli, gave her a rock-hard smile, and ignored her with a snobby vengeance. As the salads were being served, a couple timidly took the last chairs across from Gant and Molli.

"I'm Al Schmidtke. Used to call me Butterball. I think we were in physics together," the man said. "This is my wife Alice." He turned to his wife. " This is Jake Gant, honey."

Gant shook Al's hand and belched at Alice. "Can't say as I remember you." Molli nudged him. "Oh, yeah, this is Molli."

"I love your hair," Alice said to Molli. "I wish I had the nerve."

"I saw your motorcycle," Al said between bites. " I don't know much about them, but I recognized the name, Harley Davidson. Some of the guys who go to our church have them. Did have them up until a few weeks ago. A gang held them up with guns right on the church parking lot. Rode them off. About a dozen of them. I guess they must be valuable, huh?"

"You say they held them up with guns?" Molli said.

"That's what I heard," Al said.

"At the church?"

"Right."

"What is the country coming to, really?" Molli said loudly, drawing disapproving looks from their neighbors, who were listening to the speaker.

"Amen," Alice said. "God will get them."

Gant heard the senior class president name some teachers who waved to the applause. Their aged faces returned to Gant as the ghostly keepers of his discarded memories. The speaker made a joke about the double-wide size of the ex-star quarterback who laughed the loudest and told his classmates the name of his real estate company. He felt Molli tugging at him, saying stand up. He heard his name over the PA.

"...wins the award for biggest surprise. Reminds me of that old ad about the ninety-eight pound weakling on the beach who bulks up like Schwartzenegger. I bet he's got plenty of stories. And Jake found quite a companion as well. Molli, right? Stand up, Molli, so everybody knows who you are. "

Molli called his challenge and raised the bet by climbing onto the table and bowing low, aiming her buttocks at the face above the diamond cross on her left. From her impromptu stage, Molli impersonated the woman who stalked off, unaware that her classmates laughed at her.

Molli's performance destroyed any chance that the president could continue. His audience wanted to party. His gratitudes and platitudes were muffled by the sounds of voices loudly making decisions.

"Let's roll," she said to Gant. Walking in step and promising R-rated stories, Molli and Gant led their contingent of the curious into the hotel's main lounge.

"Remember not to let them too close. An actor doesn't fraternize with the audience until after the show closes," Molli said to Gant casually, as if discussing tomorrow's weather, as she searched the room for the two stools which would be at the focal point for the greatest number of people. She ordered two Jack Daniels and water.

A crowd drew near.

"Jake, remember the way that cop looked when you tore up his ticket? God, that was funny. You ever tear up a ticket?" Molli said to a man in a peach golf shirt whose eyes followed her hands as she pretended to slowly wind her watch.

"No," he said. "Did you really tear it up?" he said to Gant. And they were off.

Make it like working a jury, he said to himself. Molli leaned against him, smiling. He recalled Mouse's description of an incident several years ago.

"It was three tickets, not one," Gant said toughly. "Loud pipes, balding tire. What was the third? Bent license plate. All bullshit. Small town cop in the middle of nowhere in Texas. I tossed the pieces to the wind. He pulled his gun to arrest us. We rode away laughing at him standing by the road, gun in hand, impotent as a castrated bull."

"Was it worth it?" a woman said. "He might have shot you."

Gant thought of Flick and looked scornfully down at her. "Fuck, yes. I stand up for what I believe in. My bike was legal. No small town cop's going to hassle me. If he kills me, I'm dead. Not such a bad way to go."

It went on like a TV game show. Molli picked the topic. Gant made up the story. The audience voted by their continued presence. He told them the stories they wanted to hear — rambling, imaginative stories of wild parties full of drugs and sex and formations of bikes blasting down some high plains highway and the tale of the good timing run to Lake Tahoe when fifty cases of beer didn't last the first day. Three bikers passed out in a tree and fell, like ripe fruit, to the ground during the night without waking up. Gant captivated them with his rendition of the biker chick myth complete with the clubhouse parties and the room with mattresses for a floor. He confirmed a fantasy that they wanted no part of except in books and movies.

"Let me buy you a drink," the ex-quarterback said.

"Since you're buying, make them doubles," Molli said, giving the realtor a knowing wink. "Jake, tell them the one about when I got so wasted from the acid someone slipped in the New Year's punch."

Gant glanced quizzically at Molli.

"You remember. In New Orleans."

"Oh, yeah," Gant squeezed Molli's thigh tight enough to make her jump, "but you tell that story better than anyone."

She gracefully chased his hand away. "We were guests of another club. Hell's Angels, I think. They'd started partying hard day after Christmas and were just getting up to speed when we got there. Drugs everywhere, right?"

"Everywhere. But that's usual," Gant said knowingly.

"And as usual, you were doing pot and wine," Molli said.

"Yeah, good shit, too."

"Back then I was trying to stay clean. There was this huge punch bowl. People emptied bottles into it and used cans of fruit juice to fix the flavor. I figured it was the safest thing around. Someone dumped in some acid. Like as a joke. Brutal. The next thing I really remember is getting ready for a Super Bowl party in San Antonio. Honest. Jake had to get stoned to get on my wave length, isn't that right?" she said.

"Yeah. Otherwise you were talking in a foreign tongue. It was strange," Gant said.

"You could get work writing scripts for TV. What a life you two have," the ex-quarterback said.

"And what's the point?" the woman said.

Murmuring among themselves, the classmates turned away from Molli and Gant, like a carnival crowd no longer curious about the two-headed man and tattooed lady. A baker's dozen arranged themselves in chairs around a conference table constructed by clumsily dragging three tables together. The mood was anxious, expectant, as if attending the grand opening of a new wing in the museum of their lives. Each person's life was a part of a larger exhibit with individual achievements and flaws condensed into a judgment of the whole. The reunion provided an eerie preview of their generation's place in history.

Gant and Molli sat at the bar listening to his classmates discuss the problems of their lives with the candor of a confessional until they stood up and dispersed after about a half an hour.

Gant remained on the barstool contemplating the aptness of his role as spectator. Based on his personal experience, he had nothing to contribute.

Molli intentionally spilled the tepid remains of her drink on Gant's knee. Startled, he looked crossly at her.

"I'm so sorry. It slipped," she said, using a bar rag to blot him with uncharacteristic daintiness. "We're getting visitors."

Gant squinted against the dim light in the direction of her nod. Is that D'Oreo? he wondered. Wow. She's certainly stayed away from the pizza, he thought.

"Can we talk with you outside?" the ex-quarterback said, looking about furtively.

"You're Andrea D'Oreo, right?" Gant said as they followed him into a vacant meeting room.

"You got it. I hate wearing name tags," the woman said.

"So, how have you been?" Gant said. "You look great."

"Terrific. Three restaurants, four kids and a great husband."

"Still D'Oreo, though?" Gant said.

"How could I give up that name? You married? Kids?" D'Oreo said.

"No. None of that."

"You know, I've got to tell you," she said, "I never, in a million years, would have figured you for a biker."

The ex-quarterback cleared his throat. His fat face glistened as he smiled his realtor's smile.

"Don't be offended. It's that, you know, what we hear about bikers is that they have, what do I say? Access to drugs. Like I said, don't be offended, but some of us, well, we were wondering —"

"Just say it, for God's sake," Molli said, pulling out her watch.

"Yeah, right. Well, can you sell us some coke? Just for our use. Get the party rocking. Now if you can't, we understand."

"Shouldn't be a problem," Molli said and turned to Jake. "They seem okay to me. I'd be for it. But they're your friends. Whatever you say. You just want a few ounces, right?"

"Yeah, few ounces. Whatever you can do," the realtor said earnestly.

"Please, Jake, for old times," D'Oreo said.

"There's no reason you can't sell them some, is there, darling?" Molli said.

"Yeah, I suppose. If I had it. But, remember, we decided to ride clean," Gant said.

"Not tonight. But tomorrow. Your stash isn't that far away. And believe me," Molli said as she dropped her voice an octave and burlesqued a lascivious wink at Gant, "I'm going to need fresh air after you and I have our party."

Molli's promise combined with the unveiled expressions of astonishment from the ex-quarterback and the once coveted D'Oreo muffled the lawyerly warning sirens in his head. It's vacation. It's a game, he thought.

"I'll get it tomorrow. Could get fucked up myself. More like a funeral than a party here," Gant said.

"Yes," the ex-quarterback said, pumping his chubby right fist. "You're great. Say, if you don't mind me asking, what kind is it?"

Gant played another portion from his Flick tape. "I don't deal like I used to. I always buy from the same source. Mexicans now. For a few regular customers, personal use. An emergency stash for friends in need. Like you. Lowers the risk. Colombian. Very smooth. Very nice. Right, Molli?"

"Absolutely. Jake always has the best stuff. Blows you away," Molli said.

"Great," the ex-quarterback said. "I'm in four-twenty-nine."

"Tomorrow afternoon sometime," Molli said to him, taking hold of Gant's arm. "Bedtime, darling."

In their room, Molli carefully hung her vest on the chair by the bedside. She seduced from slightly beyond the reach of Gant who sat on the bed. Head held proud, she outlined her breasts, belly and hips with her hands. Her fingers undid the two top buttons of her blouse before she spoke.

"Call Flick," she said.

"Tomorrow." Gant bounced up, close enough to touch her, and tossed his vest over a chair arm.

Molli stepped back. "Now." She unbuttoned one more.

The small triangle of flesh beneath her black bra dully glistened a smoldering tropic white. It electrified Gant's body. He sucked air, searching for his cool.

"It can wait." He stripped off his shirt and thrust his chest at Molli to hide the slight paunch. He had no control over the love handles which bulged over his jeans like fresh baked dough.

Molli returned to the previous button. "Please, Jake, call now." She flipped her hair for the dramatic effect "I couldn't bear to have my thoughts wander elsewhere while we're experiencing coital ecstasy."

Gant laughed and spread his arms foolishly, exposing the pale under parts missed by the tanning lamp.

"You're funny," he said tenderly, "come here."

Molli buttoned herself up. "You aren't listening. Pay attention. I don't want to be thinking of anything else when we screw. That clear enough?" With provocative toughness, she cocked a hip at him.

She's a phone call away, Gant thought. What the hell. I can always change my mind. "Get back to work on those buttons. What's his number?"

Molli got rid of the blouse as she danced toward him. He held the phone away from his ear so she could hear the ringing. On the fifth ring he gestured pessimistically. She held up ten fingers. Flick answered after the next ring. At the instant Gant spoke, Molli popped the snap at the front of her bra. Bracketed by fluttering silk, her breasts dropped free inches from his moving mouth.

"Jake Gant, Flick. I need your help with something," he said, his voice wobbling and his eyes feeding on Molli's skin. "No, the bike's fine. Molli, too."

Molli leaned over him. He looked to her for the words.

"I need to buy a four ounces of coke to sell here," she mouthed.

"I need to buy a four ounces of coke," Gant said to Flick.

Molli heard Flick tell Gant he didn't catch it all, to repeat it. She simultaneously unsnapped their jeans.

"I said I need to buy a four ounces of coke," Gant said very quickly. "To sell here. I'll pick it up tomorrow. You got that now?"

She pushed Gant back onto the bed and pulled down his zipper. The phone fell from the night stand.

"What's going on there?" Flick said.

"Nothing," Gant said. "Around noon okay? You have to speak up. I'm having trouble hearing you. You say you want to speak to Molli?"

Breathing heatedly, she shook her head.

"She's busy. Can't get to the phone. I sound weird? Must be the phone. I'm fine. Okay. I really have to go. See you tomorrow," Gant said.

Molli smiled dreamily at Gant as she slid her right hand under his pants and began to massage him. Her left hand stroked herself. Eyes shut, she swayed like an apple tree in a hot August breeze.

Later, Gant broke his own rule about not smoking in bed. He heard Molli's breathing steady and shallow next to him. I don't care if she's asleep or pretending, Gant thought. I expected a forest fire of passion. More like a bonfire. So much for the biker girl myth. I'm about done with this reunion. Maybe one more day. Maybe.

*

In the morning, Gant didn't know Molli was up until he heard the shower. He ran his tongue over the ridges in his mouth. They tasted like wet corrugated cardboard. His pubic hair was matted and snarled. He desperately wanted to soap yesterday away and had intended to be the first to shower. But it had been so long since Gant had shared his morning with a woman, he hadn't considered the possibility that Molli would dare leave the bed without speaking and occupy the bathroom without asking.

The skull on the back of his vest gave him a wrinkled smile from the floor. He shook it smooth and hung it up with the disinterest of a discount store clerk. Gant realized he had nothing else to wear. He tugged on his leathers and ordered two continental breakfasts and extra coffee. The black leather fully covered his front from waist down, but exposed his buttocks and the backs of his legs.

Molli emerged from the bathroom wearing one towel wrapped around her hair and another loosely about her waist.

"Aren't we gay this morning," she said playfully, ogling his outfit.

"I ordered food," he said, ignoring her. "Money's on the table."

She lazily snapped a towel at his passing rear. He growled and closed the door. Moments later he reappeared, dumbfounded.

"You used both big towels, Molli."

"Sorry. Here" She tossed him her body towel.

"It's wet."

"But clean wet," she said.

"I can't believe you."

She opened the drapes. It was gray and drizzling.

Except for her boots, Molli was dressed when Gant came out of the bathroom. He put on underwear and jeans, then ate his breakfast without looking at her. After he grunted off her attempts at light conversation, she quit. Both acted as if last night had never happened and that they didn't want it to happen again. She pulled her boots on and brushed her hair.

"I'm going out," she said. "We need to leave for Flick's at ten-thirty."

"No, I'm not doing that. No more about drugs," Gant said.

"But you promised your friends." She turned briefly to the window. The rain had diminished to a light sprinkle.

"Hardly my friends. Why do you care about them anyway?" Gant said.

"I don't. "

"You've seemed so concerned all along about this deal. Encouraging me to agree. Making me call Flick last night."

"Don't be that way. Personally, I couldn't care less. I thought it would make you popular. I thought you wanted that," Molli said.

"With these guys? Who cares?"

"But what are you going to tell them?"

"I don't know. Maybe blame the rain."

"Yeah, that is a hard sprinkle. Whatever. You better call Flick."

"Why?"

"What do you mean 'why?'"

"Why? That's what I mean," he said.

"Because he'll be waiting," Molli said.

"So?"

"Jake!"

"You're concerned about Flick, you call him. He's your guy, anyway."

"My guy? What's with you today?"

"Just regular me."

"Yeah, right. What, last night wasn't as good as you anticipated?"

Gant shrugged.

"That makes two of us," Molli said disgustedly. "I'll call Flick from the lobby. See you for lunch."

"Don't bother."

"No, I'm on duty until it's over," Molli said.

"If I need your help, I'll ask," Gant said grimly.

He checked the morning calendar of events — tour of the athletic facilities, program for kids, a mini-tennis tournament. TV wasn't any better. He skimmed a third of a magazine Flick gave him before discarding it for lack of interest. He finally found refuge in a heavily underlined book about contemporary India that he discovered toward the top of Molli's travel bag. By skipping a few chapters, Gant finished it by lunch time. As he tucked it back into the bag, curiosity overcame him. He pawed amidst clothes until he hit a hard object wrapped in plastic which he withdrew to examine. The baggy held two miniature nine-volt batteries. He studied them momentarily before tucking them back in the corner of the bag.

Gant waited to go downstairs until he was quite sure Molli wouldn't be joining him. He loaded his plate in the buffet line. His fierce biker scowl kept the table empty until he finished eating. On his way out, the ex-quarterback and D'Oreo cut him off. He let them escort him to an empty room.

"Do you have it?" the ex-quarterback said eagerly.

"No," Gant said staring cold and flat into his eyes.

"Oh. What time will you have it?"

"I won't," Gant said.

"I don't understand." The friendly tone disappeared from his voice. "I thought —"

Gant looked toward the window. "Too wet too ride."

D'Oreo and the ex-quarterback exchanged incredulous looks. "Too wet?" she said. "What are you saying? A shower maybe, but we didn't even cancel the kids' outside games this morning."

"Is that supposed to mean something?" Gant said.

"I guess it means you haven't changed, Jake Gant. Pizza D'Oreo, remember?" She gave him the grown up version of the laugh which haunted him in high school. "Still Mr. All-Talk-and-No-Action."

"You couldn't make the team in high school, Gant," the ex-quarterback said, emboldened by his classmate. "Tough biker or not, you couldn't make my team today."

"Fuck you and who cares," Gant said at their departing backs. In the hallway, he saw the pair talking to a small group. The conversation stopped as he walked by. They all stared at him and grinned. Familiar legal terms caused him to stop at the fringe of another cluster. They glared at him with the disdain reserved for discredited witnesses and non-lawyers generally until he left. A slender man popped up from a lobby chair from a lobby chair. His name tag said "Fred N." He told Gant, and everyone else in the room, that he was a mechanic and a born again Christian. He said he quit working on bikes when he found Jesus because the bikers were too dirty and foul and profane.

"They weren't like you, that's for sure. Say, your bike is a beauty. Eighty Lowrider, right?"

"Right." Gant nervously looked to escape.

"One of the Shovelheads. What have you done about the oil leak? You have to replace the valves? What about electrical problems?"

"Get out of my way." Gant, sweating, pushed roughly by the startled mechanic.

"Sweet Jesus, save his soul," he said loud enough to be heard out on the highway. "He doesn't know what I'm talking about. I know it from the look in his eyes. Praise the Lord. Never knew a biker who didn't care for his own bike."

Gant focused on the elevator. He desperately wanted an empty car direct to his floor. He would pack his bags and go, Molli or no Molli.

"Jake Gant." It was the officious woman wearing the same tired blue dress. "I've been looking for you. The hotel says your motorcycle is improperly parked. You must move it into the garage immediately. You should have done it earlier. Look at it rain."

Huge drops shattered on the asphalt. The wind from the thunderstorm blew sheets of water under the portico and onto the bike. The woman folded her arms and waited expectantly as if Gant were a recalcitrant student. He dutifully pulled the keys from his pocket. Everyone watched him start for the door.

"Wait a minute. You think I'm stupid? I'm not going out in that," he said, veering back toward the elevator.

"They said they'd tow," she said.

Gant raised his arms without pausing.

"And they wondered why you have Carolina tags if you're from Wisconsin."

Gant stabbed at the elevator button. In his first trial, a witness gave him a totally unexpected answer which made perfect sense. The surprise response obliterated his carefully conceived trial plan and left him mute in the middle of the courtroom. Everyone had stared at him as if he were an actor who forgot his lines. Eventually, the judge got a laugh by sarcastically inquiring into the whereabouts of his tongue. As his eyes darted from one floor indicator panel to another, he had the same sense of public failure. He recalled that, after the judge's cruel rescue, he recovered to win the case. Gant grimly realized that outcome would not be duplicated here. The bell mercifully dinged the elevator's arrival.

"Ah. Don't come sneaking in like that," Molli said as she came out of the bathroom. "Scared me shitless."

"Get packed. We're leaving," he said.

"Why? What happened to you?"

"Never mind. Let's go."

"Look outside. You wanted rain, you got it. No way we're going anywhere."

"I'm going. You do what you want."

"I know, you're a tough guy. Swim the Mississippi with lead shoes. Walk across the Mojave with no shoes. And I know you know almost everything. But let me have my say so I'm comfortable with myself when I hear about your suicide. In case you've forgotten, here's what happens on a motorcycle in this weather. First, you get absolutely soaked. Second, those raindrops sting your face hard like wasps. Third, your glasses keep fogging over. Fourth, the water gets in your eyes. Probably others I can't think of. You do what you want. Me, it's dry here. Room service. TV. I'm not moving," Molli said.

The rain intensified, noisily changing the window into frosted glass. Gant had difficulty distinguishing the colors of cars in the parking lot. Okay, he thought. It's like I'm at an airport somewhere between here and there. I'm on the last flight out and it's been canceled. It's out of my control. Nothing to do but wait for tomorrow.

Their relationship spent, they let the television eat the remainder of the day in half hour bites. They bedded down sexlessly, like an unhappily married couple each hoping to outlive the other. The telephone wake-up call came at five a.m. They were on the bike forty five minutes later and at Flick's by seven.

Gant dropped the keys in the mail slot. He decided against a note. "Thanks" would be a lie and anything else was too complicated.

Molli turned on Ingrid's radio immediately after she started the car. They made excellent time to the airport in the light Sunday morning traffic. She stopped and Gant got out like he was very late.

"Good luck," Molli said.

"Yeah, you too," he replied.

CHAPTER FOURTEEN

"Where is he?" Flick said.

Molli pointed at the sky as she hopped off the cycle parked in front of the shop. She made two stops on her way back from the airport and still had waited a good twenty minutes for Flick.

"They ran him out early. We would have left yesterday but for the rain. Baby-sitting him in the room from mid-afternoon almost drove me over the edge. He can be a real jerk. He wouldn't tell me what happened. Assume it had to do with him backing out of the drug deal. I'll tell you, I'm glad to be done with that."

"I dig it. My son split the rehab center. I've been searching all night. He finally showed up down at the store," Flick said. "You got the tapes?"

Molli held up a plastic bag from a toy store. "I left all your recording stuff in the van. Here's the key."

"Far out," Flick said. "Did he suspect?"

"No way. You'll take the bug out of my watch now?" Molli said.

"Yeah. Give it here."

The quality made it seem as if Gant sat with them, enjoying coffee and doughnuts, in the sound-proofed room in Flick's studio. The hotel doorman's voice created a stereophonic sense of deja vu for Molli. She demanded Flick fast forward to the drug parts and squelched his voyeuristic interest in the bedroom portions by taking over the controls. As the telephone conversation between Gant and Flick replayed, Molli flushed as Gant's excited voice stimulated her memory of the striptease. As soon as she heard the hang-up click, she mashed the stop button with the speed of a teenager hitting the accelerator.

"That's it for the drugs," she said flatly. "You can satisfy your curiosity when I'm gone."

Flick smiled. "You did great. Far out. We've got him. We really do."

"God, I hope so. So how much are you thinking?"

"Five hundred grand. I figure he earns two fifty a year easy. A year for you, a year for me. That seems right. You think he's got it?"

"Don't know. He talked about winning big cases, but I don't

know how the money works with his partners. He didn't talk much about himself much, unlike most men," Molli said. "It's a lot of money."

"Better to start high. I need it, that's a fact. We'll give a week or so to settle in before we start," Flick said.

"We all need it. But I tell you what, I earned it." She felt the heaving of Gant's body and tensed. "I'm going to sit in a bathtub for the rest of the day."

"I can dig that. Two questions. Did you copy the tapes?"

"Of course. A girl has to look out for herself. I'll give them up when I get my half. I want to go. What else?"

"How was it?"

"You had to ask, didn't you? Men. It was wonderful. Best I ever had. Satisfied?"

Flick leered like a biker.

"Don't even think about screwing with me," Molli said, angrily shaking her finger at him. "I know too much about you."

"Molli, Molli. Hey, I gave you my word, man. We're cool."

*

Flick stood over the body slumped on the kitchen floor, the back against the cabinets.

"Get up, Son," he said softly. "You have to go back."

He hunkered down, his sore knees reminding him of the night spent stumbling along country roadsides in search of Cheyenne. His feet hurt, his eyes stung and his head ached. He clasped him by the hair and shook his head gently.

Cheyenne barely opened his eyes. He touched his nose and sniffed.

"Shit." Flick nodded. "One line, one time."

In the garage, Flick unlocked his tool drawer. He pulled a small plastic bag of white powder from a worn leather pouch full of various wrenches. He had quit years ago and kept this for his son. It's the least a father can do for his boy, he thought disgustedly as he walked back to the kitchen. Flick prepared the line and held it in front of Cheyenne's face. As he began to take the drug, Flick looked away.

"Thanks, Dad," Cheyenne said.

Cheyenne slept most of the drive. The rehab center orderlies glared at Flick like he had no business being there. He glared right back until they said he had to leave. They also told him that if his son ran away again, Cheyenne would not be allowed back.

He got back home with an hour of daylight left. Flick rode his son's bike to the flat stretch in the valley and wound it up until it vibrated from a loose front end. In other times, he might have kept on riding until his life changed. This time he wheeled into his garage as the sun disappeared. It took him a while to find the phone number for Honda and more time to figure out what time it was in Japan. He would listen to what they had to say in case it didn't work out with the lawyer.

*

Molli slowly ate a piece of her mother's chocolate pie and half-listened to her describe the pros and cons of taking the advanced macramé class at the senior center. After she left Flick, Molli had sat in the tub until she shriveled, jogged to the park and back, and bathed again. She had gone shopping downtown without looking in the stores and walked out of an afternoon movie she wasn't watching. She arrived feeling disjointed for her Saturday dinner with her mom.

"I need to talk, mom," Molli said.

Her mother nodded.

"Remember how well I was doing in Miami before I came back?" Molli said.

"I don't know what I would have done without you," her mother said.

"I was glad to come, but now you seem settled. You have friends. Go to classes."

"A few," her mother said. "You want to leave, that's it, isn't it?

"I don't want to leave you. And I wouldn't if you didn't want me to. But I may have to," Molli said.

"Have to?" her mother said. "For what reason? Trouble?"

"No. No trouble. For my career, but only if it's all right with you. I want you to come with me. Get out of this place."

"Where? Miami again? From what I've heard, I don't think I'd like it."

"Overseas. Somewhere with a big film industry," Molli said.

"Overseas? What about our house in the country?"

"I'm sorry," Molli said. She brightened. "We could get a house in the country overseas."

"Where overseas? That'd be expensive, wouldn't it?" her mother said.

Molli shrugged and scraped the crumbs into a last bite.

"This came up sudden, didn't it?" her mother said.

"I've been thinking about. Some things happened that made me think a little harder, that's all," Molli said. "You don't want to know, so don't ask. It's not trouble. Don't worry. It's just, you know, I don't feel too good about myself right now."

"It's trouble. It's in your face."

"No, it's not. Really," Molli said. "Actually, it might be the break I've been waiting for. Honest."

Her mother wiped her eyes with a tissue.

"If anything happened to you," her mother said.

"Momma, momma, don't cry. I'll be fine. Think about whether you'd like to come. Just think about it, okay?"

*

From boots to vest, each piece of clothing went directly from his body into the black plastic garbage bag. He gathered the bag and twisted the tie tight, as if to prevent escape. Naked, he peeked outside the condo door and set the bag in the empty hallway. He would drop it in the trash on his way to the office.

He had taken a cab directly home from the airport, planning to change quickly and to go to the office. Instead, he settled back gratefully into his home by eating a delivered pizza in his bathrobe and skimming and scattering the week's worth of newspapers.

He arrived at the office after sunset. Except for the ever-burning exit lights and the few timed night lights, his floor was dark. Gant went from hall to office opening doors and flipping switches until he had the place as bright as a department store before Christmas. He touched something solid in every office and cubicle, appreciating that the furniture, computers, files, and the personal photographs and mementoes represented his reality.

Immensely satisfied, Gant sorted the pink message slips Joan had left neatly on his desk. The duplicates and the ones from sales people he sailed into the wastebasket he had efficiently stationed by his right leg. He started the message from Mouse concerning a new case in that direction and changed his mind. Instead, he placed them on the Rotten file with a note reminding himself to tell Mouse to find another lawyer. Rotten, he had decided, would be his last biker client.

Gant worked his way through the mail, dictating steadily for more than an hour. The computerized tickler system printed a reminder to follow-up on the medical reports on the day care fire case and to schedule depositions in a grisly and complicated case involving a water heater explosion. He added these to his short list of projects for Monday which began with a note to plea bargain Rotten. Finally, everything not connected to these files went onto Joan's desk. Gant's desk looked like it couldn't wait for tomorrow to begin.

With his paperwork totally under control, Gant moved into his greenery. He snipped off dead leaves and expended flowers. The amaryllis was in full bloom and he thought briefly of Rebecca. He was misting the thick flat leaves of the rubber tree when Joan cautiously entered the office.

"Gosh, I'm glad it's you. What are you doing with all the lights on?" she said.

"What are you, paying the bills now? It's not your problem." Gant had never seen Joan in shorts and couldn't believe how skinny her legs were. "What the hell are you doing here, anyway?"

"I saw all the lights. I couldn't figure it out."

"You figured it out yet?

She ignored him and went to her desk, challenged by the piles Gant had left in military orderliness.

"What did you do with the one from Mouse? He wants you to call immediately. Said it was important."

"I've got it. No more biker cases. I'll tell him tomorrow."

"But you've always done their work," Joan said.

"Look, don't argue with me. I'm done with bikers. We're not representing any of them now except Rotten. Good time to cut it off clean," he said, marking each word with an extra drop of time. "Got it?"

Joan nodded. "You didn't give me any work for the Rotten trial. It's a week from tomorrow, you know."

"Not if I can help it. I'm going to settle it. It's a loser."

"That's not what you were saying a few weeks ago. Before Rebecca got the case."

"That's not it," Gant said. "I don't want to try a loser, that's all. Who needs it."

"I don't suppose you want to tell me about the reunion?" Joan said.

"That's right."

"Well, I'm going, then. You sure you don't want me to get some of these lights?" Joan said.

"Leave the damn lights alone," he said angrily. "And come ready to roll tomorrow. We have a lot to do."

"You know better than that, Jake Gant. I always, always, am ready to work."

The slam of successive doors imprinted her fury on the quiet office, but left Gant unmarked. He didn't think of her again until he switched off the lights to darken the floor.

CHAPTER FIFTEEN

Gant returned to work shortly after seven a.m. before everyone except Latisha, who arrived early to distribute overnight faxes, start the coffee, and answer the telephone until the receptionist came in. His somber, driven behavior created a discomforting sense which wafted through the offices like the aroma of an unfamiliar spice, creating curiosity and anxiety among the arriving employees.

On the third try, Gant got through to Rebecca's secretary. Her voice iced over at his name. She told him Ms. Varner was in court and would return the call.

In mid-morning, Larry cruised into Joan's office on his way to Gant's like a baserunner rounding third on his way home, oblivious to her signals to stop. Instead of his usual dress slacks and shirt, he wore jeans and a T-shirt emblazoned with a Disney cartoon character.

"Hey, biker boss," he said with cheerful cockiness, "how was your vacation?"

Gant snapped his head up as if accused of a crime and found himself confronted by a giant, grinning mouse. He didn't look at Larry, but addressed the mouse in the harsh and contemptuous tone used to skewer the evasive or naïve witness.

"I used to have a law clerk named Larry. Nice kid. Hardworking, loyal, dressed the part. If you see him, tell him to bring me some cigarettes. Now get out."

After lunch, Gant still was waiting for Rebecca's call when his partners visited as he had requested. Gant explained his aggressive and well-conceived plan for the day care fire case which included hiring a myriad of experts. He was as serious and single-minded as an engineer constructing a tunnel.

"I meet with the fire marshal tomorrow," Gant said. "If he says what I expect, we've got liability. We know there's plenty of available insurance. I say let's go for it all. We'll need to invest money — reconstruction experts, doctors, do a mock-up, day-in-the-life videos of the victims. I estimate one hundred thousand dollars for openers. If we do it right, let them know we'll spend whatever is necessary to see the last card. We can make a huge fee. Huge."

"What do you mean by huge?" Jeb said.

"Permanently crippled kids. Horribly disfigured. Like I said before, millions," Gant said.

Jeb nodded, impressed. "You convinced me. I think it's a good investment."

"This isn't going to interfere with your biker work, is it?" Rich said, unable to resist.

"For such a we-shall-overcome kind of a guy, you sure are prejudiced against the bikers," Gant said evenly. "But I'm not doing bikers any more, even though I feel like I should just to piss you off. I don't have time for them."

"Don't worry, you already piss me off," Rich said. "The party's searching for another candidate because I can't get free."

"From what I know of your chances, maybe we're saving you from yourself," Gant said.

"I don't want you messing with my life any more. I want you out. You give me a figure," Rich said.

"Me? Out? Get serious," Gant said. "I'm not going anywhere. This is my firm."

"You get serious," Rich said. "You won't buy me out, I'm offering to buy you out. Give me a number."

"One third of the world. That's my share," Gant said.

"You think you're riding so sweet, so high, that you're with the angels," Rich said. "You've become a gutter creature. You just don't know it yet."

As usual, none of the men backed down, apologized or tried to make things other than what they were between them. Just business. They agreed Gant would not need approval for each expenditure if he provided them a memo for each expense. They did not exchange cordialities when they parted.

*

Rebecca didn't call until almost everyone had left for the day.

"Thought you were avoiding me," Gant said.

"That would mean I cared," Rebecca said. "Just busy. The message says you want to settle Rotten."

"Yeah. I think we've got a good case, but there are risks. What's the best you can do?" he said.

"Hasn't changed. Plead the charge and agree to seven years in prison," she said.

"Come on. Be reasonable. It was an accident."

"Woman's dead. He was drunk."

"Three years," Gant said. "I'll tell him to take it."

"And he's out in one. No. Our case is too good. I'll go six. That's it. Need to know in twenty four hours," Rebecca said.

"How about five?"

"Six, that's all. And Bartley won't like that."

"I'll try," Gant said, "but I'm doubtful."

"Tell him I'll ask for ten when he's convicted. Harris will give it to me. You know that," she said.

"If he's convicted," he said. "Look, we don't really want to spend next week trying this thing, do we?"

"I'm ready," Rebecca said and hung up.

*

Mouse and Willie parked themselves on the white and floral print stuffed sofa with the swashbuckling audacity of rogue truckers crashing a garden party. Mouse caught the receptionist's eye and intentionally dropped a cigarette ash on the plush carpet. He belched loudly. Willie put his grimy boots on the coffee table and vigorously picked his nose.

"Gant," Mouse said to the receptionist, sounding like a bullfrog.

An hour later Gant returned from an early morning hearing in court. He had not quite figured out how to convince Rotten to accept Rebecca's offer.

"These gentlemen —" the receptionist said.

"Boys," Gant said. "I don't remember you having an appointment."

"Here's how it is," Mouse said. "You didn't call me back. We figured we better come see you, what with the trial next week and all."

"I was meaning to call you. Been busy since I got back," Gant said.

"We've got to talk." Mouse swept his arm toward the lawyer's office. "After you, counselor."

Mouse stopped on the way to his chair to smell the hibiscus and admire the hand-blown glass sculpture. "You've got some good shit here."

"Message said something about a new case. I'm too busy. You'll need to get someone else. If you want names," Gant said.

"Figured that," Mouse said. "We already got someone."

"Good. I'm shifting my emphasis. Won't be able to do you guys any more," Gant said. "Time to move on."

Mouse nodded. "How'd the reunion work out?"

"Let's put it this way. If I had paid cash, I'd want my money back. That Flick was worthless and the woman twice as bad. Where'd you find him, anyway?" Gant said.

"That's not what I heard," Mouse said.

"What do you mean?" Gant said.

"When you didn't call me back, I made some calls. Heard you were a real fuck-up, and more," Mouse said.

"What? Who said that?" Gant said.

"Doesn't matter," Mouse said. "So where does this leave Willie?"

"I talked to the DA last night. Willie, you and I got to talk," Gant said. "You'll have to wait outside, Mouse. Lawyer-client privilege."

"Wait a minute," Mouse said. "Lawyer-client privilege is for the client, right?"

"That's correct. What I say is between him and me," Gant said.

"Then the client decides, not the lawyer," Mouse said. "If Willie wants it me stay, then you don't give a shit, do you?"

"That's right," Gant said, grudgingly.

Mouse looked at Willie. "You want me to go or stay?"

"Stay, man," Willie said. "I never trusted this fucker."

"This is a serious case. You should have a lawyer you trust," Gant said. "I'll withdraw and they'll set a new trial date."

"That ain't happening. You've been paid in full," Mouse said. "What did the DA say?"

Gant glowered at Mouse.

"You've got a tough case, Willie. Less than fifty-fifty chance to win, in my opinion. Breath test hurts you bad. DA told me she'd ask for ten years if she gets a conviction. The judge probably will give her what she wants. I talked and talked to her. Got her down to six. Good behavior and you're out in less than three years. Again, in my opinion, you should seriously consider taking this," Gant said.

"I didn't kill that chick, man. It was an accident. I ain't going to prison for that," Willie said.

"The law requires us to prove it was an accident. It'll be difficult," Gant said.

"If that other DA hadn't gotten sick, I'd be done and have my bike back. I ain't pleading to nothing," Willie said.

"Ten years is a long time," Gant said.

"Don't say that, man," Willie said. "What should I do, Mouse?"

Mouse ran his fingers lightly along the polished wood desk. "You do have nice shit - especially if you think about your first office. That little closet three flights up. Be a pisser to lose it all."

"What are you talking about?" Gant said.

"You know what I think has happened here, Willie? A few weeks ago Mr. Gant was ready to kick ass, now he wants you to take it in the ass. Why the change in Mr. Gant? He had a bad trip playing biker and doesn't want us in his life. You know what to tell him?" Mouse said.

"Uhuh."

"Tell him tough shit. Tell him he better try your case like his world depended on it because certain people might be interested in how he used your fees to get to his reunion," Mouse said.

"All right," Gant said, pointing his finger at Willie. "You get your trial. You do and say exactly what I tell you, including get yourself clean. I'll do my best. But it will be damn near a miracle. If you wind up doing ten years, I'm going to tell you 'I told you so.' Be here noon Sunday. Now get out. You stink."

"Your best ain't good enough, counselor," Mouse said. "You win it."

CHAPTER SIXTEEN

"I'll do some things to make the jury think that I like you Willie," Gant said. "For example, I'll put my hand on your shoulder. Don't jump. When it seems natural, you do something for me. Pick up a pencil if I drop it or pour me a glass of water. The jury is sitting with nothing to do except look around. They'll spend a lot of time checking you out. Any questions?"

"No."

"Here's what happens this morning. First, we pick the jury. She gets to ask questions. I get to ask questions. Then we each get to cross off five names. Before I do that I'll ask you if you're getting bad vibes from any of them. You know, they're giving you the evil eye. Don't stare at them or give them funny looks. Don't react to anything the DA says. Appear calm, like a rock. Don't say anything to me unless I ask you. Got it?"

Willie nodded.

"After the jury's selected, she and I give opening statements. She'll probably say some things that piss you off. Don't react. If you act guilty, the jury will figure that you are. Then she calls her witnesses — investigating officers, someone from the lab. Her case won't take long. Might even finish today. Our witnesses will start tomorrow. Questions?"

"Yeah, is this the same judge?"

"What do you mean?"

"You know, the same one that gave that guy twenty years?"

"Oh. No, that was somebody else." Gant scanned his client who stared back like a freshly shorn recruit at boot camp. A half circle of extra-pale skin replaced his beard. Plaid short sleeve shirt and brown work pants, pressed with a tight crease, draped loosely on his slender body. Red blotches on each ear marked earring locations.

"You look all right today, Willie. Like a regular guy. Let's go get them," Gant said.

Gant had secured the counsel table nearest the jury box. Across five strides of floor, the counsel tables faced the judge's elevated bench and the witness chair and were perpendicular to the jury box. Jurors, sitting in two rows of mounted swivel chairs, could view the proceedings without moving their heads.

Gant put Willie in the chair nearest the jury. He arranged the books in short, even stacks along the front edge of the table and removed his trial notebook, three black pens, a red pen and three fresh yellow pads from his case. He placed a black pen and pad in front of Willie.

"If you have something to tell me, write it down. Don't even tap me on the shoulder," Gant said.

Gant moved behind Willie to the back wall. Deliberately, like a big cat, he paced the perimeter of the courtroom. His personal ritual, solemnly taking possession of the space by marking it, was like new owners walking through their house. He ran his right hand along the back of the last row of spectator benches and lightly drummed his left hand on the far wall. Gant paused for emphasis before the district attorney's table, the judge's bench, the witness chair, and the jury box. Rebecca waited for him there, her white fingers like talons spread possessively along the front railing.

"It goes something like, 'this is mine, you can have the rest,'" she said coldly, indicating the rest of the courtroom.

"How long has it been, Becky?" he said.

"I don't remember either, Jacob. What difference does it make?"

"You're looking good, Rebecca."

"You look like shit, Jake, seriously," she said.

"Seriously? Well, seriously, Ms Varner, I'm going to bury this case in that secret spot I remember so very well."

The door to the judge's chamber opened, stifling her response. Bailiff, court reporter, clerk and Judge Harris filed in.

"More settlement discussions? Do we have reason to be hopeful?" Harris said.

"No," Rebecca said, "Mr. Gant is as obnoxious as ever."

"Just protecting my client's rights from the outrages of the state, your honor."

"Enough, you two. We won't tolerate such behavior. Bring in the jury panel, please," Judge Harris said to the bailiff.

Gant glared and shook his head as Willie mouthed, "You and the DA?" Yeah, Gant thought, me and the DA. You should be so lucky, punk.

Gant heard the thirty six prospective jurors rustle in. The

courtroom seemed to weigh more when they sat down on the spectator benches. Their eyes crossed the back of his head like search lights. He didn't turn to look because he knew what he would see. Impassive faces of citizens selected by chance. He imagined their surprise at the letter from the clerk of court summoning them for jury duty, followed by resentment of the "why me" variety, followed by resignation. He knew that a few would volunteer to be here, but most would not. Twelve would be chosen to put their lives on hold for the next three or four days to decide if Willie killed the girl. It was part of the package of citizenship.

*

The clerk rotated her little cage and extracted one small ball. She called out loud the number written on it. A young woman in a university T-shirt and jeans self-consciously made her way to the jury box. The bailiff told her where to sit. Gant quickly found the three-by-five card containing basic information about her in the stack provided him by the clerk. Twenty two years old. Single. Grad student in bio-chemistry. He put the card on the table as the clerk called the next number. By the time she called twenty-three names, Gant had their corresponding cards arranged in front of him in the same order in which they sat in the jury box.

The judge asked questions seeking to expose reasons why a prospective juror wouldn't be able to fairly decide the case. Answers to the judge's questions brought two dismissals, one for a medical emergency in the family, the second because no one was available to milk his cows. They were replaced by two more people from the jury panel.

Gant and Rebecca sought more than fairness from the jurors. They wanted jurors favorable to their position included and hostile jurors excluded. Like picking out fruit, their inquiries probed gently, respectfully, and with the knowledge that the selection process produced unpredictable results.

Easy to understand why, Gant knew. These people didn't check their biases, prejudices, likes and dislikes at the door as if they were coats and hats. They were uneasy responding to personal questions in front of strangers. What motivated their answer?

Honesty? Embarrassment? A need to please or show off. A desire to stay or to go?

Rebecca asked few questions, creating the impression that any twelve people would be acceptable to her. When she inquired if anyone knew Gant or Rotten, Rebecca didn't look at the pair. She wrinkled her nose and pointed at them as if they were two containers of garbage she wanted hauled away.

Gant smiled, as if she were joking, and noticed a man with a blond mustache shared his amusement.

"Willie and I want to thank you all for being here," Gant said. "I'm sure that the judge and prosecutor join with me. I understand it may be an inconvenience for many of you. But without people like you who are willing to serve as jurors, we wouldn't have this great system of justice in this country. The prosecutor has accused Willie of a crime. He has a constitutional right to have a jury of his peers decide his fate.

"My job is to make sure Willie has the fairest possible trial. We want a jury who will decide the case strictly on the evidence. All of us, including myself," Gant said, putting a hand on his chest, "have biases. It's natural. We don't have to apologize for them. I don't want any of these biases getting in the way of Willie's right to a fair trial. I'm sure you can understand and respect that."

"Objection, your honor," Rebecca said. "I believe defense counsel must be confused. This sounds like his opening statement. I haven't heard a question for the jury yet."

"Just thanking these people, your honor. Thought the prosecutor would agree. I'll get right to the questions," Gant said.

"Please do," Harris said.

"Thank you, your honor. One more thing, ladies and gentlemen. I'm sure I'll ask more questions than the judge or the prosecutor. I take my responsibility seriously. If I try your patience, blame me and not Willie. Okay?" Gant tried to remember the faces that nodded.

"Now, how many of you have ridden a motorcycle, or have a close friend or relative who has ridden a motorcycle? Raise your hands please. Keep them up until I mark you down. Thank you." Gant wrote the letters "MC" on his seating diagram next to the names of the eight persons with hands in the air. "I'll start in the back row. Ms. Garth? Did I pronounce that right?"

"Yes," said a middle-aged woman in a print dress.

"Tell me your experience with motorcycles," Gant said.

"I have a daughter who rides one."

Gant skillfully mixed basic questions designed to identify traditionally unfavorable jurors, such as those related to law enforcement officers, with inquiries designed to educate about Willie's defense. The judge excused a man whose son had been seriously injured in a motorcycle accident and another who said he would not listen to evidence about any defense.

"When I hear drinking and driving, that's it for me," the man said as he exited the jury box. "I say throw away the key."

"I appreciate your honesty, sir," Gant said, sure that the man's pronouncement delighted the prosecutor.

Rebecca used her five strikes to eliminate potential jurors who resembled Willie. Out went two truck drivers, an old man with a pony tail, a woman with tattoo of a goddess on her upper arm and a woman who owned a country tavern.

Gant sent home two who admitted they were afraid of motorcycle gangs, the sister of a police officer, a big guy who liked to talk and an accountant who kept his sport coat buttoned and who Willie said looked at him funny.

That left eight women, four men, including the one with the mustache, and another woman as the alternate. An advertising agency could not have done a better job assembling a portrait of the middle of America.

Judge Harris instructed them not to talk about the case and sent them out to lunch under the care of the bailiff.

"We'll start at one-thirty," she said, departing with her entourage.

"Hey, man, what happened to the ones who're like me?" Willie said with concern.

"Wait a second. I'll tell you a another story," Gant said, nodding toward Rebecca who was leaving the courtroom. "The DA always does that."

"Several years ago I represented a black man accused of burglary. The only black guy in the district attorney's office crossed off all three potential black jurors, even though he was black. He thought the black guys would go easy on their own. So I've got an all white jury and, guess what? They acquit my client. I still give that DA grief about doing that. You can't ever tell for sure, but I think your jury is all right," Gant said reassuringly as he routinely did, strictly for the client's benefit. In reality, Gant graded the jury pass/fail at the time of verdict. "Be back here at one-fifteen."

Outside the Courthouse, Gant saw Willie climb on the back of Mouse's bike and ride away. He looked around for jurors and hoped none saw the defendant put on his black jacket. Mouse, he thought, would scare them into a guilty verdict.

On the way back to the office for lunch, Gant pondered the possibilities. If he won, the bikers would be nothing but a memory. If he lost, they could become a nightmare. Mouse might go to his partners about the fees. He knew a personal check for the difference would make it right with Jeb, but Rich's reaction concerned him. He had seen Rich mercilessly act on principle before. This uncertainty put a three-corner tear in the closely wound fabric of Gant's personal life.

He began his repair effort by knocking before he entered Rich's office. Rich was finishing a container of yogurt and motioned with his spoon.

"And people think we take two hour lunches," Gant said. "I brought you copies of a couple of kids' medical reports. Just came in. Also, remember I told you the insurance company lawyer wanted a copy of what I got from the fire marshal. I sent it to him last week. Today, he called and wants to meet. Joan set it up for Friday. After Rotten's done."

"What's the meeting for?" Rich said.

"Don't know. It's unusual so early in the case. He's coming here at three if you want to sit in."

"Good," Rich said. "Did Rotten pay all his fees?"

"Yeah, finally," Gant said. "What flavor was it?"

"Blueberry. How's Rebecca?"

"She's beautiful, but what a cold-blooded shark she's become. She'd shred me like an old file if she got the chance."

"Lot of people in that line," Rich said.

Gant swallowed his initial response. "I want to work it out with you. Don't do anything. After the trial, we'll talk."

"Do? What would I do, poison your coffee? You know what I want. You know where I am."

"Got to get back to court. We'll talk later."

Standing outside his office like a sentinel, Larry, freshly scrubbed and wearing his best clothes, greeted Gant with a salute.

"Sorry I missed this morning," Larry said. "I had an exam."

"No big deal. The trial is like a play. You missed the first scene. You have a bit part. No lines. Sit, watch, listen. According to the script, some parts of a trial are calm - boring really - other parts filled with action. The DA puts on her case this afternoon. She'll put in evidence that Rotten had been drinking, the girl was a passenger on his bike, it crashed, and she died. I concede all that, so her case isn't really the real case that brings us to court. Except for the photographs, it'll be boring, for us and for the jury. I want to keep it that way. I don't want to bring any life to her case by showing off for the jury. I'll ask one, maybe two, questions so the jury knows I'm still breathing. That's it. We'll see more action tomorrow when Willie and the experts testify. I don't want any surprises. Follow the script. It doesn't matter what the DA thinks of me, or of Willie. Only the jury matters. Let's go. You carry the file."

*

"Didn't sound good to me, man," Willie said after the first day of trial as he sat with Gant and Larry in the lawyer's office.

"Why? They didn't do anything I didn't expect. The first day's always the worst for a defendant," Gant said.

"I don't know. That DA, she made me feel like a creep. Like I meant to cut off the chick's head. She don't like me, I can tell," Willie said.

"Probably not. But who cares? It doesn't matter what the DA thinks of you. Jury, Willie, that's who's important. And, you know, some of those jurors didn't like it that the DA made them look at those photos. You see some of those faces?"

"That DA is something to look at." Willie's grin exposed a missing bottom tooth making his face look like a crudely carved pumpkin. "You and her use to get it on?"

Gant came across the table like a Marine over an obstacle. "Keep your fucking mouth shut about my life. Never again. I'm the lawyer. You're the client. Don't forget it. Got it?"

"Fucking relax, man. I didn't mean nothing."

Gant tossed a twenty toward Larry. "Get some sandwiches and something to drink."

"What kind would you like?"

"Jesus Christ," Gant said. "Can't you make any decisions? Just get some sandwiches. Who cares what kind."

Gant reviewed with Willie the carefully planned order of questions he would ask him on direct examination — had a few beers at a party, wasn't intoxicated, stranded girl asked for a ride home, driving carefully, tire blew, bike left the road, did the best that could be done.

"I'm not going to tell you the questions exactly. If the jury thinks you're just saying what I told you to say, they won't like it," Gant said. "So if you have to ask me to repeat a question or say you don't understand, that's all right. Makes it more real. Another thing. I don't think that she will - she's too experienced - but if she asks you whether I told you what to say, you answer 'Yes, he told me to tell the truth.' Got it?"

"He told me to tell the truth," Willie said.

"Like I said, she's going to do everything she can to get you to lose it. Call you a liar. Talk down to you. Trash the Vipers. Ask the same question from a dozen angles. She's keep coming until you either break or she realizes you aren't going to." Gant towered over Willie. "Now I know you're lying to me, Willie."

"What do you mean, man?" Willie said startled.

"True story goes something like this, doesn't it? You and your biker buddies got drunk and thought you'd take this girl back to the clubhouse for some fun. You were fooling around on your cycle and lost it. Your drunken crash killed her. Isn't that what happened?"

"No. What's the matter with you?" Willie said loudly.

"That tire blew out after you left the road, isn't that right?"

"No. You calling me a liar?"

"You were drunk weren't you?"

"No," he said angrily. "I —"

"You don't remember how many beers you had. It could have been fourteen, or forty. You just don't remember, do you?" Gant said.

"Hey, it wasn't no forty." Willie stood. "What are doing to me, Gant? Cut it out."

"I'm done. Sit down," Gant said, sliding his chair so close he could see that no hair grew in the shallow pock marks in Willie's face.

"That's what she'll do to you tomorrow, only longer and harder. Get angry with her like you got angry with me and you're picking up a go directly to jail card. The jury has to believe you're telling the truth. You have to stay calm. And polite. 'Yes, ma'am. No, ma'am.' And firmly stick to your story. If she tries to get you to say you had more than four beers, you keep saying four. 'No ma'am, I had four.' Say it right to the jury. You don't care what the DA thinks. She believes you're guilty. You can't change her mind. But what you say can and will help the jury make up its mind. So talk right at them. Got it?" Gant said.

Larry entered with two white paper bags with grease-stained bottoms.

"You're unbelievable," Gant said. "You were away so long I forgot about you. Where did you go?"

CHAPTER SEVENTEEN

Four casual spectators, idle as old men on a park bench, sat scattered at the back of the courtroom, watching the jury shuffle back to their seats after lunch. One of them coughed twice, catching the noise in his cheeks and hand. The judge watched Gant, holding her pen by each end. The clerk, oblivious to the tension, made notes. Rebecca, alone at her table, gathered her papers for cross examination. Behind her, Sherry Dobler's parents and sister rearranged themselves, causing the bench to squeak. Mrs. Rotten sat behind her husband's chair motionless as if watching her favorite TV program. Willie leaned forward expectantly in the witness stand. Except for one man whose head drooped like a wilted flower, the jurors stared at Gant. He read nothing from their faces and was glad for that. In a display of inclusion for the jury's benefit, Gant bent down to ask Larry if he thought of any additional questions. The surprised young man shook his head.

"No further questions, your honor," Gant said, and sat down. "That was as good a direct as you'll see," he whispered to Larry. "Now hang on."

At full height, Rebecca remained short. She wore a tailored black suit with straight skirt and slightly flared jacket, a blood-red tea rose on the lapel as much for scent as color. The white blouse had discreet ruffles and her black hair was held in place with plain gold clips that shined like the moonlit ocean. Her face came close to beautiful, but, in court, the coldness in her eyes created the fearsome look of an inquisitor. Willie nervously massaged his lips with his tongue as the heels on Rebecca's pumps clattered toward him.

Rebecca had spent the better part of two of her precious weekends getting objective about Gant. It was like stuffing more into a full suitcase. Each time she went to close it, she found a small fragment of a memory hanging out the side. Finally, the Sunday before trial, she had packed away and locked up everything she felt about Gant except that he was the lawyer on the other side of the Rotten case. For Bartley, for herself, and because she believed Rotten deserved prison time, she wanted to win this case more than any other since she won her first murder trial.

Initially, Rebecca spared gently with Willie on the witness stand, asking questions about work and family. When she saw his shoulders relax, she attacked.

"You testified on direct you drank four beers, is that correct?" Rebecca said.

"Yes, ma'am," Willie said.

"You belong to the Vipers, don't you?"

"Yes."

"That's a motorcycle gang, isn't it?"

"Object. Irrelevant," Gant said.

"Overruled. Answer," said the judge.

"Well —" Willie said.

"That's what you call yourselves, isn't it?" Rebecca said. "A motorcycle gang?"

"Yeah."

"A gang like the Hell's Angels, right?" Rebecca said.

Gant stood like a man defending the family honor. "I object. Irrelevant, your honor."

"Sustained," Harris said.

"When your gang has a party, there's always beer, isn't there?" Rebecca said.

"Yeah," Willie said.

"And you always have beer at the gang's clubhouse, don't you?"

"Yeah, unless someone forgets to buy it."

"Nobody keeps track of how many beers other people are drinking do they?"

"Excuse me, ma'am," Willie said. "I didn't understand the question."

"Nobody counts how many beers you drink," Rebecca said.

"Oh, right."

"You can drink as many as you want?"

Rebecca walked from the witness stand to the jury box. Willie's eyes and his words followed her so that he spoke directly to the jury.

"Yeah, pretty much. If someone flips out we'll, you know, cut them off," Willie said.

"No one was counting the beers you drank that Saturday, right?" Rebecca said.

"Right."

"Including you, right?"

"Right," Willie said. "Wait."

"So you —" Rebecca said.

"You mean was I counting my beers?"

"You answered the question, Mr. Rotten. We're moving on."

"Let him finish his answer," Gant said loudly. "Your honor, the prosecutor —"

"He had finished, you honor. Just because Mr. Gant didn't like it —" Rebecca said.

"No, I hadn't," Willie said.

"Mr. Rotten, don't speak unless someone asks you a question. Mr. Reporter, read the question and answer back," Harris said.

With an apologetic smile at the jury, Rebecca stepped aside so that all of them could see the reporter. She ignored Gant's gaze which locked onto her like radar.

"Finish your answer, Mr. Rotten," Harris said after her reporter read the previous question and answer.

"I did count my beers. Four," Willie said.

"I see. Did you count them by marking them down on a piece of paper?" Rebecca said.

Willie looked at Gant for help. Gant nodded at the jury as if he thought it was a fair question and gestured encouragingly at Willie.

"No," Willie said.

"Did you tell someone each time you had a beer, 'this is number one, this is number three,' like that? Rebecca said.

"No."

"Isn't it a fact you don't know how many beers you had the night Sherry Dobler was killed?

"No."

"Isn't a fact that on that Saturday at the party you didn't count them at all?"

"No, ma'am," Willie said.

"Then tell the jury, Mr. Rotten, exactly how you counted those beers on that Saturday," Rebecca said.

"I object, you honor," Gant said. "He's already answered that question."

"Overruled. Answer the question, Mr. Rotten," Harris said.

"I remembered," Willie said. "Four."

"You remembered?" Rebecca said.

"Yes."

"I see," Rebecca said.

As if she were contemplating Willie's answer, Rebecca rested her pen between her teeth and, eyes on her pointed toes, deliberately paced the distance between the jury box and Gant's table. She rested her right hand on the corner of his table and clattered her fingernails like a snare drum roll.

"Isn't it a fact, Mr. Rotten, that the first time you remembered four beers was when you talked to your lawyer?" Rebecca said, pointing at Gant and moving away.

"Object, your honor." Gant smelled the scents of perfume and rose Rebecca left behind.

The judge hesitated. "No. He can answer. It's a when question, not a what question. Go ahead, Mr. Rotten."

"Yes."

"And isn't it a fact, sir, that this is something you and Mr. Gant figured out?"

"Don't answer. Totally improper and irrelevant. Object, your honor. Strenuously. Want to be heard. She knows better. Prosecutorial abuse. Move for a mistrial," Gant said indignantly.

"Calm down, Mr. Gant. Objection sustained. Motion denied," Harris said. "I assume, Ms. Varner, we're not going any further down that road?"

"Of course not, your honor," she said innocently. "Mr. Rotten, you spoke with the police at the scene of the accident and again at the hospital, correct?"

"Yeah," Willie said.

"You truthfully told them everything?"

"Yeah."

"You told the jury on direct that your front tire blew out and that caused you to leave the highway. Was that your testimony?" Rebecca said.

"Yeah. That's what happened," Willie said.

"I'm giving you state's exhibits F and G, the police reports. Look them over. Then tell the jury whether the blown tire is mentioned in either report. Take your time."

Rebecca returned to her position near the jury box. Gant noisily shuffled though papers to distract the jury from Willie, who was slowly reading the reports he had never seen before.

"Finished, sir?" Rebecca said.

"Yeah," Willie said.

"And is there a single word about that tire?"

"No. No, nothing about the tire."

"Not by you, not by the other gang members who were there, this VD and this Hairball?"

"Yeah."

"Nothing further, your honor," Rebecca said.

"We'll take a fifteen minute recess," Harris said. "Let the jury stretch its legs."

Lucky break, Gant thought. Immediately after the last juror left, he herded Willie into a tiny conference room and lit a cigarette.

"You did good," Gant said. "She hit you with some rough questions"

"What a fucking bitch, man. I'd like to get her in the clubhouse."

"Stay calm. You're not done. We need to go over a few questions I need to ask you on redirect. Then she gets one more shot. So hang in there."

*

Gant sensed that Willie was about drained of patience. Smoothly and crisply, he repaired the damage of Rebecca's cross examination. Carefully crafting his questions to avoid objections, Gant had Willie repeat his version of the incident. He smiled at Rebecca as he gave the police reports to Willie.

"Look at Exhibit F, about twelve lines down. It starts 'Cummings stated...'", Gant said. "Read that line and the next one to the jury, please"

'Cummings, also known as Hairball, stated that he was riding point and he heard a noise behind him. He turned and saw Rotten fly off his bike in the ditch.'

"'Heard a noise,' is that what you read?" Gant said.

"Yes, sir."

"Thank you. At the bottom of page two of that report, do you see the reference to Diruski?" Gant said.

"Let's see. Yeah," Willie said.

"Read those lines to the jury, please."

"Diruski, also known as VD, stated he was in the middle and heard Rotten yell 'Oh, shit.' By the time he looked Rotten was in the ditch."

The sincerity of Willie's next answer was critical. If the jury believed him, he'd be halfway down the road to an acquittal. Gant paused to signal its importance to the jury.

"Willie, do you know why you didn't mention the blown tire to the officers?" Gant asked solemnly.

"No," he said. 'I was pretty shook up. Looking at Sherry and all. I honestly don't remember what I told them. But I know that tire blew."

Rebecca had no further questions. Gant patted Willie's back twice. Rotten was trembling.

Go either way, Gant thought.

*

Off the record, before the jury was summoned, Rebecca explained she didn't have the tire because Gant hadn't specifically requested that it be in court that afternoon. The judge regarded her with the practiced skepticism of a parent listening to the excuse of a tardy child. Gant sat upright, smug as the prompt sibling. Dr. Herbert van Appen —goatee, wire rimmed glasses, and high forehead — followed the dialogue from the witness chair with detached politeness of the moderately curious.

"Your honor," Gant said, affecting a slow patronizing drawl, "Bartley, that is Mr. Suss, her boss, and I agreed to stipulate to the admission of the tire to save an officer from taking time to come into court to identify it. The DA's office kept the tire. Miss Varner knew I'd need the tire for Dr. van Appen's testimony. I know we're off the record and I don't, at this point, want to make too big of a thing out of this. But, your honor, I do believe this is a part of her continued attempt to sabotage Mr. Rotten's defense."

"That's nonsense," Rebecca said frostily, "Mr. Gant is as deluded as he ever was."

"Why, Becky, I didn't know you cared," Gant said sarcastically.

"I don't," Rebecca said.

"Enough, both of you." Judge's Harris' voice slapped like a ruler against a desktop. "No more, I mean it. Where is the tire, Ms. Varner?"

"In my office, your honor."

"Go get it, please. Now," Harris said.

"Go with her, Larry," Gant said. "I know she won't want to get her hands dirty."

"Mr. Gant, I meant it," Harris said.

"Of course, your honor. I was just trying to be helpful," Gant said.

"One more thing, your honor," Rebecca said. "I apologize for this. It was unnecessary. I got caught up in the game playing among attorneys."

*

Gant obtained permission for van Appen to conduct his demonstration on the front rail of the jury box. The expert described in detail the difference between a blowout caused by tire failure and one caused from hitting an object. He demonstrated by sticking a gloved finger through the black cords from the inside and waving it at the jurors.

On cross examination Rebecca asked van Appen how much the defendant paid him to testify. The witness squirmed as he reluctantly admitted to receiving twenty-five hundred dollars. Rebecca raised her eyebrows.

"Twenty-five hundred? I see," she said. "Dr. van Appen, you don't know whether the tire blew out before or after the motorcycle left the highway, do you?"

"Well, the testimony is that it happened on the highway," he said.

"But your opinion is based on your tests, correct?" Rebecca said.

"And my experience," van Appen said.

"Twenty-five hundred dollars worth of experience," Rebecca said.

"Objection," Gant said

"Sustained," Harris said.

"Your tests don't establish where the blowout occurred, do they?" Rebecca said.

"No, that's correct," van Appen said.

"So you can't tell the jury where the blowout occurred, can you?"

"No, I'm sorry I can't."

"Thank you. Nothing else," Rebecca said

"Mr. Gant?" Harris said.

"No more questions, your honor," Gant said. "Dr. van Appen, put the tire there by the clerk. Thank you."

Gant put a pleased mask on and nodded to Willie and Larry, exhibiting the false confidence of a pilot with a sputtering engine.

*

Gant next called Roy Ogden who testified that he had given the tests for state motorcycle licenses for fifteen years, taught motorcycle safety classes at the community college and was the immediate past president of the local chapter of HOG, the Harley Owners Group.

"Let's get right to it, Mr. Ogden," Gant said. "Assuming the tire on Mr. Rotten's motorcycle blew out on the highway, do you have an opinion to a reasonable degree of certainty what effect that would have on the operation of the motorcycle?

"He would have lost control of his bike," Ogden said.

"In your opinion, was Mr. Rotten's description of what happened to him that day consistent with losing control of the bike because his tire blew out on the highway?" Gant said.

"Yes. Absolutely."

"Assuming the blowout occurred on the highway, what could Mr. Rotten have done differently in your opinion? Anything?"

"Nothing," Ogden said. "I can't think of anything."

"Thank you. That's all," Gant said.

"Cross?" Harris said, looking at Rebecca.

"You taught motorcycle safety for many years, correct?" Rebecca said

"Yes," Ogden said.

"A motorcycle is dangerous if not operated safely, correct?"

"No more than a car."

"Exactly, no more than a car," Rebecca said. "Therefore, Mr. Ogden, it is as dangerous to operate a motorcycle after drinking alcohol as it is to operate a car, correct?"

"Sure," Ogden said.

"That's because alcohol affects the driver's ability to control his motorcycle, isn't that right?"

"Object. Goes beyond the scope of direct, your honor," Gant said.

"We're not going to belabor this point, are we, Ms. Varner?" Harris said.

"Oh, no, your honor."

"Overruled," Judge Harris said. "You may answer."

"Yes," Ogden said.

"And this could cause some innocent passenger to be killed?" Rebecca said.

"Object. Irrelevant. Lack of foundation. Beyond the scope. Your honor, come on," Gant said. "She's not only belaboring the point, she's making a career out of it."

"Settle down, Mr. Gant. Let's move along, Ms. Varner," Harris said sternly. "Objection is sustained."

"Assume the tire didn't blow out on the highway, okay?" Rebecca said.

"Object. Lack of foundation. Calls for speculation," Gant said.

"I'd like to be heard, your honor," Rebecca said.

Judge Harris excused the jury.

"We'll hear you now, Ms. Varner," she said.

"Judge, the only evidence that the tire blew on the highway comes from the testimony of the defendant and the gang members. The jury has the right to disbelieve them. The jury is entitled to know whether Mr. Ogden's analysis and opinion is consistent with not believing these witnesses."

"Mr. Gant?" Harris said.

"Your honor, Miss Varner is attempting to get the expert to exceed what he can do. By that I mean he —any expert —must have a foundation before they can give an opinion. This foundation must be made of facts, which are admitted into evidence. There is no evidence that the blowout occurred anywhere other than on the highway."

"Don't let Mr. Gant fool you, your honor," Rebecca said. "He's trying to say that a coin only has one side. The other side of his client's testimony is that the blowout didn't happen on the highway.

Either the jury should have both sides, or they shouldn't have either side."

"We understand your positions," Harris said. "We're going to let him answer the question. We don't consider the defendant's friends —Mr. Cummings and Mr. Diruski —to be distanced enough from the defendant to be considered independent. The defendant's credibility always is an issue for the jury. The witness may answer the question. Anything else?"

"Mr. Ogden," Rebecca said, "please make these four assumptions. One, the tire didn't blow out on the highway. Two, the motorcycle left the highway because Mr. Rotten lost control. Three, the motorcycle was going 55 miles per hour at the time it left the highway. Four, the conditions at the scene generally were the same as when you visited. Okay, got all that?"

"Yes. Okay," Ogden said.

"Good. Now, tell the jury how difficult it would be to control the motorcycle after it left the highway?"

"First, the driver would be trying to keep it upright. Tough. Because of the slope of the ditch and the soft dirt. But definitely possible. Second, the driver would be trying not to hit anything. Even more difficult. Pretty well stuck with the direction the bike takes. Minor changes, maybe, but that's all.

"You heard Mr. Rotten's testimony about his difficulty in controlling the bike after it left the highway and about the direction it went, correct?" Rebecca said.

"Yes," Ogden said.

"Isn't that consistent with what would happen if a bike left the highway because the driver lost control?

"Well...."

"Isn't it, Mr. Ogden? Be honest, now," Rebecca said.

"Yes, I guess I would have to say it was," Ogden said.

"That's your opinion to a reasonable certainty?"

"Yes."

"Thank you. No further questions, your honor," Rebecca said.

"Mr. Gant? Anything additional?" Harris said.

"No, your honor," Gant said.

As Ogden left the witness stand, Gant snuck a look at the jury.

They were impassive, except for a quizzical grimace by the man with the mustache.

"No further witnesses, your honor," Gant said pleasantly.

Willie's face shifted from slender to sunken, as if he had a vision of a cell filled with fat, brown rats. Larry slumped like he had been fired. Quitters, Gant thought.

"Either sit like a winner or get out," he whispered savagely to Larry. Willie looked too fragile to restore.

If she's smart, she won't call anyone in rebuttal, he thought. She turned both experts or at least neutralized them. He watched Rebecca's fingernails turn the pages in her trial notebook. The interstate system those fingernails once mapped on his body on Sunday mornings remained, badly in need of maintenance.

Why leave it to the jury, Becky? Tell you what, flip the coin. You win, and Willie and I go away forever. I win, Willie walks, and you be my toy — leathers, feathers, lotions, and oils. You repair the interstate. My tongue will trench a canal system for your delightful enjoyment. When I'm done with you, your job will be waiting because you're so good, he thought.

"The state is convinced it will get a conviction without producing further evidence. It rests, your honor," Rebecca said.

"Wishful thinking, Miss Varner," Gant said. She gave him a rare look. Her blowtorch eyes incinerated his nostalgic travel guide of the erotic senses. The ashes made him cough. He cleared his throat. "If words could make it so, you might have something. The defense also rests, your honor."

"Earlier than we expected," Judge Harris said. "We're pleased. We're sure the jury is, also. We're going to send you home for the day," she said to the jury. "We'll work with the attorneys this afternoon to finish the instructions and other matters. When you return tomorrow morning, you'll hear their final arguments. Thank you, and have a nice day, what's left of it, anyway."

*

After surviving the ordeal of closing arguments and the judge's instructions, the jury seized absolute control of the case and solemnly left the courtroom to deliberate. The jury had no forms to fill out or format to follow. The jurors would repeatedly pour what they heard and saw in the courtroom and the comments of each other through a sieve to refine it into a decision. Their method would remain unknown and their reasoning a secret.

"Wait for me in the hall. Both of you," Gant said to Willie and Larry after they respectfully watched the jury exit their box. "I want to talk to the DA."

"Why?" Willie said.

"To see if she's ready to be reasonable," Gant said.

"Bitch probably wants twenty years now," Willie said.

Gant shook his head and walked to Rebecca's table. "Can we talk a minute?" he said.

Rebecca did not look up and continued to pack up her file.

"Rebecca," Gant said. "Can't we work something out? Neither of us wants to lose."

"My position hasn't changed," she said. "Your man can plead to the charge and I'll recommend seven years in prison."

"That doesn't make sense. This is a reasonable doubt jury if I've ever seen one," Gant said. "The blowout on the highway may have caused it all. This jury will agree this argument creates reasonable doubt."

"They're not going to buy that story about the blowout any more than they'll believe he spent all afternoon at a motorcycle gang party and only had four beers," Rebecca said. "Your magic trick isn't going to work."

"I don't want to argue. Look, I think Willie's ready to plead if you are reasonable on the sentence. Give him a year, maybe two, and I think I can sell it," Gant said.

"Seven," Rebecca said.

"Come on. You get the plea. He does time. Two. Seven. What difference does it make to you?"

"A woman's dead because of what he did. Seven is the appropriate penalty."

"This isn't personal, is it? You know, because I'm his lawyer?" Gant said.

Rebecca hastily inserted the last part of her file into the carrying case and snapped the latches. She lifted it with a jerk and turned to leave. Gant partially blocked her way.

"Not personal at all. It's exactly what our sentencing guidelines call for. I checked with Bartley. He agreed," Rebecca said. "Now, excuse me."

"I'm in a bad place, Rebecca. I can't afford to lose this one. Can't we go talk somewhere?"

"Sure, I'd like to talk. Sometime. I'd like to know what the hell happened that night. But not now. This is business. I can't help you." Rebecca stepped toward him. "Get out of my way."

Gant moved aside. He heard the door open and click closed and he was alone in the courtroom. If we lose, he thought, I'll try to keep him out on bond until the sentencing and use that time to get next to Rich. He rubbed the rail in front of the jury box for luck.

As with most other lawyers, Gant found it impossible to do any real work while his jury was out. Earlier in his career, Gant, alternately wound tight by the expected ecstasy of victory and paralyzed by the fear of probable defeat, joined other lawyers at a nearby bar for the traditional wait for the clerk's call.

Now Gant preferred the freedom of his cell. He left Willie at the courthouse and wandered. Three hours later, the clerk caught him at the Dew Drop. With a wave at the owner, he took the call on the sidewalk.

"We have a verdict, Mr. Gant," the clerk said.

CHAPTER EIGHTEEN

Secrecy and anonymity seemed most important, although Flick wasn't sure why. He hired a biker's sister, who transcribed doctor's notes at the local hospital, to type the transcripts of the tapes.

He slipped the transcripts, one of the photos, and a note into a plain brown envelope. Feeling a little foolish, he clumsily cut with kitchen shears from a random selection of old magazines and newspapers small letters for Gant's name and address and glued them onto the envelope.

Cheyenne picked up the envelope off the kitchen table and snickered.

"What's with the funny letters. It looks like kids' TV," he said.

"Man, put it down. Your prints are on it," Flick said. He pinned it to the table with his elbow and vigorously rubbed the package with a dry cloth. "It's for that lawyer."

"He's going to know where it came from. It's not like there's more than one source for those tapes and shit. You really think he'll pay?" Cheyenne said.

Flick ignored him. It's the drugs, he thought.

"And what were you talking to Honda about?" Cheyenne said. "Those fucking riceburners."

"My movie," Flick said. "They're very interested."

"You're talking to Honda about making your biker movie? That's fucked up."

"They got the bread to do it right."

Flick put a plate with two pieces of peanut butter, toast and jam down in front of his son.

"So what?" Cheyenne said. "Only tool to use on those things is a sledgehammer."

"It gets the film made. That's what's important."

"That's bullshit. Who we are and what we stand for is what's important. Starts and ends with Harleys. Man, I can't believe you're saying this."

"Eat your toast," Flick said.

"Everything you've told me about bikers, you don't believe that any more?" Cheyenne said. "You've made some major changes."

"I got to do what I got to do," Flick said. "Right now, I got to get you straight. You're fucked up on dope. We need money to get into something new. Harley doesn't answer me, maybe the lawyer doesn't come through, and so I'm talking to Honda. I'll do whatever it takes. Tough if you don't like it"

"You're the one who's fucked up, not me. I'm doing what I want to do. I'm a biker. Freedom. Loyalty. 'Live to Ride. Ride to Live.' You taught me that and now I live it. Same as my brothers in the garage. Drugs are part of it and I don't care. I don't want to live forever. And who are you to come down on dope. You've made your living selling it." Cheyenne angrily stalked form the kitchen.

*

Molli was talking to Cheyenne when Flick returned from mailing the envelope.

"She said you let her ride my Harley while I was gone," Cheyenne said.

"Yeah, we did an ad," Flick said. "No big thing."

"Pisses me off, dad. She's not a brother. And a woman. No offense," Cheyenne said to Molli. "You're cool."

"I said no big deal. It's a screwed up time, that's for sure." Flick said. "Now split for awhile."

"A little hyper, isn't he?" Molli said, after Cheyenne hurried away.

"It's the dope. I've got to get him out of here," Flick said.

"Away from your bikers?"

"Don't you fucking start on that. He's telling me I'm selling out. Idealism of youth. I'm only doing it for him. He doesn't see that."

"What about our deal? That's why I'm here. I hadn't heard from you," Molli said.

"It's cool. Just got back from mailing it. I didn't want him to get it while he was trying that biker case. So I waited. You got a problem with that?" Flick said.

"You guys really do stick together," she said. "No, no problem. What's next?"

"I call him Saturday."

"Then what?"

"Who knows? Depends on him."

"Think he'll pay?"

"Not the half million. Fifty-fifty maybe he'll pay something," Flick said. "I'm going to squeeze him good because I need it. Did I tell you I've been talking to Honda about the film? Honda. Makes me want to puke. But it's a way for me to get my boy out of here. That's number one right now. If Gant pays, I can kiss Honda off."

"I can use it, too," Molli said. "I'm looking at film opportunities overseas, like Europe and India."

"Far out," Flick said. "Think about Asia. Singapore. Japan."

"I've got screen tests. Wanted to tell you I'll be gone for a week," Molli said.

CHAPTER NINETEEN

Willie's wife sat surrounded by every member of the Vipers except Hairball, who couldn't get off work. Every member and their wives or girl friends, kids, hangers-on, recruits, wannabes, and extra women of every description. A nighttime sky of black vests, boots, jackets, hats, pants, shades, mascara, beards, hair, fingernails, gloves and belts filled the seats behind Gant and Willie and spread into the section behind the prosecutor's table. Wallet chains rattled, babies cried, and an occasional belch or laugh punctuated the low murmur, as persistent and discordant as rush hour traffic.

Gant saw Judge Harris twitch, as if Attila and the Huns had invaded her courtroom, as she came through her private door. She cocked her head like a bird at him. He read her eyes.

"Evening, Judge." A voice called from the back accompanied by tight-knit laughter and louder mumbles.

"How nice to see so many familiar faces," Judge Harris said forcefully. "We know you all remember our rules."

She called the attorneys up to her bench.

"What is the meaning of this, Mr. Gant?" she whispered angrily.

"What do you mean, your honor?" Gant replied innocently. I'm going to make you say it, he thought, congratulating himself for telling the bikers not to attend the trial.

"All those, those, people. Why did you bring them to our courtroom?"

"I didn't bring them. They want to hear the verdict, that's all. They're concerned about their friend."

"Are we safe? Should we get extra bailiffs?" Harris said.

"I feel safe. It's up to you," Gant said.

"We won't tolerate disruption in our courtroom," Harris said.

"Of course not, your honor," Gant said.

"Does the district attorney have a position?" she said to Rebecca.

"No, your honor," Rebecca said. "Typical Gant move, I'd say."

"Where are the Doblers, Becky? You send them home, or they couldn't get out of the bar?"

"Enough, Mr. Gant," Harris said. "Just enough. One more time and we'll sanction. Understand?"

"Yes. May we get the verdict?" he said frigidly.

Sometimes, Gant knew, he got a clue from their faces. They strode in purposefully, led by the woman in the print dress. Gant watched her blink at all the bikers. Four more poker faces. His man with the mustache entered sixth. Gant saw his lips turn up as if he realized they'd been fooled, or that they knew it all along. Shit, Gant thought, I'm going to lose.

With the solemnity of slower times, the proceeding continued.

"You have been elected foreperson?" Judge Harris inquired of the woman in the print dress.

"Yes."

"We understand you have reached a verdict, is that correct?"

"Yes."

"Would you hand it to the bailiff, please."

A baby gurgled insistently as a spring, the only sound except for the pad of the bailiff's shoes as he carried the piece of paper to Judge Harris. Absolutely stone faced, Gant thought. She began to read.

"We the jury find the defendant Willie Rotten...." Harris paused."...not guilty."

Rebecca went rigid. Gant jumped up, both arms raised above his head in relieved delight like a boxer who retained his title by split decision. Rotten whooped and traded high fives with some of the Vipers before hugging his wife and kids.

"Order," Harris said repeatedly, banging her gavel. The tumultuous back slapping, hand shaking, foot stomping celebration grew. Women and men kissed. Kids danced in the aisles. Someone opened a beer.

Harris cupped her hands around her mouth like a coach and screamed at the jury members who moved toward their door like frightened sheep.

"Is that your verdict?" she said and they nodded and escaped, not hearing the judge's customary words of thanks. The judge glared at Gant and abandoned her courtroom to the pandemonium.

"Good fucking job, man," Mouse said to Gant. "Nice win."

"Yeah, thanks. So we're square, right?" Gant said.

"Relax. I understand nothing's forever. We've had a good run. Now it's party time, man. Let's go."

"Yeah, maybe, I don't know." He saw Rebecca detour around the celebrating mass like it was a herd of diseased animals. "Son of a bitch," he said to Larry. "This is a sweet one. Haul it back, will you." He flicked his hand at the scattered files and books.

Gant chased Rebecca down in the hallway by the drinking fountain near her office. "You could have won that."

"Cut the crap," she said.

"Seriously, could have gone either way."

"Jake."

"Reasonable doubt case. Who knows about juries?"

"If that case had been tried on the truth, the jury would have convicted in about five minutes. I know what you did and you know I know."

"What I did? I don't have a clue. I presented the evidence. That's it," Gant said.

"Not all the evidence was true," Rebecca said.

"What are you saying here? That the evidence was manufactured?"

"Something like that."

"You've lost it."

"Someday your luck will disappear like the truth at a liars' convention. I hope I'm there." She pivoted toward the door.

"You're pissed because I kicked your butt in there," he said abusively. "You've become a loser, Becky, a bad loser."

CHAPTER TWENTY

Gant entered the office the next morning to accolades befitting the leader of a single party country —thumbs up, waves, demurely dropped eyes, words of praise. He enjoyed congratulations as solid as particle board and warm as yesterday's leftovers. Unoffended, Gant responded with the graciousness of a disdainful dictator. He stopped last at Joan's desk.

"Your conquering hero is home, covered with fame and fortune. Where are the flowers, the music, the dancing girls? Why are you not prone at my feet, offering yourself to quench my every desire?" Gant said.

Joan made a face like she had tasted wine gone bad. "I can quench your desire for messages," she said, waving a small bunch of pick slips, "that's it."

"You know what they say. Win when it's expected, you're a winner. Win when you're supposed to lose, you're a myth. Don't I at least get a hug and a kiss?" Gant said.

"Isn't that what you get paid to do, win cases? It's not like Willie Rotten was that big of a case."

"Okay, Miss Sunshine, what do you have?"

"Congratulations, mostly from attorneys. Look at them later," she said as she gave him slips one at a time. "This one is Channel Four. She wants comments. Call before eleven. Same with this radio person. Mouse called about getting the bike back."

"I'm done with them. Let Mouse get it back. Wait," Gant said. "Get Rebecca on the phone instead. I want to talk to her, but tell her it's about the bike. And see if Bruce can have lunch today or tomorrow. He'll appreciate my win."

Joan calmly took notes. "New PI clients at three and four-fifteen. That Joy Friendly called. She wants to take your deposition," Joan said.

"Who?"

"She's the woman who suing you to pay her ticket, the parking space."

"Take my deposition? In that case? Crazy. What else?" Gant said.

"I cut out the article in the morning paper," Joan said. "It's on your desk. It's good, I think. Let me know if you want it framed.

Finally, Rich came by. Tried to make me promise to buzz him as soon as you came in. He and Jeb want to meet with you today.

"Now what? God. Late this afternoon is okay. Put Rebecca through no matter what."

"Are you taking calls?"

"What do mean am I taking calls. Of course I'm taking calls. When don't I take calls?" Gant said sharply and shook his head in disgust. "Stop giving me all this crap and send in Larry."

He motioned Larry to a chair as he finished the telephone interview. District Attorney Suss has lost control of his office, he told the television reporter. Wish him a speedy recovery, of course. He files ridiculous charges. It's an unnecessary waste of taxpayer dollars and court time. Unfair cost to innocent citizens who are wrongly charged. Appear on a panel? Glad to. Anytime, he said and hung up.

"Good job on the brief. So, you all set to be a trial lawyer?" he said to Larry.

"It was great. Thanks for letting me come. I knew you were good, but I had no idea you were that good," Larry said, gushing. "It opened my eyes."

Gant nodded.

"I heard what you just said about the DA," Larry said. "A friend of mine clerks there. She said Ms. Varner was really steamed after the verdict. Said all kinds of bad things about you. Accused you of fixing the evidence."

"Becky always was a bad loser. What did you say to your friend?"

"I didn't know what to say."

"I see," Gant said, disappointed. "Go get me some cigarettes... Please."

"Excuse me," Larry said. "Do you have a minute?"

"What?" Gant said.

"Next Friday will be my last day. I've decided trial law isn't for me. Got a job with a tax firm. Sorry. Learned a lot from you. Thanks for everything." Larry said, rising quickly from his chair.

"You're gone today. As of now. Tell Joan to cut you a check," Gant said, staring fiercely into Larry's eyes. "Good decision. You're not tough enough for this work."

Gant dismissed Larry's abrupt departure as unimportant, except that it meant hiring another law clerk which was a task he hated. He searched his wall for a suitable spot for the clip from the morning newspaper, reading occasional paragraphs praising his abilities in some of the yellowing articles. He put that on his list for Joan to take care of.

Gant normally went through a detached stage, like a traveler with jet lag, immediately after a trial. This time he had slept it off. Gant felt particularly good about his life this morning. The reunion fiasco was a distant memory. He was back in control and could clearly see what he had to do.

Gant had no doubt that Mouse would leave him alone. He intended to forget that he had spoken words of reconciliation to Rich. His partner could either continue to suffer in well-paid misery or he could walk out with his family photos. Gant believed Rich was too concerned about his image to go to court.

He would meet Friday with the insurance lawyer on the day care fire case. As he had expected, the fire marshal had unequivocally blamed the woeful negligence of the building owner for the fire in the day care center. Gant assigned a team of eager young associates from the litigation department specific tasks to be completed promptly, including the preparation of a list of potential experts. If the insurance company wanted to admit liability and talk settlement, fine. If not, he'd be ready. Gant intended to prepare this case perfectly.

The verdict had not changed his mind. After he got Willie's motorcycle back, he was done with bikers. And he was only doing that because it gave him an opportunity to talk to Rebecca. Her courtroom comment about wanting to discuss their last night together had grown in Gant's mind until it became an invitation. He decided he'd wait until her anger over the verdict subsided, then they'd go to dinner.

Later in the morning, Gant and Joan were doing their mail-opening ritual when the phone rang. Gant motioned for Joan to answer and heard her tell the caller that he was right here. He reached for the receiver. She shook her head and turned her back on him.

"I'll tell him," she said before hanging up. "Ms. Varner," Joan said. "Mr. Rotten can pick up his motorcycle at the police property section tomorrow. She specifically said she didn't want to talk to you."

"Still pissed," he said. "She'll come around."

*

Rich remained in Gant's office after the Friday meeting. The insurance lawyer condescendingly spoke of a full exchange of information leading to an orderly, prompt, and fair settlement process.

"Translate that into a time frame," Rich said.

"Can't," Gant said. "Too many unanswered questions yet, including whether he's being serious with us. Depends on when the docs release the kids from care. Could be a year for some, maybe more. Then there's the question of whether we can settle them one at a time or whether we have to settle them all at once. That depends on the amount of insurance. One thing that's sure is that each settlement has to be approved by the court because they're minors."

"So, we're not going to see any money for awhile?" Rich said.

"I don't see it happening. And our fees aren't automatic," Gant said.

"What do you mean?"

"The court doesn't care if we have a contract giving us one third of the settlement in fees. If it thinks we've been sitting on the couch clipping coupons, it will knock our share way down. So we have to go ahead as if we never met this guy today. Hire the experts. Make the videos. Do the legal work. We need to justify higher fees."

"You're saying this money won't be available to help us resolve our other deal, right?" Rich said.

"What other deal?" Gant said.

"Letting me go. Or you getting out. Remember, you said we'd work it out after the trial. It's after the trial, let's get it done."

"No. Either you misheard or I misspoke."

"Come on," Rich said disbelieving.

"Options haven't changed. You can stay, walk, or, if you have the guts, sue," Gant said.

Rich grinned like he had learned the secret of the universe. "You're a sick man. Very sick. Here's what's happening. I will sue your ass. Be after you low and hard. And for the duration, you got something to say to me, put it in writing. You hearing me?"

Amused, Gant wrote three words on his pad and held it up for Rich.

"Yes, sir, boss," it read.

Gant trailed Rich out of his office. Joan's desk was clean except for the bundle of mail and empty salad container. She was changing into her walking shoes.

"Leaving early?" Gant said.

"It's after five," Joan said without raising her head. "Have a nice weekend."

"You, too," he said automatically. "Bruce call yet?"

"No."

"That's unusual. Wonder if he's on vacation."

He left soon after Joan. A man was photographing his car in the parking garage. He nodded as Gant approached him.

"Nice car," he said, continuing to point and shoot.

"What are you doing?" Gant said.

The photographer looked at him like he had asked a stupid question and handed him a business card which identified him as a private investigator.

"My client needs some pictures of your car," he said.

"Your client? Who's that?"

"Joy Friendly," the man said. "I'm done. Thanks. Have a good weekend."

"You, too," Gant said. He could not recall who she was until he was on the street. Talk about crazy, he thought, I need a drink.

At the Dew Drop, a balding man with a waxed mustache mixed him a vodka gimlet.

"Where's Lola?" Gant said.

"Who's Lola?" the man said.

"The night bartender."

"I'm the night bartender. They call me a lot of names, but Lola isn't one of them. Sorry, partner."

The owner explained that Lola had left in the middle of her shift two nights ago with her ex-boy friend who drove a new Cadillac convertible practically into the bar. He flashed some bills and said his brother in Tallahassee has jobs for both of them.

"I promised her I give you this," the owner said and handed Gant a photograph.

It was from her old modeling portfolio, taken many years ago. Wearing white shorts, vest, and cowgirl hat, she was standing next to a horse. In big, scrawling, script she had written —"Mr. Gant - Love and kisses forever. Lola."

Gant emptied his drink, laid the photo on the bar, and headed for the door.

"Hey," the bartender said. "You forgot your picture."

"I don't want it," Gant said. "She's yours."

The bartender stuck it behind the row of bottles. "Have a good weekend," he said as Gant went out.

*

Gant knocked over the glass sitting next to the phone. It fell without breaking on a pile of clothes. It was dark out and the digital clock glowed five-twenty.

"Hello," Gant said. He had the beginning of a headache.

"Did I wake you?"

"Who is this?"

"Joan."

"Joan?" Gant said. "Oh, yeah. What do you want?"

"Have you heard?" she said.

"What?"

"Bartley's dead. You told me to tell you, remember?"

"But it's Saturday morning. I didn't need to know," he said.

"I'm following your orders. You going in today?" Joan said.

"Yeah. Maybe. I don't know. Christ. It's early. Don't do this to me again."

Gant blamed Joan for not being able to get back to sleep. Lying in bed, he recalled his early trials against Bartley. The DA could kill defense attorneys with his fairness. He'd capture the jury by giving in on all the little points. Then he'd ask for a crucial concession. If the attorney didn't agree, Bartley's betrayed appearance asked the jury to punish. If he was on, it was tough to win a case against him.

Gant assumed the governor would appoint Rebecca to succeed Bartley. She'd paid her dues, did quality work and was widely regarded as his heir apparent. Gant lit his first cigarette. He could give up doing criminal work without missing it. That would eliminate the conflict problem. He thought about how it would feel to be back together. How could she say no?

CHAPTER TWENTY ONE

The cemetery held memorial services in a large auditorium attached to the administration building and in a small chapel on the older part of the grounds. The chapel was constructed of gray stone in a style so European it appeared to have been moved directly from Germany. Bartley had specifically requested the chapel, disregarding his wife's concern that it would be too small.

Inside the chapel at Bartley's funeral late Monday afternoon, the Suss family occupied the first two pews, their space protected by a discreetly positioned black rope. Three tiers of huge flower arrangements provided the backdrop to the podium. Politicians and lawyers signed the guest book and found seats where they could among Bartley's friends and neighbors. In silence, they paid their respects to Bartley, comforted by the sweet, sad organ music and the steady sobs of Mrs. Suss.

The day was warm and still and the mourners were fanning themselves with their programs when Gant arrived. He came to meet Rebecca. From the back of the crowded room, Gant located Rebecca's head in the row immediately behind the family. There was no place to sit near her. He would have to wait until the service concluded. When she stood to give a piece of the eulogy, Gant tried to catch her eye. He heard her voice break and wondered if she would cry.

At the conclusion of the service, the flow of the exiting crowd forced Gant outside. He nodded abruptly at familiar faces as he waited by the door. Rebecca came out in the middle of the Suss clan with her arm around the widow. Gant confronted them.

"We have to talk," he said.

Rebecca looked at him like he had crawled out from under a rock.

"Now?" she said. "Have you no sense?"

"Okay. I'll wait over there." Gant pointed at one of the tall fir trees that surrounded the chapel.

"Leave us alone. You're awful," Rebecca said, pushing by him.

"I thought you wanted to talk," he said.

On the way home from the funeral, in the privacy of his car, Gant admitted it hurt to be called awful by Rebecca. He would give her one more chance, then to hell with her, he thought. A song on the radio reminded him that Thursday was poker night and he wondered why Bruce had not returned his calls. On the way into his building, he retrieved his mail from the box by the front door. A thick tan rubber band held magazines and full-sized ads curled around the envelopes. Gant pitched the bundle untouched onto his bed.

In his underwear, shirt on but unbuttoned, Gant slipped off the rubber band and snapped it on his dresser. The packet flopped open. The phone bill was on top, followed by two solicitations and a brown manila envelope without a return address postmarked in Carolina. His name and address were printed childlike in random sized letters. Perplexed, Gant set it aside momentarily while he scanned the remainder of the mail. He looked a long time at the envelope before he picked it up again. He hefted it and drummed it against his free hand. It was thick enough to require a third stamp. Gant worked his finger under the flap and split it open raggedly along one of the ends. He shook out the six sheets and one photograph.

Its format was similar to a deposition transcript. He didn't comprehend until he read a portion of the first page. It was the exact conversation that he'd had at the hotel with the ex-quarterback, D'Oreo and Molli when he agreed to supply drugs.

Gant frantically shuffled through the rest of the pages. It was more of the same. An unsigned note in the same awkward printing fell from between the fourth and fifth pages. "Be at your phone between six and seven p.m. your time Saturday."

Fuck, Gant said to his bedroom. It was as if he had called three days after the doctor ordered the test and the nurse told him to come in. So Molli recorded everything, he thought. He knew why Flick was involved, but he couldn't figure Molli's angle. He raged profanely at both of them, Mouse and the Vipers, bikers and women in general, and his classmates who were responsible for the whole debacle. If they all died, he wouldn't mind.

Gant poured vodka over ice, took one sip and dumped it in the kitchen sink. He spread the pages on the table and read them as objectively as possible. It was professionally prepared on good quality paper. The order of the dialogue had been rearranged into a classic inverted pyramid with the most potent paragraphs at the top.

Not good, he admitted, but at least he never actually bought or sold anything. They're meaningless words. A joke. He realized he had been set up. But in context it's not bad. If he said this on a stage, the audience would know that they were only lines in a play. That's all these are.

He considered taking this to the cops and having them take the call Saturday. Blackmail across state lines was a federal offense. Gant pictured the skeptical reaction of the authorities to this anonymous and self-incriminating evidence. When he phones, I'll tell him to stuff it. Call his bluff. That will end it.

*

Gant discovered that his work blotted out the transcripts for substantial periods of time. He spent most of the next three days at the office, growing increasingly distant and ill-tempered. People avoided him, except for Joan who had no choice.

Gant went to the poker game for distraction, like the victim of a gnawing disease. As a man facing surgery, Gant tried to spin it into the realm of the inconsequential. He'd laugh it off and become calmly fatalistic. It's not as bad as it seems.

Bruce had canceled dinner. Although he was loose with the others at the table, he treated Gant like a stranger.

"Thought you'd want to hear about my latest triumph," Gant said finally. "You getting your messages okay?"

"Yeah. Been busy," Bruce said. "I read about it in the paper. That's good enough."

Gant's feigned unconcern lasted until the sixth hand when he found himself foolishly chasing a pair of aces. His mind had heard the testimony and wouldn't let it go, despite his attempt to declare the transcript irrelevant and bury it in the special file in his head for things he wanted to forget. After he carelessly folded a winning hand face up, he quit playing.

"We appreciate your charity tonight, Jake. Hate to see you go," Bruce said, chortling.

By Saturday morning Gant had succeeded in making Joan cry at the office for the first time in many years. She threatened to quit. In the solitude of Saturday afternoon, he outlined several scenarios for the phone call. No matter who called, what they said, and how they threatened, Gant was determined to tell them he would give them nothing.

At six-fifty that evening, Gant let the phone ring three and a half times before he answered.

"Gant?" Flick said jovially.

"Yeah. Is this Flick?"

"Good to talk to you, man. I had a far-out time with you. So did Molli. Said to ask you how it was hanging. What did she mean by that? Anyway, we got some cool photos I'm sure you'll want to show your friends. I sent them out yesterday along with a couple more pages. It's as good as the first package."

"Let's be clear, I'm not paying anything," Gant said.

Flick flattened Gant's well-rehearsed refusal like it was a pebble on the highway. "As they say in the movies, counselor, I'm only going to say this once. Five hundred thousand cash in ten days. If not, I send a complete set to your partners. No money in another five days, copies go to newspapers, TV, bar association, and, of course, district attorney. I'll call tomorrow same time for your answer. Report this, and we all go down. You know I keep my word."

Gant laughed at the dead phone as if it were to blame, a laugh which verged on hysteria before screeching into a wail and dying out as a cough-punctuated moan. Flick's voice made Gant feel alone in a small windowless room with two doors, one bearing the dollar sign, the other a picture of a ball and chain. A half a million dollars, he said softly, a half a million. He didn't have that much. That son of a bitch will do what he says, he thought. There must be a way.

Gant knew Flick would call in twenty-four hours. If he didn't agree to pay, Rich and Jeb would get a package and Rich would love it. What would they do? Maybe the partnership breaks up. He knew he could survive because other lawyers had. The bar association may give him a reprimand, but no charges could be filed. They couldn't prove he bought or sold anything.

*

During the next twenty four hours, Gant manipulated these possibilities innumerably as he methodically did petty tasks in the safe environment of his condo. By the time the phone rang, he had almost convinced himself that everything would work out.

"You think you've got me, you fucking nobody," Gant said. "Think again. I'm Jake Gant. I can take a hit. Tell my partners. Tell the TV. I don't care. I didn't do anything. All just talk. Trying to squeeze me for that film. It didn't work in the restaurant, and it's not working now. Fuck you. And that bitch Molli, too. You do me, and I'm going to the feds on you two."

"Fuck you, too, you fucking phony." Flick said, not angrily but like he was giving orders. "You'll get a copy of Flea's statement tomorrow. You read it closely. You'll be begging me to take your money."

"What? What statement? Who's Flea?"

"He tells me you sold him coke. Quarter pound," Flick said. "He wanted to talk to the DA here. Thought it might help him out with another problem he's got. I convinced him to wait. Anybody asks me, I'll say you two spent time together. Face it, Gant, you're, like, dead meat."

"You're bluffing," Gant said.

"It's your bet. But, I'm telling you, I never bluff and I always keep my word. You're going to be snuffling with the hogs unless I get my money. I figure you can earn five hundred grand in a couple years. That's cheap for the rest of your life. Dig?"

"Goddamn it, you're framing me. I don't have that kind of money. You cock-sucking, motherfucking, camel-humping, ass-licking bastard. I'm not paying you fucking anything. You fuck with me and I'll turn your life into pure shit. You got that, you pond scum?"

"The money is here this time next week. Otherwise, we'll play out the hands," Flick said tersely and hung up.

*

Because Gant very rarely left the office except for business, Joan looked quizzically at him early Monday afternoon when he told her he'd be back in a little while.

"Where are you going?" she said.

"Out," Gant said viciously, his face red. "Out. That's all you need to know. I'm about done with all your prying, stupid questions."

In the waiting room, he glared at several staff members and clients who were openmouthed at his outburst. He weaved and cursed his way through traffic to his condo.

"Home early today, Mr. Gant?"

Gant grunted uncivilly at the security guard's question and rushed to his mailbox. He let three of the four pieces fall to the carpet and opened the manila envelope with closed eyes. He extracted the paper clipped-white sheets and photographs. More transcripts, but no statement. I knew he was bluffing, Gant thought exultantly.

"The rest of your mail, sir," the guard said stiffly, as Gant spun around to leave.

"Thanks. I appreciate that. You have a nice day," Gant said, picking it up and waving clumsily.

Limp and sweaty with relief, Gant sat in his car in the parking garage, radio and air conditioning on. Flick was bluffing, he thought. Thankful for having survived, like the chronic drunk the morning after, Gant compiled a to-do list of personal changes to be made in tribute to those responsible, as if they kept score. He'd make it right with Rebecca. He'd let Rich and Jeb buy him out and he'd start his own practice. He'd find out what's wrong with Bruce. He'd start exercising and eat better. He might even quit smoking.

Gant grimaced at the glossy photos. I look ridiculous in those clothes, he thought. He studied the bored look on Molli's face as he held her breasts. The media will love these. It's obviously a joke. No one in the right mind would seriously do this.

CHAPTER TWENTY TWO

Molli received Flick's message when she got home from her trip and called him back the next day. She listened to the summaries of his conversations with Gant, disregarding the name-calling and profanity. Flick described him as determined not to pay.

"Of course," Flick said, "he hasn't seen the statement."

"What statement?" she said, surprised.

"Flea's statement. You know him. He works for me."

"Guy who wants to look like Elvis?" Molli said.

"That's him. He says Gant sold him a quarter pound of coke."

"Right, and I'm Marilyn Monroe. I'd be shocked if Jake could taste the difference between coke and baking soda."

"He swears it happened. Wrote it out. Was going to the DA until I stopped him."

Molli thought for a minute. "Let me guess. He's going down anyway, and you offered financial support for his wife and kids while he's gone."

"That's close."

"It's more than the money now, isn't it?"

"Right on. Gant's a first class prick, excuse my language."

In some ways, my friend, she thought, you two belong to the same fraternity. "So, where are we at?"

"He'll get the statement today or tomorrow. It will change how he thinks. He said something about not having the money. Maybe he'll call and want to deal. What do you think about that?" Flick said.

"You mean should we take less?" Molli said.

"Yeah. If he offers."

"Not by me. I think you set it right. Five hundred grand. He's either got it, or he can get it."

"Cool. I dig it."

"If he doesn't pay, it's because he doesn't think anyone can beat him." She paused. "How's Cheyenne?"

"It's a bad scene getting worse," Flick said. "Got me worried. Guys in the shop don't help any. They heard that I'm talking to Honda about the film and agree with Cheyenne. But he's not their kid, you know? I'm about ready to throw him over the back of the bike and split."

"That would make him happy," Molli said, dryly.

"He'd thank me later. Drugs have him screwed up," Flick said. "How was your trip?"

"Good. They loved the screen test, but it will take money, especially if mom comes along."

"What kind of film?" Flick said.

"Period romance in colonial India." Molli picked Meryl up. "You know, I did all this crazy shit with you to be a star. Now I might have a chance, but it might mean leaving mom. I thought it would be no problem. I mean, kids leave their parents every day. But now when it comes down to it, I'm not sure I can. Not sure it's worth it."

"That's heavy," Flick said.

"Too heavy for this phone line," she said. "Stay in touch."

*

On his way back to the office Monday, Gant had bought Joan a wildflower bouquet. He gave the flowers awkwardly and she took them suspiciously, leaving immediately to dry her eyes under the pretext of filling a vase with water. He allowed her to punish him with silence and with a wounded look which reminded Gant why he didn't have pets. He knew he'd need her if the partnership exploded.

By noon on Tuesday, Gant had fabricated on paper his safety net, a new law practice comprised of clients too thick skinned or desperate to care, young attorneys grateful for work, and Joan. He worked the numbers to calculate the approximate value of his share of the firm – conservatively, more that four hundred thousand. He'd let them pay him over time.

He surprised Joan by authorizing settlement with Joy Friendly in the amount of her ticket. He sent a handwritten offer to buy dinner to Bruce. Gant choked down plain yogurt and a bran muffin for lunch and set an appointment at six that evening with the personal trainer at the athletic club. At his instructions, Joan had been trying to reach Rebecca, but could not get past the receptionist. Gant had two tickets to Saturday's football game. For openers, he planned to offer them to her without suggesting that he go along.

"I can't even get through to her secretary," Joan said. "As soon as I say your name, she cuts me off. Sorry."

"They can't do that to Jake Gant," he said. "Watch this."

"Ms. Varner, please," Gant told the receptionist. "This is Mr. Martin from the funeral home. Something unexpected has come up regarding Mr. Suss and I must speak with her."

"Oh no, Jake," Joan said, mouthing the words.

"Rebecca," he said. "Sorry to do this but they wouldn't put me through. Know you're busy. Congratulations on the appointment. We need to talk. Have two football tickets for Saturday's --"

"Stop it," Rebecca said. "You used Bartley? I can't believe you. You can't treat people like nothing matters. Like you're the one and only."

"I want to tell you about that night. We have to talk."

"Not now. You've lost your way. You think you're special, but you're not. Watch out. You're going down and the fall will hurt."

Joan took the beeping phone from him and hung it up.

"Don't look at me like that," Gant said. "How else was I going to get through?"

After his workout, he decided not to stop at the Dew Drop. It wasn't the same without Lola's delighted squeal. At his condo, Gant forced a dry whistle as he inserted the key in his mailbox, convinced it was again benign rather than a breeding pit for razor-jawed surprises. He thought he'd shut the little door and go have a drink on his balcony.

A single envelope slanted diagonally from bottom to side. Gant knew what it was before he touched it. Still, he drew it out slowly with his fingertips, reading his name written with the same adolescent letters.

The statement was almost two pages long, single spaced. Signed and notarized, it detailed a transaction in which a person who identified himself as Jake Gant sold one quarter-pound of powder cocaine to Hobart Hilltop, also known as Flea. According to the statement, they had met at Straight Ahead Cycle, although the transaction took place down the road. It went on to say that Gant had bragged of past sales and offered to supply more from his Mexican connection.

Gant sat catatonic, unaware of the passing of time. He thought of nothing, as if the road of his life had come to a vast desert without guideposts or familiar landmarks. He looked at the phone when it rang, but didn't move to answer it. He heard Molli telling the answering machine that she had to talk to him. She'd call back in one hour. He got up and went to the bathroom. The statement kills me, he thought. He could go confront him, but with a name like Flea, he's got to be a biker. They'll all get up, one after the other, and swear he's telling the truth. The phone rang again.

"This is Molli. How have you been?"

"Molli, I can't find the words to express how fucking delighted I am to hear your voice. I am wonderful," he said.

"I know you're angry. Don't blame you. Sounds trite, but it's true. But, please listen to me. I want to help you. Really."

"You want to know trite?" Gant said, "Here's trite —with friends like you, I don't need enemies. I did what you wanted and you taped me. I can't believe people like you exist."

"Damn it. I know, you feel I used you and all of that. You can beat on me all month and that won't help. Do you want to listen, or should I hang up?" she said.

"Go ahead."

"Now don't interrupt. Flick and I expected a schmuck who would get off on investing in his movie. When you said no, Flick flipped out. So we bugged you. I admit it, I tricked you into talking about drugs. We got lucky with your classmates wanting coke. What jerks. Now Flick has someone who swears you sold drugs. I don't believe that at all about you. 'He's financing, dig it.' That's all he says. You know how he talks. He thinks you're loaded and will pay if he puts on enough pressure. It doesn't help that he can't stand you. On the other hand, I find you attractive."

"Stuff it." Gant said.

"Seriously. You don't have to believe me, but it's true. You have this intense way about you, like you have to win everything. That turns me on. Anyway, I know you probably don't have five hundred thousand dollars. But Flick's got the packets ready to go. I don't think he realizes that once he drops them in the box, that's the ballgame, as they say. That stuff will ruin you, and I don't want you to go to prison.

"Here's the deal. I kept the negatives and the tapes as my insurance against Flick cutting me out. He and I are supposed to split fifty-fifty. You come up with three hundred fifty thousand and

I'll give you the tapes and negatives. I'll cut my share so that Flick gets what he wants" Molli said.

"Hang on. First, I don't have that kind of money either. Second, if you have the tapes and negatives and feel so bad about what's happened, why not give them to me?" Gant said.

"You know how violent Flick can be. He wouldn't care that I'm a woman. If he couldn't find me, he'd go after my mom. I know he would. He's got this honor thing. He expects everybody's word to be as good as his. Cross him and you pay. I've seen it."

"I can't get that kind of money."

"With all those big cases you told me about? I mean, that was a lot of money," she said.

"Most of it went back into the firm. I have my condo and car. Some in retirement, but it would take too long to get it out. Some mutual funds and stocks, but not three hundred and fifty grand."

"Listen to me again. You're the lawyer. You've read all Flick's stuff. You know what it looks like for you. I'm telling you Flick will send it. He does what he says. If you don't care, then I'll say good night. But if you want to keep it secret, then we have to reach a compromise. That's what you lawyers do, isn't it? I'm willing to do whatever I can to make that happen, but Flick won't quit without money," Molli said.

Pragmatically, Gant knew she was correct. The only way that makes sense was to pay. Otherwise, he'd be lucky to get a job as an insurance adjuster. I'll reimburse myself with extra fees from the day care fire case. There was so much there, they'd never miss it. It's just business, he thought. Get the best deal and get done with it.

"Truth is, I'd be lucky to raise two hundred thousand. If I decided to pay. And those words taste like rotten meat in my mouth," Gant said.

Molli sighed as loudly as she could into the phone. "Well, I guess we'll have to let it go," she said hopelessly. "I'm positive Flick won't take less than two hundred fifty thousand which is his full share. I can live with fifty. That makes three hundred thousand. I really feel like I'm giving up a lot."

"What do you mean, you can live with fifty thousand? That's my money! Why should I pay you anything after what you've done to me?"

"If I don't get something, it means Flick wins and you win and I lose."

"I win? I pay two hundred fifty thousand dollars and I win? That's absurd. I'll tell you what. I'll pay the two fifty, but that's it. If that's what it takes to make Flick go away, then you don't get anything. And so you understand, if I go down, believe that I'll do all I can to take you both with me. Remember, your voice is on that tape, too."

Molli sighed again. "Okay, but it's not fair," she said, her voice cracking. "This is a very bad deal for me. But I have to get out of it before my mother gets hurt."

"You want me to feel sorry for you? You're absolutely demented," Gant said bitterly. "Give me Flick's number. I want to make sure this works for him."

"I'll give you the number, but I don't think you should call," Molli said tensely. "He hates you. As soon as you say you'll pay only two hundred fifty thousand, he'll stop listening. Even though it all goes to him. He'll think you're pulling a deal on him."

"He's even more demented than you. The hell with it then," Gant said.

"Wait. Let me talk to him. He listens to me. And, more important, I have leverage. I have another tape of him that he doesn't want played for the outside world. He'll go along with this deal. I'm certain of it."

"What's on that tape?"

"Doesn't have anything to do with you."

"Why couldn't we —"

"Look," Molli said wearily, "there's only one way this works. Flick gets his money, you get to go on about your life making tons of money, and I get out of a bad deal knowing my mom won't get hurt. That's it. Yes or no?"

"How can I be sure Flick, or you for that matter, won't come around again?" Gant said.

"I get out of this, I promise you won't see me again," she said earnestly. "Like you said, I'm on that tape with you. You think I want them playing that on the talk shows? No way! As for Flick, once he starts his dream film, he'll have too much to lose. But, I'll tell you what, I'll give you the tape I have on him, just in case. You boys will be even."

"I don't know," Gant said.

"What else is there? We're like legs on a tripod. If one collapses—"

"I know that," Gant said impatiently, thinking of his partners. "It's difficult for me to trust you. I'm sure you understand that."

Molli was quiet.

"Shit, what choice do I have? Call Flick and call me back," Gant said sullenly.

CHAPTER TWENTY THREE

He began raising the money early the next day by requesting an equity loan on his condo and Porsche. He explained he needed one hundred thousand dollars immediately for an overseas investment opportunity. Gant complained to no avail when the banker said that, because he was a preferred customer, he could get seventy five thousand. A larger amount would require committee approval, which would take a week.

"I need it in cash. One hundreds. I'll pick it up this afternoon," Gant said.

"I don't know if we can do that," the banker said, starting in about reporting requirements, available currency, and forms.

"Report it to whoever you need to. I'll sign the forms. You get the cash by three. If I don't get the cash, I'll lose the chance to make a lot of money. And I'll sue you personally and your bank, I swear it," Gant said forcefully.

He assured his mutual fund representative that he would replace the seventy-five thousand dollar withdrawal with a one hundred thousand dollar deposit within thirty days. He confided to her that he expected shortly a very large sum, perhaps as much as one million, from the settlement of a case and asked her to do a preliminary investment plan for him. As a favor, he asked her to expedite processing and arrange for him to pick up the cash at her company's bank the following day.

He withdrew twenty five thousand from his emergency savings account, virtually cleaning it out.

By late Thursday afternoon, 1,750 one hundred dollar bills were locked in Gant's trial briefcase behind his desk. He needed 750 more by Friday night. After carefully searching all the possibilities, no matter how remote, he found the one viable source.

He would set up a new business account at the firm's bank. He would write checks on the day care fire case special contingency account to potential experts. Gant would forge endorsements of these checks, deposit them to the new account, and immediately withdraw the money in his own name. Later, as quickly as possible, Gant would replenish this account with personal money from salary and bonuses. As the money became available, he could hire the experts as they were needed. It's a loan from my company to me, he thought. If my partners were reasonable men, I wouldn't have to go through all this.

Gant took the checkbook from the locked cabinet in Joan's office. More than once, he had sought for a client leniency and compassion from judge and jury by invoking the phrase, "desperate men commit desperate acts." As he sat at his desk writing the checks, these words visited him as a black-cloaked admonition to slow down.

Gant was traveling too fast to hear it.

*

The flight Saturday morning was uneventful. Gant paced in front of the terminal until he spotted Molli's car three rows deep in traffic.

"Where's Flick?" he said, ducking his head through the open passenger side window.

"Not with me," Molli said with a shrug. "I meet him at one at his place. That's all I know."

Gant scrutinized nearby cars for a familiar face. "I want to see it before I get in."

"Here it is." Molli unzipped a nylon file carrier and exposed the tapes and a small envelope with the negatives for Gant to see. "I assume you have the money?"

Gant nodded and got in quickly, aware of the approaching traffic cop. "Where are we going?"

"There's a park not too far from here," Molli said.

"No," Gant said quickly. "I'm not going any place you pick. I don't trust you or Flick."

"Oh, boy. Where then?"

"Downtown."

"Downtown? Are you nuts? I'm sorry, but no way do we want to take this money into the city. I mean —"

"Okay. Okay. There's a motel near here. Flick can pay for the room," he said, hefting the briefcase on his lap.

In the room, Gant, feeling enraged and helpless, did what little he could to inspect the goods. He held the negatives to the light. His bony hands covered Molli's breasts, invisible as soft tissue on an X-ray. The tape cassettes had been punched out to prevent copying. But who knows for sure, he thought. Gant fast-forwarded through each one, pausing haphazardly for snippets of conversations, too vividly recalled.

Molli dumped the money onto the bed and solemnly counted as she transferred it to an old-fashioned hard suitcase. She clicked it shut and hauled it to the door.

"Here's the tape on Flick. I'm keeping the original for my protection."

"I hope I never have to listen to it," Gant said.

"Jake," Molli said sweetly, "would you carry the money down for me? I'm not going to ruin my back for Flick, and I don't really want the bellboy involved."

"I can't fucking believe it. I don't do anything wrong. You take advantage of me. And I wind up carrying my own money downstairs for you to give to some biker. I've got to get out of here."

"I do know how you must feel. But, believe me, it could have been worse. I'm so glad we were able to work it out," Molli said sincerely. "Should we go to the airport?"

"I'll put the bag in the car. Then I'll call a cab."

Back home, Gant worked for the rest of the weekend to stuff Flick, Molli and his money into boxes destined for cold storage in the deepest recesses of his mind. The people went easily. The money, he couldn't think about for very long without frustration and anger spraying over his life like boiling water, from an erupting geyser, which he could cap only by concentrating on the day care fire case fees.

*

Molli delayed visiting because she knew her mom would beg her not to go. There would be tears and she would leave her mother's feeling terribly guilty. Molli had the plane ticket to India and the unsigned contract promising her a starring role in exchange for investing in the film. She didn't think she could refuse, even for her mom. It was too close to everything she wanted. She gave notice at the bar where she worked, wrote notes for her instructors at school and made arrangements for Meryl and Ingrid.

"Sorry, I'm late," Molli said to her mother.

"That's okay," her mother said. "I know you're busy. I kept it warm. I have to leave soon, though. Macramé class is having a going away party at Vi's. I'll miss her."

"You think I'm busy. You're the one. Miss Go, Go, Go."

"I try to stay busy. I feel like I have my own life for the first time since before I was married. They still haven't come about the bugs. Maybe when the weather changes, they'll leave." Her mother smiled. "What's up with you?"

"Remember that screen test? They want me to star in it. Starting right away. I want to do it, but I worry about you. Will you come with me?"

"How soon is right away?" her mother said.

"Soon. Like this week," Molli said.

"How are you going to pay for this?"

"Don't worry about the money. Will you come? Please."

"I'd be a burden to you. You'll do better without me," her mother said.

"No. I want you to come. Really," Molli said.

"I have my life here. A few friends. My macramé. I'm too old to start again. Don't worry about me. I'll be fine."

Molli looked at the tiny apartment. Her mother had made bright curtains to hide the view of the littered vacant lot from the kitchen window. She tucked the roach hotels behind discreetly placed potted plants which she faithfully rotated to a place in front of the only other window. A small pan remained strategically located in the corner to catch the drip from the upstairs neighbor's leaky sink. Her mother's constant cleaning and clever and colorful decorations made the efficiency barely livable. Molli saw her mother as a survivor who was tiring of the struggle. It doesn't have to end this way, she thought, and wrapped her mother in her arms.

"You still want that house in the country?" Molli said.

"Don't," her mother said. "I can't think about it. I'll cry."

"Let's start looking tomorrow. I'm tired of the city, too," Molli said.

"Your career. You've worked so hard."

"I've already given up too much for my career. Honestly, doing this with you will make me the happiest." Molli shuddered as a roach skittered across the kitchen floor. "Unless you'll miss your little friends."

"How?" her mother said. "What about money?"

"You can't ask about it. That'll have to be our deal. It's nothing to worry about. I just don't want to talk about it."

"I'm late for Vi's," her mother said. "Lock up when you leave, will you please?"

"I'll pick you up right after church," Molli said. "I love you."

"I love you, too, dear," her mother said.

I'm glad I made the tape before I changed my mind, Molli thought. It will sound more authentic.

*

Flick didn't hear the full urban myth until months afterwards.

Apparently, his son in Japan told a mid manager for Honda who mentioned the film while practicing his English on an Australian consulate employee at a sushi and saki party in Osaka. This snippet of his conversation was overheard by a visiting economics professor who used it as another example of the decline of American culture during a discussion with his seat mate on the flight to Los Angeles. The seat mate, a golf ball salesman from Dallas, told his know-it-all brother-in-law who worked in customer services for Harley Davidson who told his supervisor who told his manager who told her vice president that the film was almost finished.

The vice president used a pay phone to call the executive director of the Open Road Foundation who immediately directed the foundation truth squad to Flick's repair shop. The five men who rolled up to the shop's front door looked enough like real bikers to cause the real bikers to casually pick up chains and wrenches. What the men said made Flick rise up on the balls of his size thirteen feet.

"Let me see if I've got this straight," he said. "Like, you want me to suspend discussions with Honda and do the film with you?"

"Close. We want you to stop making the film with Honda. Do it with us and you get cooperation. Do it with Honda and you get grief," the leader said.

"Are you from Harley?" Flick said.

"No legal connection. We are a separate and distinct non-profit. However, we do have a certain relationship," the leader said.

"Spiritual?"

"That works."

"I dig," Flick said.

"Not completely, you don't," the leader said. "I don't know this, you understand what I'm saying. It's just my opinion. But I think some of Harley's stockholders might object to the company doing business with you. We've checked you out. Drug dealing, violence, extortion. On the fringe, and maybe directly involved. We don't want to know any more. On the other hand, people like you are responsible for the Harley myth. We like the idea for the movie. It will capture and perpetuate this myth. You've been at it a long time. With your connections, we believe you can make it happen, with professional help of course. It's about Harleys, but the company's not involved."

"Far out," Flick said. "What's the catch?"

"No illegal drugs. Zero tolerance. No second chances. Full prosecution and maximum penalties," the leader said. "Doesn't include booze, of course."

"Check out my studio if you want," Flick said to the truth squad. "We've got to talk."

The bikers who were listening twitched, and metal objects clanked against each other like manacles against the bars of a cell. At a meeting after the truth squad rode off as suddenly as they appeared, four of the bikers decided to stay in Carolina' safe hills, rather than risk jail. The others would ride North with Flick. Cheyenne didn't vote.

"Let's walk," Flick said to Cheyenne and they went outside.

"Out of sight," Flick said. "Like a dream come true, man. We get to play the part of the universal biker, which is who we want to be. We'll be history. It's too much."

"I'm afraid," Cheyenne said.

"I was bluffing with Honda. You know that. "

"Whatever. I don't want to go to prison."

"You're not going to prison," Flick said.

"I won't be able to stop. They meant it. It won't matter that it's your son," Cheyenne said.

"He had to say it that way. Be different once we get there. We'll be real cool about it. You'll be okay. Give you a chance to get off dope. You can do this. You know what it means to me?"

"I do. I'm going because I know you won't stay. But I'm a doper," Cheyenne said. "I'll die in prison."

Flick walked to the edge of the parking lot. Concerns about his son vibrated like static, disrupting the harmonic euphoria he felt about his film. The film was too important, but the odds favored him visiting his dying son in jail.

"Your studio's impressive," the leader said.

"Thanks. I want to be straight with you," Flick said. "I've been wanting to do this film for years. I can see it, feel it, smell it. Give me the chance and I'll give you something you'll be damn proud of. But I got a problem. My son is a righteous biker, but he's a doper. We can't risk prison. So I can't do this film with you unless you can do something for me."

"What?" the leader said. "No drugs. We can't compromise that."

"No. I understand. I want you to sponsor Cheyenne for the rehab program you operate that's special for bikers. It can be part of my salary," Flick said. "If you won't do that, I'll stick with Honda."

"We can do that," the leader said, "but it's strictly voluntary. Does he want to get clean?"

"Right out front I'm asking you to do this," Flick said to Cheyenne. "If you don't, you better stay here."

"You'd leave me?" Cheyenne said.

"Life goes on," Flick said.

"Your program is, like, bikers only?" Cheyenne said.

"Yes. Our goal is to get them back on their bikes doing whatever they did before, except for drugs," the leader said.

"That's cool," Cheyenne said. "Can I still be in the movie?"

"I'll save you a part," Flick said.

Flick didn't get an answer when he called later to tell Molli that Gant had not contacted him before the deadline passed. Even though he no longer expected Gant to pay, he mailed the package of duplicates to Gant's partners because Flick had promised himself that he would. He imagined it would hit the partnership like a live grenade. Flick didn't think he would be around to view the carnage. It was time to move on.

CHAPTER TWENTY FOUR

Gant didn't know the purpose of the meeting hastily called by Jeb and Rich that afternoon. What a waste of time, he thought. He came through the conference room door talking.

"Do you really need me?" he said disdainfully. "I'm right in the middle...."

His words were frozen by glacial stares of his partners, as if they were judges about to sentence for a particularly heinous crime. Their hands rested on a stack of familiar transcripts. The photos were spread between them. One copy of the statement had portions underlined in green.

His blood abandoned his extremities for the vital organs. Gant fell into a chair, his face alabaster. He recovered in time to capture a confession before it left his mouth. His tongue lwent to sandpaper.

"I didn't do anything wrong," he said.

"That doesn't matter," Jeb said dispassionately. "You have to go."

"Now," Rich said. The word hammered into Gant like a stake. A clock chimed twice.

"Fuck you," Gant said.

"Jake," Rich said, "you've got no choice."

"Bullshit. I didn't do it."

"Doesn't matter."

"I'll take it to a jury. I've got that right. You can't run me out. Innocent, damn it," Gant said.

The preliminaries over, Jeb and Rich carefully watched Gant like he was an unpredictable, trapped animal searching for an way to escape. Gant's breathing slowed. He lit a cigarette, drawing a frown from Jeb.

"What's in the transcripts, jokes. All of it. Part of the act. Didn't know it was taped. The statement is a flat-out lie. They tried to blackmail me. Why should I leave? I'm not going. You guys should be with me on this," Gant said.

"You want to go to prison?" Rich said firmly.

"Prison? Give me a break!" Gant looked away. Goddesses frolicked on the papered wall. A framed firm brochure hung askew.

His partners sat patient as vultures.

"Don't look at me like that. I didn't do anything wrong."

"I could say a lot right now," Rich said. "What goes around, comes around will suffice. I'm not looking for revenge. After Keesha, I don't do those feelings any more. I do see this as a time for us to lighten our load by letting you go. If you had been more understanding and less of an asshole, maybe I'd be willing to risk more than we are to help you. But maybe not. You're in a bad spot."

"I was going to work something out with you, Rich," Gant said. "Honest. We can still do it so you can leave. Right, Jeb?"

"Too late," Jeb said. He coughed into his hand. A sharp bark.

"I'm going to take you through how it is," Rich said. "You'll see in the end it only comes out one way. Say we turn everything over to the bar's professional responsibility people. Technically we're required to, you know that. Because of the allegations of criminal conduct, they'll share information with the DA. Then your troubles really begin."

"Look, I didn't do it," Gant said.

"Tell that to Rebecca Varner," Rich said.

"Criminal? You think I'm a criminal?"

"I can't believe you'd be that stupid," Rich said. "So, no, I don't think you did it. But, that's not what the evidence says. If I wanted to make a case against you, it's sure there."

"Bullshit. There's nothing there. Jokes. Lies. I've never sold drugs to anyone," Gant said.

"That's not what it looks like," Rich said.

"I don't care what it looks like. I'm telling the truth."

"Let's keep going. So Varner gets all this and she's got enough to issue a complaint or get the grand jury to indict," Rich said.

"Not her jurisdiction," Gant said.

"That would sound good, arguing legal technicalities. What are you going to say, 'I didn't do it, judge, but if I did do it, I didn't do it here?' And what if you win the argument? Varner will take the evidence to the district attorney or federal prosecutor in whatever jurisdiction is necessary to get a conviction," Rich said.

"You think she's do that?" Gant said.

"She wants you very bad. Thinks you're a menace to the legal community" Rich said.

"I don't believe that. How do you know?" Gant said.

"That's the word in the courthouse. The motorcycle case, pushed her across the line as far as you're concerned. She thinks you need help," Rich said.

"A jury would never convict."

"Oh, no? On the tapes, you say you've bought and sold drugs. No, you brag about it. You make it sound like you've been doing it for years. You say you'll get drugs for these people like it was as easy as picking up something at a convenience store. Then there are those photographs. Smoking joints and feeling up that woman," Rich said.

"But I wasn't smoking," Gant said.

"That doesn't matter, either. The photos aren't good. A jury won't like them. You don't have to be a lawyer to know that," Rich said.

"They're jokes, too."

"But your major problem is the statement from the person who said he bought from you."

"No way. It didn't happen."

"If he says you did, the DA will use it. A big risk to you even if you devastate him on cross examination. The evidence makes it look like you've been working with these people for years. Like you were a moral bigamist, leading lives as attorney and as drug dealer," Rich said.

"That's crap," Gant said.

"Yeah, but I can hear the prosecutor say those words and I can see the jury looking at you like you should be locked up."

"I just met them at the reunion."

"I know. I found out you traded fees, which I have to tell you pissed me off and may be against the Code of Ethics. But that's another matter. You traded fees to a client who arranged through other parties for these people to teach you to be a biker for the reunion. Right?"

"Right," Gant said.

"You sleep with her?" Rich said.

"What?"

"You'll take the stand, of course, to deny it all. The prosecutor will ask that type of question. My experience is they become a crusader when the defendant is a lawyer."

"But it's not relevant," Gant said.

Rich laughed. "Not relevant. Funny you should say that. As I recall, you prided yourself on asking irrelevant questions that made the witness' face burn."

"But I didn't do anything."

"That will be for the jury to decide. Of course, you'll be asked why you went to the reunion as a biker instead of as yourself, a respected attorney." Gant sighed. Rich averted his eyes. "And the answer will be?"

"Just as a joke. I wanted to fool them."

"The jury is going to know that the people you wanted to fool are just like them. Regular people. They aren't going to like the joke. And they probably won't like you, either," Rich said.

"There's not enough evidence to convict. They have to find reasonable doubt."

"Maybe you get extremely lucky and get a judge to dismiss it before trial. But I don't think so. In fact, he'll probably bend the other way to avoid appearing like he's treating you special. If it gets to the jury, you're likely to be convicted. The evidence doesn't raise reasonable doubt and you can't manufacture it. Not this time. If you're convicted, under the sentencing guidelines, you're going to prison. You like the sound of that? Jake Gant, inmate. Could you take it? You can't risk it," Rich said.

"Those motherfuckers," Gant said. "I already paid them."

"What did you say?" Jeb asked quickly.

"I already paid them. I analyzed it the same way you did. I couldn't find a way out. They said they wouldn't send this to you. That was the deal."

"Good people, those bikers," Jeb said.

"How much did you pay?" Rich said.

"They wanted five hundred grand," Gant said.

"How much did you pay?" he said.

"Half. Two fifty."

Stunned, Rich and Jeb stared at Jake.

"You paid them two hundred and fifty thousand dollars?" Jeb said.

"What was I going to do? I couldn't risk prison. Didn't want to lose my license. It's all I got. Come on, guys, work with me on this. What do I do? Nowhere else. Come on, we go way back. We can cut a deal on my share. Don't put me out. One mistake. Didn't do anything wrong. See it my way. Please, guys. Please," Gant said.

"Where did you get two hundred and fifty thousand dollars?" Rich said.

"What business is that of yours?"

"Where did you get it?"

"Equity loan on the condo and car. Cashed in my mutual funds and savings."

"You had that much?" Jeb said. "And I thought I was doing well."

Rich buzzed Joan. "Bring all the checkbooks to the small conference room. Now." He paused. "Yes, Jake wants you to do that. Here, he'll tell you." He held the phone out for Jake.

"Bring the checkbooks," Gant said, avoiding Rich's gaze.

Rich made her stay as he studied the various checkbook registers. The last one was the day care fire case contingency account.

"You've hired all these experts already?" Rich said, adding the numbers quickly. "Seventy five thousand dollars. Does he always write the checks, Joan?"

"No, I mean, sometimes he does," she said.

"Do you know anything about these?" Rich said to her. "Did you do letters? Is there anything in the file?"

"No. No, I don't know anything," she said adamantly.

"You want to tell us, Jake, or should I start calling these people?" Rich said.

"Okay. It's a loan. That's all. I needed the money right away. I'll pay it all back before we need it. Nobody gets hurt. I knew I couldn't ask you guys. I had nowhere else to go," Gant said.

Movement as essential as breathing stopped as if someone had pulled the power plug. Gant's eyes shopped unsuccessfully for understanding, but found only disgust.

"Excuse me, I'm leaving," Joan said, breaking the silence. "I quit."

"Joan -- ," Gant said.

"Don't. I could put up with how awful you are, but not this. I quit."

"Jake will be leaving," Jeb said smoothly. "Rich and I would like it very much if you would stay. You're a valuable member of our team."

"No, thank you," she said. closing the door on her wake.

"For the best, I imagine," Rich said. "This will change what we do. We'll be right back. Don't go anywhere." They left and returned a few minutes later.

"This gives us no pleasure. You were our friend. We made all this together. But, simply put, you've betrayed our trust. You have to go." Rich gave Gant some papers. "You will sign these documents giving up completely, for now and for all time, your rights and claims to any interest in the firm. We will give you ten thousand dollars compensation. You can thank Jeb. I said zero. All of what you've done, the drug statement and all, including the embezzlement from the firm, will stay with Jeb and I, and no one else. We'll risk the consequences of our failure to turn you in. After we leave here, I'll walk you to your office and watch you pack your personal items. We never want to see you again. If you don't agree right now, I'll keep my appointment this afternoon at the bar and disclose everything. Do you agree?"

Gant's world disintegrated section by section. He frantically grabbed at them as they flew into space. "Rich, give me a break. I can't decide that right now. Maybe I'll talk to a lawyer. Ten grand for my interest in the firm? That's robbery! I'll tell you tomorrow."

"Now," Rich said low and hard. "Not tomorrow. Not five minutes from now. Now. The only reason we're doing this is to avoid scandal to the firm, and we're taking some risk. You're a thief. You have no say in how it's done."

"Let me stay until the fire case is done. I'm the one who can get the most money. I promise, when it's finished I'll leave quick and quiet. You need me for it. You don't want it to leave the office," Gant said.

"No. You're gone. I'll get help to try it if it doesn't settle," Rich said.

"I don't know," Gant said.

"We talked about making you give up your license. Decided against it. You're a damn fine lawyer. Go to work for something you believe in. It'll be good for your soul," Rich said.

"And, once, you were a damn fine person. Where'd it go?" Jeb said.

Rich picked up the checkbook and slid the photos and documents into an envelope. "I'm on my way to the bar, unless you sign it now."

"What choice do I have?" Gant shook his head. He had ventured where consequences were swift and uncompromising. Powerless, he could only do what he was told. No deals. No settlements. No negotiations. He signed the release without reading it. "Do I get handcuffs? Shackles?" he said.

No one laughed.. Uncomfortable with the gasps and croaks of Gant's imploding life, his ex-partners attended him with the tolerance reserved for the dying. Rich checked his watch. A fat Rolex

"Will you care for my plants?" Gant said finally.

CHAPTER TWENTY FIVE

After turning his back on Rich's hand outside the office building, Gant stopped on the way to the airport to get something from his bedside table. Its silver weight filled his palm. It tossed it lightly and dropped it into his pocket.

Impulsively, he punched in Rebecca's number aware that he'd get her after-hours voice mail. On command, he gave his apology.

"My life is in the shredder, but I put it there," he said. "Had some help right at the end from a couple of people. I'm going to make it right with them. It wouldn't be wise for me to give the details to the district attorney.

"I'm calling primarily to tell you why I did what I did that night. I made it up. I knew then you would never repeat what I told you in confidence. I did it because I was enjoying too much the time I spent with you when I should have been at the office. I knew that I had to put in extra hours or I'd always be like the shopkeeper in the old Western who hustled behind locked doors at the first sign of trouble. I wanted to be on the street with the crowd watching me draw my gun. White hat or black hat, it didn't matter. Our relationship had to go. Looking back, it was a bad decision.

"You're right. I am lost. I'll go take care of this business, then try to find myself. I know I'm done here. I don't know where to go next. If I get my life back together, I'll give you a call. You'll be a great DA."

On the last night flight to Wilmington, however, Gant didn't appear different from the other exhausted and bedraggled passengers. He had withdrawn deep inside himself, to the place where he stored the memories of Flick, Molli and his money. All else, like the plane ride and the car rental, became hazy and transient. Unless he found them together, Gant planned to get Flick first, then find Molli and do the same to her.

He split the gaggle of bikers like they were ghosts.

"He ain't here," one said.

"I'll wait," Gant said.

All morning, Gant and Flea warily watched each other with nothing to say, like the only two people on a late night subway car. Gant sat on a straight back chair, an unlit cigarette caught between his lips and his hands hidden under a lightweight jacket tossed across his lap. Flea slouched against the wall next to the door, splattering tobacco occasionally into a rusty peanut can.

Flick came in without a word. He looked back and forth between Gant's concealed hands and his face which glowed with the fire of a zealot.

"What are you doing here? You don't look too cool, man," Flick opened a coke. Dirty foam pooled on the desk.

"My money. Give it here," Gant said around his cigarette.

"Money? What money? What are you talking about?" Flick said.

"What are you talking about? What are you talking about? What are you talking about?" Gant said, screeching like a parrot.

"Just relax. Stay cool," Flick said as he very deliberately walked to his desk, opened the drawer, and got his gun which he pointed at Gant. "Move your hands slowly from under that coat. Slowly."

"Shoot me," Gant said, agitated. "Shoot me two hundred and fifty fucking thousand dollars worth. Big man with a big gun. My word. My word. Your word is worthless as rat dung. My money or I'll turn you in to one sorry fucker, I swear it."

"Stay calm, now. I want to see your hands. Slowly."

"A gun. I thought about it. I really did. Figured I'd get close enough and keep shooting you until you stopped moving. Then I'd be in prison. And that would be a joke. Ha. Ha. Ha. Because, you fucking lowlife, because that's why I paid you the money. To stay out of prison."

"What money? Damn it, Gant, you're not making sense." Flick sighted down the barrel at Gant's cigarette.

"But here's what I brought instead." Gant whipped a cassette player out from under his jacket.

Reflexively, Flick ducked toward his desk He squeezed. Nothing happened. Safety on.

"You dumb shit. Almost shot you. You're lucky, man."

"Oh, yeah, the luckiest man alive." Gant laughed unnaturally. "I know I should thank you. Thank you for not shooting me. Thank you for destroying my life. Thank you for destroying my partnership. You know how long I put up with those bastards? And thank you for stealing my two hundred and fifty thousand dollars."

"I stole two hundred and fifty thousand dollars? Is that what you're saying? Man, you are wasted," Flick said.

"Wasted? I'll waste your life up so bad that money will seem like tips on the table. Personally. In business. You'll never know when. Something's broken. Missing. Maybe you have an accident. Drink some bad water. Over and over until you think you live under a dark cloud. You and your films. Think of a lifetime of bad endings. Big mistake, sending those lies out," Gant said.

"Man, I told you I'd send them if you didn't pay," Flick said.

"I did pay, you son of a bitch."

"Honestly, I don't know what you're talking about. Man, if you'd paid me any where near that kind of money, I would have eaten those papers before I sent them. I thought you'd call Sunday, maybe Saturday, and offer fifty or seventy five thousand, and we'd work something out. I got no pleasure of mailing it. But what I say I'll do, I do. That's how I am."

"Oh, yeah, right. Your word is your bond." Gant sneered as if rabid. "You're a liar. A fucking god damn liar."

"Nobody calls me that." Flick came hard at Gant. "I don't know what planet you're on. But, dig this, I don't have one penny of yours. Now get out."

"No, not until I get the money I gave Molli."

Flick stopped as if at the edge of a cliff. "Molli?"

"Yeah. And she gave it to you. It was set."

"Molli? You gave Molli money? When?"

"Saturday. She met you here at one. You...., " Gant said.

"I haven't talked to Molli for a week. Over a week. If you paid her, man, I never saw any of it," Flick said.

"She thought you might try this," Gant said, energized, as if he had trapped the witness and, with clever questions, would expose him before the jury. "So, she gave me the tape about your criminal activities."

"Tape? What tape? You're talking more nonsense."

"This," Gant said, shaking it at Flick. "Play it. Go ahead. I have duplicates. Go on, play it."

"This is too weird, man. You pay Molli. She gives you a tape about me. She never had a tape about me. Really, I never saw the money," Flick said.

"Play the tape, God damn it," Gant said.

Uncertain, Flick cued it up. Tense, they waited through the lead-in, as if they were the two finalists for the last seat on the last plane out. Flick unconsciously tapped his leg with the barrel of his gun. Gant chewed at the cigarette paper stuck to his lips.

"Hello, boys," Molli said. "It's quite warm in Bombay this time of year although they promise me that the studio is air conditioned. Oh yes, my dressing room door will have a star. The Indian film industry is booming. Plenty of roles for a tall Anglo woman, although I'll have to improve my British accent. Well, I know you two have a lot to talk about. Bikes and women and sex and drugs and all that. So I'll let you go. As the saying goes, thanks for the memories. Cheerio."

Gant abruptly shriveled inside his clothes, as if the gods had run out of patience and pulled the plug on the person, reducing him to skin and bones. He rattled when he shivered. He gummed the air wide-eyed, like a frightened fish flopping on the hot sand. Noxious gases passed from orifices and pores.

"India! Far out," Flick said. "Gee, I wonder how far your money will go in India. Nice twist, don't you think?" He shouted to the bikers. "Hey, this dumb fuck lawyer gave Molli two hundred and fifty grand and she split to India. Is that a great movie , or what?"

Gant heard the raucous laughter. He knew every person in the world would join in, if they knew. I cannot laugh at myself. I have lost my senses. I am a dead man without a grave, he thought.

"You shouldn't have tried to rent a life, Gant. I knew you were on your way down when I first saw you. Whatever you were, you're not shit now. Two hundred fifty grand. Man, it's hard to imagine."

Flick circled Gant disdainfully. He prodded the tasseled loafer with the toe of his boot. "I want you out of here, Gant. You stink. Come on. Let's go."

"Wait," Gant said hoarsely. "Nowhere to go."

"Not my problem." He picked Gant up by the scruff of his shirt as if he was a bartender dealing with a drunk who had soiled himself.

The bikers formed a macabre honor guard as Flick towed Gant across the parking lot. He propped him against the car, found the keys, and started it. Flick wedged Gant behind the steering wheel of the dull gray sub-compact.

"Now, get! or I'll call the cops," Flick said.

Gant rolled down the window as if to retch. He slowly rotated the knob on the radio until he found a rock 'n roll station and turned the volume all the way up. He licked the accumulated spittle off his lips. It began to rain. Big drops pocked Flick's denim shirt.

"Get Nicholas Cage for my part," Gant said.

The End

Denlinger's Publishers, Ltd., "The InstaBook publisher for tomorrow's great authors... today!", hopes you have enjoyed reading this book.

We will forward your emailed comments to the author upon request. [support@thebookden.com].

Visit our on-line bookstore for additional **InstaBook** titles, electronic book titles (**eBooks)**, and **GemStar** edition titles (formerly known as Rocket eBook and SoftBook).

Contact:
http://www.thebookden.com

This book was produced by **InstaBook** system technology.

Mission Statement

We will earnestly strive to enrich and entertain our customers through reading by promoting one of our constitutional rights, "freedom of speech." And, with honesty and integrity, strive to recognize and promote authors by publishing their works.

Denlinger's Publishers & Bookstore

P.O. Box 1030 – Edgewater, FL 32132-1030